Beyond the Sea

ANNIE'S JOURNEY INTO THE EXTRAORDINARY

NINA PURTEE

PORTO BANUS
PUBLISHING

PORTO BANUS PUBLISHING 2024
St Pete Beach, FL

Originally published by Page Publishing 2023

ISBN 979-8-9898529-0-1 (Paperback)
ISBN 979-8-9898529-1-8 (Digital)

INTRODUCTION

*B*eyond *the Sea: Annie's Journey into the Extraordinary* has evolved from the storyline written within the fashion catalog *Porto Banus* from the 1990s. The colors, textures, and flavors found in Annie's sea travels would embellish the coordinating fashions filling the pages throughout with excited snipets of her story entertwined. The story was a tribute to the loss of my original business partner, Anne Kraft, who unexpectedly died of natural causes while sailing in a regatta having the time of her life.

When the catalog closed after the September 11, 2001 tragedy, I received letter after letter asking what had happened to Annie. It was over fifteen years later that I asked myself the same question and set out to find out for myself.

I began writing at sea. It seemed only fitting. On a transatlantic cruise to Spain, I charted the map of the story while sitting on my balcony listening to the waves. Who would have thought that Annie's story would turn out to be a four-book series (with another book on the way)? Writing about young women embarking on their own journey of self-discovery is something I cherish.

Discover Annie as she navigates her journey and gathers an unforgettable cast of multicultural characters around her in a story of family, friendship, intrigue, and romance.

Caught up in the moment, it is impossible to see the designs in motion or the webs being woven. A pause at a fork in the road, choices made, future path rerouting...

Chapter 1

Boothbay, Maine, USA—Early Spring 1995

The crisp Maine morning began so innocently...the sun was shining, the sky a deep cobalt blue. Annie rose early, making sure not to wake either her mother or her cousin, who had arrived the prior evening, and quietly slipped out of the house. Her ever-contemplative spirit thrived on the solitude of these early-morning walks along the rocky coast looking out over Boothbay Harbor. The sea, with its promise of excitement, voyages, and discovery, had beckoned her since she was a child. It was during these walks that her innermost thoughts had a chance to surface.

She knew the path well and walked briskly as if pushing against the wind and was soon at her favorite rock perched high on a cliff overlooking the harbor. Annie sat and gazed out to the sea beyond, contemplating her fascination with the sea and how she had come back to Boothbay.

This love of the sea began at an early age when Annie and her mother lived in her grandparents' villa on the Mediterranean Sea in Marbella, Spain. On her fifth birthday, to her delight, she was finally allowed to board her grandfather's massive sailing vessel, the *Porto Banus*.[1]

The memory of leaving Marbella's port for her maiden voyage with Captain Luis at the helm always made her smile. He spent hours teaching her about sailing and the

---

[1] The name *Porto Banus* is derived from the port at Marbella, Spain, Puerto Banus.

sea. From that first day, she used every charm a young girl has to invent excuses to sail with the captain and feel that familiar rhythm of the waves, at least until her father arrived suddenly and moved them to Maine. But it was those sailing trips, combined with her grandfather and father's tales of international travels, that implanted those early seeds of adventure and intrigue, knowing the sea was the path. Into her teens, with many visits back to Marbella, Annie's desire to see the world, learn of its history, and immerse herself in foreign cultures took root and grew.

Annie sighed. Although the sea still beckoned, she couldn't shake the feeling that somehow her life had been put on hold. Was it guilt over her breakup with Jeffrey just before he returned to active duty in the Persian Gulf and his subsequent death? Ever since receiving that heart-wrenching news, the shock and pain left her grappling with a mix of emotions, struggling to find meaning to his shortened life and how she might have handled things differently.

Or was it her father's mysterious whereabouts? Given his involvement in the British military, he'd carried out many dangerous missions over the years, but he'd been out of touch for longer than ever before with no word. She knew how worried her mom was, home alone in Boothbay.

After graduating college with honors, Annie landed a dream job as an architect at a renowned firm in Portland. Her ability to create designs that evoked a sense of nostalgia had caught the attention of both her peers and upper management. She loved to give modern structures a timeless feel by blending contemporary elements with historical references. Her promising career almost made her lose that need for the sea and the restless urge to see the world. *Almost...*

But Jeffrey's death and her endless worry about her father left Annie searching for answers that weren't there. The day came when, in the midst of a drawing, she packed up her bag, walked into the manager's office, and handed in her resignation. Her heart told her she needed to be there for her mom.

*****

"Annie, *ma cousine!*" A familiar voice shook Annie out of her reverie. "I thought I might find you up here among the rocks."

Annie smiled at her cousin, confidante, and closest friend she so loved. "*Oui*, Sabine, I'm here. I hope I didn't wake you."

"*Non, pas du tout*, I'm still on French time," Sabine said with a grin.

As always, she looked adorable. She had found a little fedora straw hat with colorful seashells around the brim. Paired with capris and a sweatshirt, the hat seemed very tropical with her long chestnut-brown hair. She was visiting Annie and her aunt Celeste for a few weeks before returning to France by way of a visit to Marbella. Although Sabine was pure French, Annie always felt herself to be a bit of a European mutt. Both grandparents on her paternal side were British. On her maternal side, she had a Spanish grandfather, Don Marco, married to her French grandmother, Genevieve, whose sister, Claudette, was Sabine's grandmother. Annie and Sabine were about the same age and grew up seeing each other at all the various residences, becoming inseparable and sharing their love of sailing. Friends forever, they understood each other's moods. Even now, Sabine sensed Annie was brooding and tried to brighten her spirits.

"What is it, *chérie?* Why do you look so serious?"

Looking back out at sea, Annie shook her head. "It's nothing." She knew full well her cousin wouldn't be satisfied with that answer. Sabine had always been able to read Annie like no one else. They had talked last night, catching up on their lives, but, with Celeste close, kept the subjects light.

Annie didn't want to go deeper now either, but Sabine persisted, "It's the job, isn't it?"

"No, it's fine. The Maritime Museum here is..."

"I'll never understand why you took that position! I know you! You aren't challenged enough, especially after the career you started in Portland. And you probably miss Portland with all of its cosmopolitan amenities as well, *n'est-ce pas*? Annie, you are a brilliant architect, and now you're dealing with old ships? *Mon Dieu!*" Sabine said dramatically.

Annie smiled at her cousin. She could rant and rave as much as she wanted, as long as she didn't mention Jeffrey. At that thought, Annie's face fell; and Sabine, of course, noticed.

"Oh no! It's not still Jeffrey, is it?" Sabine asked, putting an arm around Annie. Knowing she had found the problem, she added, "I'm sorry, *chérie,* but I worry about you."

"No, don't be sorry. I mean, he's been gone now for almost a year, Sabine," Annie said. "I'm...I'm fine, really... and I needed to be here for my mom."

"Honestly, you are the worst liar. Aunt Celeste is used to coping on her own. Annie, it is past time to get over this and move on with your life. Have you considered that staying here might not be the answer?"

Annie sighed. It was hopeless trying to keep anything from Sabine. "I feel as though a brake has been pressed on my life, and I can't get it to release. Being in Portland just didn't feel right. And, Sabine, I can't leave Boothbay and my mom. There was something during Dad's last stay here. He took me aside and asked me to take care of Mom while he was away. I've been home for six months, with his words still echoing in my mind and no word from him, I know something isn't right. I had to be here. I thought it would be for a short time. But now I just feel like everything has been put on hold."

The two women were silent for a moment while they both gazed out at sea. Then Sabine sought to change the mood. With a smile, she said, "Why don't we go for a sail? You always feel better out on the water...and there's a clambake over at Cabbage Island this afternoon!"

"How did you find that out? You just got here." Annie laughed.

"Oh, I have my ways," Sabine said, eyes twinkling. "I also learned they will serve lobster rolls."

Annie rolled her eyes. "And you cannot resist those..."

"Of course not! After all, I am French, and we have exquisite taste," Sabine joked. "Oh, and why don't we ask that sailing friend of yours, Robert, to come along?"

Annie had met Robert at a sailing club during a college vacation. He had been a good friend and steady rock when she decided to start her career in Portland, but even more so when she heard of Jeffrey's death. Since her return home to Boothbay, he had become like a brother to her.

Annie raised her eyebrows at her mischievous cousin and laughed. "Hmmm...is something brewing between you two?"

"*Pas du tout*," Sabine replied sassily.

Annie laughed. "Not at all, indeed. Yes, of course, we can ask him. It's a great day for a sail, don't you think?" That settled, they headed back to the house to invite Robert, happy with their plans for the day.

Chapter 2

Sailing to Cabbage Island

Later that morning, Annie reached the dock first and began to ready the twenty-six foot monohull sailboat. She noticed the winds were steady and should give them an exhilarating sail across the bay. Sabine was picking up a few items to bring with them, and Robert was expected to join them shortly. Annie, ready for a distraction, was in high spirits and anxious to be out at sea for the afternoon. She looked up to see Sabine sashaying down to the dock, waving and grinning.

"*Bonjour, ma capitaine.*" Sabine said with a salute.

"Indeed. Now quit standing there, looking as if you just stepped out of a fashion catalog, and help me get this boat ready," Annie joked.

"Aye, aye, Captain." Sabine laughed and began helping Annie check the mainsail rig.

"This was a great idea, Sabine! I'm sorry I've been so out of sorts. We should have the boat ready by the time Robert arrives," Annie said.

Giving Annie a sideways look, Sabine broached another subject. "*Alors*, has any man even come close to winning your heart since Jeffrey? Someone you might be keeping from me?"

Annie busied herself with the sail. "No one, silly. I don't have the time, and I am not that interested anyway. I have my sailing friends, and I refuse to get back into the gloomy conversation from this morning."

"There's always time for *amour*, Annie," Sabine said softly. "Have you thought maybe it's time for you to take care of yourself and live up to that potential you so clearly have? Romance doesn't have to be a dream. You deserve a bigger, richer life, Annie, and it is time to fill your heart again. After all, we never know what life will bring, so you must truly live it, *ma cousine*, as we all should."

Annie sighed. "Sabine, I just...oh, look, there's Robert." Relieved not to be pressed further by Sabine, Annie called out, "Hey, Robert."

"Hi ladies," Robert called back, looking less than dapper in his baggy jeans and parka as he clambered aboard and smiled over at Sabine. No matter what Annie suggested, Robert never seemed to be able to achieve any sort of fashion sense, but he was a gem of a friend and Annie found him to be easy company.

Soon, they were ready to set sail. Annie was at the helm, as usual, with Sabine at the bow. Robert released the ropes from the dock, and they motored out of the marina past the old lighthouse. Annie smiled at the sight of Sabine. With the wind blowing back her hair, Sabine's face glowed with pure joy. As the boat rounded the rocky point, Annie said, "Heading for Cabbage Island."

"*Bon!* Clams and lobster. Can't wait." Sabine said, clapping her hands with delight. "What is your favorite, Robert?"

"Oh, er, both," Robert said and busied himself with stowing the buoys. Annie noticed Robert blushing and grinned. Sabine had that effect on men. Annie noticed the winds rising but felt them still well under control. She loved the symbiotic relationship she had with the sea. Her distractions from the morning walk were at rest for now. Everything was secure for the moment, so Annie and Robert discussed the upcoming regatta later that month. They were trying to determine who would crew with them, and each suggested several names. It was a longer course than usual. Having the right crew that worked well together was essential.

Minutes later, Robert called out, "Annie, we've moved into the downwind stretch."

She nodded and let out the sail to catch the wind behind her. When it came time to jibe, she called out loudly, "Standby to jibe."

Too late, Annie saw the wires to Sabine's earphones. Sabine hadn't heard the warning. As if in slow motion, the boom and mainsheet violently crossed the boat, hitting Sabine in the head and knocking her off her feet and into the water.

"Oh no. Sabine!" Annie screamed.

Robert released the sail in record time as they quickly maneuvered toward Sabine, floating face down in the frigid water.

Thankfully, Sabine had a life jacket on, but she was clearly unconscious. Annie rapidly secured the helm. Timing was everything now. When they got close to Sabine, Robert plunged the boat hook into the water to grab her life jacket. Every second counted. He strained to get her on board. Once she was on deck, Robert started CPR with his own heart pounding.

Annie grabbed the tiller, revved the motor, and raced back to the dock while radioing, "Mayday! Mayday!" *Please, God, make her okay*, Annie prayed.

Minutes felt like hours. Once she finally heard Sabine's gurgled inhale and cough, Annie realized she'd been holding her own breath. Paramedics met them at the dock by the lighthouse, shortening their trip back. Once they saw the gash on Sabine's head, they hurried to prepare her for the forty-five-minute ambulance ride to the nearest hospital.

Annie and Robert secured the boat and followed the ambulance by car, finally reaching the hospital, anxiously awaiting any news about Sabine's condition. They were both in a state of shock. After several hours and one test after the next, the doctors finally confirmed a brain injury. Annie finally called her mom and Celeste arrived in time to learn

Sabine's body had induced a self-protective coma. The only good news was that she had her life preserver on, and Robert got her out of the water before acute hypothermia could add to the damage. Leaving the hospital that night, Annie's guilt and grief were debilitating. Robert was a wreck himself and could offer her no solace.

Celeste had immediately contacted Sabine's parents. Francoise and Marta, grief-stricken, arrived in Maine the next morning to be by her side. Annie's devastation sent her into a very dark place. Day after day, she sat in the hospital waiting room, praying for a miracle.

After a few days, Annie tried half-heartedly to return to her job at the Maritime Museum but couldn't find the focus or a purpose for being there. She didn't want to leave the hospital in case there was any news.

Seeing Robert at the hospital somehow made it worse, reminding her that her careless distraction had caused this. He knew it was a tragic freak accident, but Annie put all blame on herself. By the second week of Sabine's hospital-ization, Annie knew she needed to go back to Boothbay if only to speak with her employer. During an early morning walk, she stressed over what to say to them. She knew that she simply couldn't go into work and decided to ask for a prolonged leave of absence. Annie had now quit a second job in the span of six months.

Her mother, very much like Sabine and always in tune with Annie's moods, was seriously worried about her. Whenever she was not at the hospital, Annie continued to sit around the house in a deep depression. No matter what she tried, Celeste couldn't shake her out of it.

Finally, the doctors released Sabine to return home to France with her parents for follow-up care at home. Facing her aunt and uncle, and watching an unconscious Sabine carried out by stretcher, Annie reached her lowest point. In all fairness, they were so distraught they were not thinking of Annie. They wanted to get Sabine home to France and

9

their own doctors there.

It was several days later when a letter arrived from her grandparents, Don Marco and Genevieve:

> *'Dearest Annie, the beginning of the season is coming, and we could use your help at the villa. Won't you come? It will do you good to be back in Marbella. Much love, Dom and Gennie'*

Celeste, very concerned about Annie's well-being, encouraged her to go, but Annie hated to leave her mom alone while her father was still away. Annie pleaded with her to come too, but Celeste insisted, "Annie, the timing couldn't be better. You have got to snap out of this. It was a horrible accident. No one blames you, and this is not Jeffrey. Sabine will pull through...she is a strong girl."

"Mom, you're wrong. I blame me," Annie replied. "I should have seen the earphones and done more to keep Sabine safe."

Her mother pulled her close. "Sweetheart, you come from a long line of mariners, storytellers, and explorers. It is time...I want you to put this pain and guilt aside and try to embrace a new direction. Sabine would be the first to tell you to do so, wouldn't she? Don't waste this opportunity. It might be just the answer. As for me, I will be fine. It is important I remain here in case Alex tries to reach me."

Annie nodded and recalled that strangely, Sabine had said almost the same thing to her the day of the accident as they readied to sail when she leaned close and whispered, "It's time to release the brake, Annie."

Chapter 3

Marbella, Spain

Embarking on a plane ride that Annie hoped would start a new chapter in her life, her final glance back at her mother in the airport filled her with both sorrow and anticipation. Her mother's words of encouragement had helped her take that first step forward to accept her grandparents' offer. But what Celeste didn't know was that Annie was now more determined than ever to learn the whereabouts of her father, Alex. If she could do so, her mother could get on with her life, and she, with her own.

As the plane ascended, Annie closed her eyes and allowed time for introspection. Throughout most of her youth, she often traveled to Marbella to spend time with her grandparents at their seaside home. She loved helping them at the villa, so deciding to start her journey there made sense. As young children, she and Sabine were fascinated by Don Marco's love of the sea; his curious nature to embrace all cultures; and, of course, his sailing vessel, *Porto Banus*. The interesting coming and going of the visitors who frequented the villa fascinated the young girls, and it was those experiences that ingrained the love of international travel in Annie, especially aboard *Porto Banus*. As she reflected upon those early adventures, she realized each day at sea had planted yet another seed of how important sailing would be to her. *How could it be such a cruel twist of fate that the one thing I was so passionate about could be the demise of Sabine and perhaps the collapse of my mariner's spirit?* She couldn't help but wonder.

But her worries turned to hope as she absorbed the beauty of the Spanish countryside through the windows of the high-speed train from Madrid to Malaga. Andalusia had always held a special place in her heart, and now that she was getting closer, she could feel the excitement rise to see her beloved grandparents...and of course Marbella.

As she exited the train at the Malaga station, she stretched her legs and barely had time to look around before she heard her name being called by a familiar voice she knew well.

"Annie, *hola, como estas.* How are you?" Her cousin, Tomás, rounded the corner at the station, looking as dashing as ever. His slim, muscular physique was accented by his brown knit shirt and black jeans. But it was his affable boyish charm, heightened by his wavy light-brown hair and inviting blue eyes, that made him a delight to all who knew him.

Growing up, Annie, Tomás, and Sabine, each as only children, found siblings in one another. The three of them, although living in different countries, had managed to always be there for one another.

After a welcoming hug, she said, "Ah, Tomás, it's so good to see you. I see you have grown a beard. I've missed you so much!" With a deep breath, she added, "How are Dom and Gennie?"

"They're well and can't wait to see you. Any more news about Sabine? It was such a tragic accident."

Tomás was as close to Sabine as Annie was. As she looked up at him, tears began to flow, and he saw the pain that was so raw in her.

"Dearest cousin," he hugged her tightly. "Let's get out of here and take you home."

And before she knew it, Annie was bundled into Tomás's silver four-door coupe, her luggage stowed, and heading toward the villa. The silence during the ride felt right, especially with Tomás holding her hand, and Annie absorbed some comfort. As they entered the old stone gate to the villa, Tomás gave her hand a squeeze of encouragement. Her grandparents eagerly awaited her arrival, and Annie's spirit lifted as soon as she saw them standing on the veranda.

Dom (Don Marco de Patron) was a distinguished and highly respected patriarch and *cuentistos* who wore his Spanish heritage well. He had made his fortune knowing the exact property to acquire both in Spain and abroad. And he now had many. His hair and short beard were almost white now, which only made him look more distinguished. His tie was tucked into his sweater, and his casual toss of a natty blazer and khaki pants signaled that the weather here in Marbella was still somewhat cool. Her grandmother, Genevieve, affectionately called Gennie, seemed like Dom's polar opposite. She radiated warmth, and the twinkle in her eyes belied her impeccable blend of French passion with a natural fashion sense. Annie was always envious of how her grandmother could so casually pull off a total look. It was clear why she made such a good hostess to their myriad of guests and dignitaries who frequented the villa throughout the year.

For now, it was just them, and Annie rushed into their arms with warm greetings. Tomás took her bags to her usual guest room and retired to the carriage house on the back of the property, where he now lived.

Before leaving, he told Annie, "I will be traveling over the next week, but we will catch up when I return."

Nodding, Annie gave him a huge hug and mouthed the words, "Thank you."

"*Chérie*, let me look at you." Gennie intervened, scrutinizing her granddaughter.

"You've lost weight...such a long trip. You must be exhausted! Don't worry. You are here now, and it will be our pleasure to spoil you."

As her grandmother lovingly clucked over her, Dom took her face in his hands. With an understanding only great wisdom brought, he said, "Annie, let your time here soothe your weariness. We will get through this crisis. I think you will find that at the end of this dark tunnel lies clarity, self-forgiveness, and gratitude. Allow yourself to find your way."

Dom brushed away the gentle tears beginning to flow. At that moment, Annie understood she had made the right decision to come here. It was time to rest her soul and re-nourish her spirit after all that had happened.

Three weeks of mornings spent watching the sea from behind a window box full of tropical color on her balcony at the villa had worked its calming spell on Annie. Built in typical Spanish style with adobe walls and terracotta tile roof, the two-story villa rambled along the large property just steps from the beach and shoreline of the Mediterranean, giving all guest rooms a spectacular view. Separating the villa from the shore was a marble-edged infinity pool and an outdoor gazebo. The landscaping pulled everything together with the perfect blend of trees, shrubs, and gardens with stone walkways meandering throughout. Annie never stopped admiring each individual nuance that made this estate so unique.

Although Gennie fussed over her and cooked her favorite Spanish dishes, it was the long walks with Dom and his magically spun tales that inspired her most. Don Marco had mesmerized Annie since she was a child with his Spanish legends and stories of far-reaching adventures, and his stories hadn't lost any of their power.

Also, during those weeks, Annie enjoyed helping to prepare the villa, which would soon be filled with an international jet-set clientele. Tomás came and went, busy attending to Dom's properties. Annie was so proud of him, and she could tell Dom and Gennie were too. Excitement was mounting at the villa. During high season, the electricity of the barefoot and sequined nightlife that lit up the clubs in Marbella took over. As the dancing heated up, the ladies often kicked off their shoes in abandoned delight, dancing until the wee hours. Exotic yachts would arrive from near and far, clustered like oceangoing chariots bringing high energy to this jewel of the *Costa del Sol*. It was a sight that never ceased to impress.

That would soon come. But for the moment, Annie enjoyed the simple lifestyle here that was a unique brand of seductive spice indigenous to the small Spanish villages bordering the Mediterranean along southern Spain. Annie took it all in...from the hypnotic music to the fresh tapas, to the late afternoon strolls.

It was one particular leisurely walk with her grandfather through the exquisite grounds of the villa that began to stir some of her old spirit. They walked along the boardwalk and met Genevieve for some traditional Spanish tapas at a quiet bistro.

Sipping an effervescent glass of local *pitarra* and listening to the soft sounds of the sea, Annie smiled at her grandparents. "These are the simple joys that lure me back to you and Marbella again and again."

Her grandmother could see that these weeks had been good for Annie. There was a new bloom to her complexion that had been missing these past weeks. But it was Don Marco who cryptically replied, "Annie, remember, the sea did not take Sabine from us, and the doctors sound hopeful. You said yourself she was at the bow with a large smile on her face. She was happy. You need to look somewhere deep down inside yourself to realize that. Try to feel the weather vane in your soul shifting with an unseen breeze, creaking prophetically toward some new point on the compass of your life."

Dom took Gennie's hand, smiling, and Annie looked at each of them inquisitively. Dom cleared his throat and began, "As you know, Annie, I have been blessed in this lifetime. Gennie and I are older now, and it is time we shared our good fortune. Your father and I sat down years ago to ensure Celeste would be financially secure. You, Sabine, and Tomás are our family. After Tomás's parents were in that horrific car accident, there was no question he would come live with us. We raised our grandson to take over the business someday, and he has exceeded all our expectations! Sabine now has the finest doctors looking after her to ensure her full recovery. If necessary, she will never have to work. We have been so proud of you, Annie. The position you earned at that architectural company in Portland was no small feat. You were able to combine both of your passions, history and architecture. We were amazed when we saw some of your renderings of what would become modern buildings with subtle influences in them from ancient times. They were astounding and showed what talent you have."

Gennie squeezed Dom's hand and said, "It's your turn, Annie."

From his leather satchel, Dom pulled out an unexpected package, a roll of ship's charts tied with a rough cord. Annie unrolled the maps and charts to see what was about to become her next great adventure. The itinerary moved through the Straits of Gibraltar, around the southwestern tip of Portugal, then on to Morocco.

Annie's eyes were wide with surprise and so many questions, which were answered when Don Marco said, "Captain Luis is bringing the *Porto Banus* to Marbella next week. Go, Annie. Take this trek to find adventure and the inner peace you seek. She's yours to sail for as long as you'd like." And with a wink, he added, "But before you leave, our first guests arrive tomorrow, and we have much planned to entertain them!"

So many thoughts rumbled through Annie's mind... excitement about Captain Luis and the *Porto Banus*, the journey about to unfold, this week's upcoming events, so much for which to prepare. Yet to her grandfather, her answer was a simple "Thank you. I love you both so dearly. Yes, I accept!"

After they hugged, they all raised their glasses in a silent but joyful toast.

Chapter 4

Last Days in Marbella

Annie sighed as she rose to another beautiful Marbella day. Today, the guests would begin to arrive, and she was pleased to greet them as they appeared. She continued to wonder how this port and the Spanish culture beckoned her as nowhere else. The high energy of Spain's music and dance lay in such contrast to lazy siestas and strolls along the Mediterranean. Amid her grandparents' intriguing friends, Annie was content in her role as the somewhat mysterious and sultry American in this foreign land, and she helped show them the hospitality the villa's reputation assured. Even with her American accent, her Spanish was perfectly fluid. Captain Luis and the *Porto Banus* would arrive within the week, and her identity would be redefined once again as she sailed away on this magnificent vessel. With a new affirmation, Annie determined, *I will turn twenty-six this summer. It's time to change direction, find a new path, and embrace the opportunity to move forward.*

As tradition dictated, there was no better way to start the season than with a bullfight, or *corrida de toros*. Her grandfather had secured a private box at the Marbella bull-ring for the opening exhibition of the season. The venue was filled with over nine thousand spectators, and the air sizzled with anticipation. Excitement building, Annie was intrigued; she would finally see the notoriously brave and handsome matador, Ramone Sanchez, face off against the bull. From Marbella to Madrid, Ramone's bullfighting skills were legendary. But was she prepared for the wildly attractive man in his "suit of lights" now center ring? Tall, dark, intense...Annie strained to see him clearly. When he began the dance with his cape, teasing the bull into a charge, Annie gasped as the crowd shouted, *"Toro!"*

Tomás leaned over and whispered, "Do you know that suit is probably worth a small fortune? The more famous the matador, the more costly his suit."

Shocked, Annie exclaimed, "How can that possibly be?"

Tomás was about to answer when he noticed that Annie's attention was back on Ramone. Tomás chuckled to himself. Then he looked at Dom and Gennie, who were also watching Annie and grinning.

Annie's heart skipped a beat when the matador glanced her way. *Is he looking at me?*

Ramone then acknowledged her with a subtle nod of his head. Blushing furiously, she returned his acknowledgment with a smile. The lavish spectacle of bullfighting held her spellbound with the determination and finesse Ramone used as he moved to victory among the roar of the crowd. And when he stood victorious with his victor's bouquet of roses, Ramone stared directly at Annie and tossed her a perfect red rose. Surprised and flattered, she caught it with a wide smile. The roar of the crowd's approval was deafening.

Despite how her heart raced as she clutched the rose, nothing prepared her for the messenger that arrived at the villa later that afternoon with a dozen beautiful long-stem red roses and an invitation for "a night to remember." Her curiosity piqued, she asked who it was from. The messenger said only the name *Ramone*.

Romantic distraction was not something Annie had sought for this journey. *But after all, it has presented itself and certainly intrigues me with its possibilities.* After a few wisecracks from Tomás, Annie made a conscious decision to enjoy the upcoming evening and spent the rest of the afternoon choosing the perfect dress and accessories to make the matador proud. In traditional Spanish custom, Ramone arrived at the villa later in the evening. She was sipping on a glass of local wine with some of the villa guests around the gazebo by the pool. Their conversation moved easily from talk of the day's bullfight to an upcoming international regatta, along with some of Marbella's finest restaurants. But one particular discussion caught Annie's attention regarding the turbulence in Hong Kong between the British and the Chinese.

Is it possible my father has been in Hong Kong all this time? If this is true, why has neither Mother nor I heard from him? Could he be in the midst of this turbulence? Before her thoughts could sort this through, Ramone was at the door. Annie took in the sight of him. She had expected handsome, of course. What she hadn't counted on was his serious demeanor. Clean-shaven, perfectly combed brown hair, dark expressive eyes, custom-tailored suit...this man was undoubtedly all male and somewhat intimidating. And when the other guests saw him, all conversation stopped dead.

When he smiled so sincerely and his features softened, Annie knew he was someone to be reckoned with. Her normal distant composure might surely be put to the test tonight.

"Ah, *querida*," he said, moving to Annie, taking her hand and kissing it as the hush continued on the patio. "How can it be possible you are even more beautiful than when I saw you earlier from the ring?" With a blush and a quick goodbye to Dom and Gennie, Annie took Ramone's arm, and they left.

The evening certainly did not disappoint! Ramone wanted to show her one of the older neighborhoods outside of Marbella where the evening *paseo*, or casual stroll, was common. Many people knew Ramone and stopped for light conversation and to speculate on his new American friend. Annie remained demure and allowed him the limelight, but when it came time for dinner, all his focus was on her. A cozy candlelit table awaited them in the corner, enhanced by magical strums of a harpsichord whispering in the background.

Why was she in Spain? How long was she staying? He had heard of Don Marco's reputation but had not known of such a lovely granddaughter. Over a lingering dessert, Ramone told her he had to leave the next day for the Spring Festival in Sevilla. He was the featured matador for their distinctive corrida de toros, where some of Spain's most intense bullfighting happened in its massive bullring, Plaza de Toros.

After dinner, Annie was captivated by the flamenco and the lightning-fast guitarists that surrounded their table. The men and their foot-tapping paired perfectly with the women's graceful turns and smooth, shuffling steps of the *solea*. Shoes were tossed against the wall with abandon.

Ramone looked across the table at Annie. "Shall we?"

They danced for hours...this amazing country and this even more amazing man having quite the hypnotic effect on her.

As Ramone escorted Annie back to the villa, the first rays of a breaking dawn showed on the horizon. When he leaned in for a kiss, she did not resist, and the kiss left her head spinning.

Close to her, Ramone said softly, "Come to Sevilla, *querida*. It is such a special city filled with Spanish tradition. Let me show you the festival and win the Toros trophy for you!"

Clearing her head, Annie then told him about Captain Luis and the *Porto Banus*. She was to leave Marbella in three days.

Ramone said with a whisper as soft as a caress, "*Por favor*, delay your departure for me, *querida*." With that and a gentle touch of her face, he was gone. It had indeed been a night she would remember for a long time.

Annie sat on the balcony of her room, staring at the sun starting to rise over the water and pondering a romantic getaway with the handsome matador. However, the lure of the open water and the journey ahead were too strong to keep her anchored. Surely, there would be another Ramone somewhere out there, perhaps. For now, she had other things to plan. A call to Sabine's parents assured her the doctors were still hopeful she would wake from the coma, and they promised to keep Annie informed of her condition.

The next call was to her mother. After catching up, Annie told her about the romantic evening with the matador and his parting words.

"Annie, sweetheart," Celeste wisely counseled, "romance will come in its own time. Take the journey Dom and Gennie have offered you. This is a once-in-a-lifetime opportunity. Rekindle your love of the sea, embrace the unknown, and find the peace and balance your soul is longing for."

"I'll try...these weeks at the villa with Dom and Gennie have already worked wonders. Oh, and, Mom, I heard something yesterday about Hong Kong and the British adversity with China. Do you think it's possible Dad might be there?"

Celeste paused for a few moments, then said, "Your father moved us to Maine to protect us when you were very young. His life as a British diplomat, active in the military, has often been a dangerous one. He loves us dearly, and I know he will contact us as soon as he is able. And as for you, my precious girl, stay alert and be careful as you travel."

Chapter 5

Marbella to Portugal

Gennie came outside to find Annie aimlessly wandering through the villa's fragrant gardens. "Captain Luis has arrived this morning and is with your grandfather." With a hug, she added, "We will miss you, *chérie*, but the time has come to plan your departure."

It had been several years since Annie had seen the captain, but she recognized him instantly! Wavy white hair and a jovial laugh that filled the room...he had to be sharing a humorous story with Dom.

When Luis saw Annie, he smiled with a wink. "Look at you, lass, all grown up. And quite a looker if you don't mind me saying."

Dom put his arm around Annie and got serious for a moment. "Take care of our girl, Luis. She needs this journey, but bring her back to us safely. Annie, this is a chance to follow your whims and trust your instincts even when there may be no rhyme or reason. And don't worry. We will get word to you if we hear any news of Sabine."

Dom handed her a letter-size journal with the image of a rather mystical woman's face on the cover. On the side were cutout letters spelling *Fearless*, and on the inside cover, it read "Embrace the Journey." Deeply touched and close to tears, Annie hugged both Dom and Gennie, knowing their generosity was beyond anything she could imagine.

After a few more pleasantries, Captain Luis said goodbye and told Annie to be at the dock the next morning at

9:00 a.m. He and his crew planned to spend the rest of the day provisioning and preparing the *Porto Banus* to sail.

This will be my last night in Spain for a while, but somehow, I feel no regret. While her grandparents were entertaining their guests, a bowl of paella at a nearby café, followed by a long steamy bath, seemed like the perfect evening. Annie closed her eyes and shuddered at the pleasurable wave of premonition that prickled her skin and told of experiences to come on this journey. Scrutinizing her new journal, she knew she had made the right choice. *Whatever the path in front of me brings, I plan to embrace the journey.*

As expected, Luis had over-provisioned the *Porto Banus,* and Annie smiled as she studied her captain a little closer and realized he had gained a few pounds around the middle since she saw him last. When introduced to the main crew, Helene and Roff, Annie found they both exuded warm hospitality strikingly in contrast to their formal dress whites. Annie quickly settled into her cabin, but she could not miss the *Porto Banus* leaving the port of Marbella. As the captain called out his orders, Roff and the other crew members operated in perfect harmony; and when the sails went up, the *Porto Banus* listed slightly as she rounded the wind-shaped point, off to the mysterious unknown and moving out of view and safety of Marbella.

Back at sea again, Annie was determined not to dwell on the recent sail that had ended so badly. She let the familiar rhythm of the waves soothe her and sighed. Standing at the bow, she concluded something important. *This is a special moment in time where there is no past or future...just the present.* A glance back at the perfectly balanced ship's wheel under Luis's expert hands gave Annie hope that she might find that same balance in her own life. Was it time to leave the past and future behind and live in the present? *I think yes.* She would not easily forget the evening with the matador, but she clung to the promise of this new adventure.

As the *Porto Banus* shouldered its way through the blue-green troughs that led the way through the straits, past the magnificent Rock of Gibraltar, Captain Luis pointed out the coast of Morocco to portside. In its strategic position between two continents, Morocco would be an intriguing and exotic destination for Annie. But for now, this time in Portugal was her focus. And given her love of history, she was excited to dig deep into how the foreign lands she was about to experience evolved throughout history to their present day.

Annie awakened to the rugged coastline and long stretches of beach along the shore of Portugal's Algarve region. After a light breakfast, Captain Luis reined in the sails in preparation for their first landing at the rustic seaport of Tavira. She had naturally been studying her itinerary and knew this region was the last to be conquered by the Portuguese king in 1292; and traces of the Moorish presence still lingered throughout the area—in the terraces, chimneys, and whitewashed structures that dotted the shore.

But it was the seven-arched bridge dating back to Roman times, the Gothic windows, and portals of Tavira's medieval houses that caught the early sunlight and winked a welcome that awakened Annie's architectural eye and set the tone for the rest of her day of exploration.

Annie wandered through the port, taking in its rich history and gaining a new perspective on the many generations before that had made this special place home. It was this enthralling perception that enticed her in college to get her second degree in history. Here was an example of the deepest part of what she sought. Equally intriguing were the various cultural influences immersed in the architecture of the buildings surrounding her. Combining history and architecture into a unique design had always given Annie an innate sense of accomplishment, and here was example after example of the same at every turn. *What an inspiring day...I should pull out my new journal and make a few sketches.*

Helene had dinner ready upon her late-afternoon return to the ship, and soon after, Captain Luis sat at his desk planning a course for Sagres at the extreme western tip of the Algarve. Preparations were made to leave early the next morning.

Annie recalled Dom's stories about Sagres and how it drew visitors who wanted to challenge nature's very existence. He said it was a region of wild environments and dramatic landscapes—the very essence of nature's raw power. An area of seemingly endless contrasts, there were raging seas that carved immense cliffs, bracing winds that created barren landscapes, and an intense summer sun. Dom used to surf in his youth, and he went to Sagres with his buddies to test its turbulent sea. He also told her it was a haven for introspective hiking along cliffside trails and cycling deserted roads. Annie couldn't wait to see for herself.

The *Porto Banus* set sail at first light and arrived at the port in Sagres several hours later. Annie's first impression was a sense of isolation emitted by the rocky terrain with its lone hilltop lighthouse. In the harbor, she rented a bicycle and set out with a map in hand. Riding past a beautiful stretch of beach along the southern coast, she noticed the crowd of surfers and stopped to watch for a while. Annie was astonished at the extraordinary skills of these surfers and became so absorbed that the minutes stretched into an hour.

Finally pulling herself away, she spent the afternoon wandering the old school of navigation founded here five centuries before, known in history for its role in the Portuguese discoveries. She was fascinated.

But it was at the town's fifteenth-century fortress the following morning where her heart skipped a beat. For there among the milling crowds, a man stood watching her with piercing eyes. She was sure of it. And then suddenly he was gone. Had he known she saw him? *Surely, Dom's vivid stories have me imagining things.* Annie knew no one here; so she shook her head, flipped back her hair, and consciously chose to ignore any possible intrigue.

She turned her attention to the *Rosa dos Ventos*, or "Rose of the Winds," a huge circular stone paving commemorating Portugal's Age of Discoveries. Captivated, Annie wandered over to the adjacent sign with an old rendering and an explanation. She read that the design replicated a magnetic compass, one of the early world-altering inventions, which included the clock, the compass, the printing press, the telescope, and the microscope. Its use as a navigational tool was undoubtedly the single most important development for world exploration.

The afternoon moved to discovering the countryside of Portugal. After an invigorating hike along the cliffs, Annie stopped at a highly recommended roadside café. The aromas of fresh fish soup; traditional fresh tuna cooked in onions; and the fig, almond, and egg sweets so loved by the Portuguese people spoke volumes about the meal she was about to enjoy. This was a time of celebration here in Sagres. The latest wine harvest had been particularly successful, and her after-dinner glass of local port was a great way to top off such a succulent meal.

On her walk back to the port and the *Porto Banus*, Annie wandered through the local marketplace and, once again, had an unsettling feeling of being watched. This time, however, she saw no one. Shaking it off, she was distracted by brightly colored ceramics at a local shop and stopped to purchase a memory of her newfound love of Portugal. Once on board the *Porto Banus*, Annie bade a fond farewell to this enticing country. Tomorrow the captain would set sail toward Morocco and the exotic port of Casablanca.

Chapter 6

Morocco—Casablanca to Marrakech

Along the shores of Casablanca, word of the *Porto Banus'* arrival spread quickly. After all, a vessel of this stature, especially with a beautiful woman alone at the bow, was hard to keep a secret in this town of many whispers. Roff oversaw Annie's disembarkation with one final warning from Captain Luis to not go out alone without a guide. Grabbing Annie's bag and hefting it onto his broad shoulder, Roff led the way as they maneuvered through the crowded marketplace to her accommodation for the next few days.

Once settled, Annie glanced at her watch, realizing there was just enough time for her to meet her guide for the next day outside in the courtyard. Crouched in the corner, the seemingly gentle older man with the typical shemagh headdress, a tuft of white chin beard, and a toothy grin called out to her.

"My name is Wadi, my lady." With a cryptic grin, he added, "Are you ready to explore these territories where life is so different from your own western culture? I will be here for you tomorrow." And with that, he was gone.

Restless for this adventure to begin, Annie felt the tempting anticipation of venturing out beyond her comforts. Writing an entry in her journal, she speculated:

> *Sometimes the best opportunities are those you don't even know about yet. This is the perfect time to discover what those possibili-*

ties are! I want to climb outside my walls of comfort in this exotic land and experience the present.

Dining that first night in Morocco was certainly a culinary experience...curried lamb stew, quail pie filled with plumb raisins, all eaten with fingers or using coarse wedges of bread as her utensil. Lost in a world of men juggling live snakes and women dancing with precious stones in their navels, Annie wasn't sure what made her glance toward the entrance. The most mesmerizing young man stood there, casually leaning against the wall.

He wore an ivory collarless shirt with matching pants and a burgundy textured scarf held by thick black cording as his headdress. But it was his face that captured Annie's breath! His piercing eyes had a golden hue contrasting his darker complexion, and his short black beard was artfully sculpted around his enticing mouth. Without a smile, he simply acknowledged her stare and left. Bewildered by the unsettling twist to the end of the evening, Annie made her way back to her door where she found a handwritten note with her name on it, held fast by the traditional pewter hand door knocker (once believed to ward off evil).

'A desirable woman should not dine alone here. I will see you at dinner tomorrow.'

And that was all it said.

The arrogance! Annie thought. *First, I don't even know who he is. And second, how does he know my room and presume to know where I will be for dinner? Forget those lethal eyes!* Convinced she would not be available tomorrow evening, she ignored the tinge of warning and fell asleep with vivid images of a dark, mysterious man with golden eyes.

After a light breakfast, she found Wadi waiting for her in the courtyard. Before they started, he cautioned her about the hustlers trying to peddle their trinkets but said for the most part they were harmless. "Stay close, my lady."

Very quickly Annie saw the bustling activity of this westernmost commercial port. Its French colonial legacy was evident in its downtown Moresque architecture accented by ornate wrought-iron balconies, carved facades, and rounded edges. Annie studied the blend of Moorish style combined with European art deco and found it both interesting and complex. She would have to make notes about this in her journal. And the Hassan Mosque, the second largest in Africa, was simply breathtaking.

But the city energy was not the sole purpose of this journey. Annie was fully prepared to stay over another night in Casablanca, but when Wadi suggested an excursion to the imperial city of Marrakech, she emphatically said, "Yes, I would love that."

She did, however, take in one *turista* indulgence...a sand-blown camel ride beyond the city walls. Amazing. During their rather uneventful ride to Marrakech, Wadi referred to it as the "Jewel of the South," and when they arrived, Annie could not help becoming caught up in its ambience and found it intoxicating. Wadi told her about its previous stature as an imperial city, which left it filled with palaces, courtyards, and vibrant souks selling their wares. Its brimming markets had survived centuries because of its unique position on ancient trade routes. But as she looked out beyond the city walls, she asked her guide about the colorful tents in the distance.

"That, my lady, is the tribal land of El Amir." Intrigued, Annie noticed her guide did not smile his usual toothy grin.

After a full day of sightseeing, Wadi got Annie settled at a cozy but mostly French-run guesthouse amid the lanes intertwined in the center of the *medina*, or old town. Annie had the good fortune to speak fluent French as her third language, so it was the perfect spot. The hospitable owners recommended the café next door for dinner, and Wadi nodded approval, then retired for the evening.

The charming little teahouse enchanted her at once with its exotic whine of Moroccan horns. Rich golds and ancient hues surrounded her, appealing to her newfound cultural images. When she asked for a table, she was escorted to a table for two. And there he was with those dark, handsome eyes commanding her attention and standing for an introduction.

Reason told her this was impossible. But here he stood as he introduced himself. He was indeed El Amir, the man of those haunting golden eyes from the previous night. With merely a moment of hesitation, she decided to sit down, remembering her journal entry:

> There are times a woman should dance with
> mystery, skirt the shadowy side, and embrace
> a bit of calculated risk.

So here she was, seated at a dinner this man had invited her to in another city—but somehow here with him now in Marrakech. The decision to join him made, Annie studied her dinner partner. *After all*, she thought, *you never know who might walk through that door and change your life completely.*

Annie was prepared to be intimidated, but he had a magnetic way about him. And when he smiled at her with those expressive eyes, she was convinced she was his only focus for the evening. All reason about the way Arab men thought about western women was cast aside. She could sense he had a dark side, but his boyish charm tugged at her. Morocco, with its mix of so many cultures (Annie learned from their discussion), was one of the more progressive Muslim countries. Regardless, she accepted El Amir's offer to order for them both, assuming he knew the delicacies on the menu better. The first priority was a glass of Moroccan tea. Next followed *harira*, a tomato-based vegetable soup, then couscous with saffron chicken, potatoes, vegetables, and spices topped off with Morocco's distinctive round flatbread, and, of course, almond cookies for dessert.

Conversation with El Amir was surprisingly easy, and his English was impeccable. He shared tales about the food they were eating and was delighted to watch her try the different flavors. Annie found herself enjoying the evening immensely.

"Annie, tell me about this journey you have chosen and how you managed to be aboard such a magnificent vessel."

Annie hesitated for just a moment, then took another sip of tea before throwing caution to the wind. She told him about her grandparents' offer giving her this chance to sail on the *Porto Banus*. A ninety-five-foot motor sailer, it did make quite an impression. She told him about Sabine's accident, hoping he would not judge her too harshly. However, she purposely neglected to tell him about her missing father, ever protective of his secrecy.

Not willing to end the evening after dinner, El Amir suggested they transition to more festive activities with a walk through the old town. Scrutinizing him, Annie attempted to assess whether she could trust this man but, in the end, followed her instinct. Filled with street dancers, storytellers, and small cafés, the medina was the perfect ending to the evening. Ever respectful of his Arab culture, Annie knew he was not allowed to touch her in public, but the volumes his eyes said were more than a caress.

As he escorted Annie back to her guesthouse, El Amir casually said, "I must exercise my falcon tomorrow morning. It can be quite entertaining. Would you care to accompany me? Wadi can bring you."

Surprised he knew Wadi's name, Annie thought for a few seconds, remembering the touring she had planned for the next day. Always a fan of the unexpected, Annie decided to relish this spontaneous gift that unfolded before her.

Pensive for just a moment, she replied, "I have never seen a falcon before and look forward to seeing him soar."

The next morning, ignoring the tiny voice of caution in her ear, Annie chose a long dark tweed skirt and brown boots with a flowing white silk blouse, then added a russet scarf at her neck to complete the look. Looking suitably demure, she greeted Wadi to tell him of her new plans, but of course, he already knew. Leaving the guesthouse with Wadi, Annie once again had that disturbing feeling of being watched but saw no one. Nevertheless, she stayed close to Wadi.

When she arrived at the edge of the forest, El Amir was waiting for her, dressed more informally today with his long solid earth-tone tunic, or *djellaba*. His headscarf this morning casually covered his hair and was swept into a side knot. Somehow his casual attire contrasted with his stern demeanor. Perched on a block, the hooded falcon had long brown feathers and a spotted chest, with jesses tied to its ankle. His restlessness showed he was expecting to be untethered soon. El Amir donned his leather gauntlet while soothingly talking to the bird. As his hood lifted, the falcon moved without hesitation to El Amir's arm.

Annie soon learned the goal of a bird of prey was to hunt. El Amir, very serious, explained the complicated undertaking of falconry. The falcon would be hunting for smaller birds or rabbits, and as he was released, Annie noticed the tiny bell attached to his ankle. She was fascinated by the skill of the falcon but also of his master. Hours seemed to pass as the falcon proudly brought home its prey, each time with a jingle of the bell.

However, once the serious business was over and the raptor was again hooded and tethered to his block, El Amir finally gave her a sideways glance with his boyish grin that smiled all the way to his eyes. "How about a picnic?"

A trip to the open market flooded Annie's senses as she wandered by vast piles of fruit, veggies, olives, countless varieties of bread, and fresh goat cheese wrapped in palm leaves. El Amir explained that the hanging chickens displayed had been plucked and hung to show they had been killed according to Islamic guidelines—drained of their blood with their heads facing Mecca. Wadi amicably followed them, collecting baskets full of delectables as El Amir instructed him. Annie quietly pondered how the two seemed to know each other.

Laying out a colorful Berber blanket, Wadi showed up with plates and napkins. El Amir had thoughtfully added utensils for Annie. She helped lay out the food, and as they were preparing their plates, a messenger arrived on horseback with a letter for El Amir. She could see mixed emotions cross his face as he read.

Looking up at Annie, he said, "I must go visit a friend for a few days. Her name is Sarah, and she is a remarkable artist. She has business we need to conduct. I think she might be a good person for you to meet on this journey of yours. Sarah is an artist living in a tent on the plains of Tanzania in the heart of the Serengeti, where she paints wildlife...primarily zebras. I will leave by plane tomorrow. Would you care to join me? Your guide could come as well. Perhaps even a short safari."

And without even thinking about it or about what to do with Captain Luis, Annie looked into those eyes and whispered back, "Yes, I'll go pack."

In her journal that evening, she wrote:

> *What is it about this man that has me abandoning caution and so easily trusting him?*

Chapter 7

Tanzania to Zanzibar

The thought of an unexplored, mysterious wilderness such as Africa seemed to mirror such a desirable picture of womanhood that Sarah's unconventional lifestyle represented. Annie decided she would love to explore the natural rhythm of the life Sarah must feel living among the animals with respect, not fear. Spending more time with El Amir also held great appeal. For all his cool and calm, Annie sensed great passion and fire as well. Meanwhile, memories of a certain matador seemed light-years away.

As Annie packed that evening, grateful she had brought extra attire from the *Porto Banus*, she also took time for some correspondence, first to her mother, then her grandparents, and the last to Sabine's parents, hoping they wouldn't think her too reckless. She wanted to share how inspired and expanded she felt by her new experiences and had much to tell. The note to Captain Luis was harder. She had to tell him that instead of coming back to Casablanca, she was leaving for East Africa the next day. She did assure him she was in safe company.

Finishing, she added:

> '*Would you and the* Porto Banus *meet me back in Marbella?*'

In a moment of reflection, the thought lingered. *Am I, in fact, in safe company?* Then on a last-minute whim, she penned a note to Ramone, thanking him for the night out in Marbella and telling him a little of her time in Portugal and Morocco, as well as her pending departure for Tanzania. Now she was ready to embark on a new adventure!

The private jet was well-appointed for a long-distance flight. El Amir was obviously its owner. Annie made a mental note to find out more about this mysterious man's wealth. The flight would take most of the day. It was after their stop for fuel midway that the view from the plane grew incredible. As they began their descent, they flew over treetops and scrubby plains, scattered with huge herds of wildlife Annie had previously only seen in books or on television. The vastness of the area was haunting, and the beauty of it stole her breath. El Amir watched her silently as the pilot took them on the most magnificent flight of her life.

When they approached the sparse airstrip in eastern Tanzania, El Amir began to speak of his friend, Sarah, and her artwork. "Sarah is originally from Southampton and I met her when she was a student working at a London gallery I supported. I became a huge fan of her talent while she went to art school at L'École des Artes in Paris on scholarship. She visited this area several years ago staying at a lodge where she painted. She was enthralled by the land and its wildlife here. When personal reasons allowed her to come back, she decided to stay. Her home is a large tent, with only one other artist close by in his tent, living among the animals of East Africa."

Annie genuinely looked forward to meeting this woman whose commitment, bravery, and inner strength fascinated her. One look at the scenery, the silence, and the brilliant late afternoon sunset Sarah enjoyed daily was enough to demonstrate the inspirational qualities of this place.

When they arrived at Sarah's camp, they found her working on her current painting...a trio of interacting zebras. However, she immediately put her brushes aside to take time to visit with Annie, delighted to have the company of another female. Her business with El Amir could wait for a bit. El Amir had mentioned a little of Annie's journey to Sarah in his note advising her they were on the way.

Smiling at Annie, she asked, "Are you aware that in all the existing herds of zebras, no two have the same pattern of stripes? I find that a most amazing fact of nature and continue my fascination with each of my paintings. There is an analogy that I particularly like that compares these zebras to indigenous cultures throughout the world where no two are the same."

Sarah looked at Annie with a certain scrutiny, then continued, "You have known El Amir for just a few days, yet you have traveled with him to this foreign land. Is this typical for you? Do you not think you are flirting with a bit of danger?"

Annie pondered her acknowledged "dance with mystery," then replied, "Sometimes instinct takes over, and I admit, I feel a sense of trust with him. Am I wrong?"

Shaking her head, Sarah replied, "No, fortunately you are not wrong—far from it."

Neither woman had enjoyed the easy comradery of a female companion for a while, and they settled into what would soon become a long and close friendship. Missing Sabine terribly, Annie was captivated by Sarah's personality and readily accepted her open offer of friendship.

El Amir gave them time to get acquainted as he arranged for Sarah to join them at their tent camp. Annie speculated that Sarah was to be her chaperone but gave it no further thought when the three of them set out for a hike. Sarah wanted Annie to see how the Masai tribesmen spread out, each with their herd of cows, and calculated with precision whose turn was next to take his cows down to the watering hole. As they stopped for a light snack along the trail, two Masai approached them, undoubtedly curious about this Arab man with these two fair-skinned women. Sarah spoke the language and took out her old Polaroid camera to take a "magic" photo of each of them.

Sarah explained, "They have never seen themselves in a mirror. Watch..." Sarah took one picture and showed it to the man, pointing at his friend who was the subject of the photo. When Annie saw the moment of recognition that the images were of each other, she smiled in wonder. The tribesmen laughed as they traded their hand-carved walking sticks for more photos, evidently believing themselves to have gotten the better end of the deal.

Once Annie was back at their tent camp, she had time to write in her journal while El Amir and Sarah discussed their business. Deeply moved by her meeting with Sarah and the vast expanse of Tanzania, Annie's journal was filling daily:

> *Being in this land gives one an impression of*
> *incredible remoteness and distance from life*
> *in both Andalusia and my home in Maine. I*
> *feel my perspective broadening.*

Sitting around the campfire as animals walked dispassionately by, El Amir and Sarah told her of the delicate balance of nature here. When Annie questioned Sarah's living conditions, Sarah wisely continued, "It is not necessarily the more glamorous parts of travel that leave the most lasting impressions, Annie."

Then almost in a spontaneous celebration of the sheer enormity of it all, they picked up their new walking sticks and headed for an elegant picnic, Wadi bringing a wagon filled with silver, china and tablecloth in tow. With a glance around, Annie noticed the local natives in charge of the tent camp remained close by with their turbans and sabers at their hips.

El Amir had planned a special surprise for Annie and Sarah the following morning. Up early, the three of them ventured along the rough path to a flat grassy field. In the distance, a vibrant colored hot-air balloon was in the process of inflating. Annie's eyes grew wide at the thought of being suspended in the air just above some of the world's fiercest animals!

El Amir smiled at Annie's concern and attempted to comfort her nerves. "Annie, you will be fine, and the experience of floating aloft over this astounding terrain is like no other. I am sure you will find it exceptional."

Annie looked into those golden eyes and replied, "I trust you...let's do this!"

Taking his offer of a hand to help her into the basket, Annie was the first in. Sarah was next, then El Amir. The pilot spoke to them in English. He went through the list of safety measures, then the lines were released. The basket adjusted, and the float began. The quiet was only interrupted by the roar of the fire propelling them upward.

Annie was beside herself with excitement. "Oh my, I have never experienced anything like this!"

Sarah began to point out the animals below them. There was a herd of migrating wildebeest, followed by perhaps a dozen zebras. She asked Annie, "Do you have any idea why the wildebeest and the zebra travel together?" When Annie shook her head, Sarah continued, "They have quite a symbiotic relationship, and they have learned to live in harmony with each other throughout time. There is no competition between them for food because the zebra like to eat the tallgrass and the wildebeest eat the shortgrass. Plus, there is no shortage of predators. The wildebeest have a great sense of hearing, and the zebra a great sense of sight. It is their combination of strengths that keeps most of them safe."

A thought occurred to Annie, and she asked, "There have to be kills every day, yet the plains are literally free of dead animals. How can that be?"

The pilot heard her question and began to steer the balloon's direction. "In fact, there was a zebra kill early this morning. A lion took him down, and they are feasting on him now."

Annie saw the scene ahead of her.

The pilot continued, "Nature works in such an amazing way here. By nightfall, the only thing left at this spot will be an indented plot of grass. The lions will get their fill. But behind them are the hyenas, the wild dogs, and vultures who will take their turn to make use of every morsel, every bone, and every hair. It is one of the most inspirational parts of living in this land among these animals."

By the end of the ride, they had seen herds of giraffe, elephants, rhinos, and flamingos. Annie thought she must have taken a hundred photos. Such an experience. All the while, El Amir watched her range of emotions mixed with wonder and delight.

Sarah's departure back to her own camp the following morning was bittersweet, but both women vowed upon their farewells to see each other again. Annie and El Amir wandered cautiously down to the river for a dip. El Amir's lack of headdress, dark tousled hair loose, and open shirt struck Annie with his irresistible appeal. He had been quiet all morning, but Annie's exhilaration and sheer sense of freedom here had kept her from noticing until now. Aside from the distraction of his handsome look, she could now see the longing that radiated from those alluring golden eyes. Was this the time to tempt fate? But El Amir smiled sadly and handed her a letter postmarked Zanzibar, just off the eastern coast of Tanzania. She looked at him, puzzled. But when she saw the handwriting, she knew it immediately, and her hand began to tremble.

The letter was from Ramone. The matador from Marbella. He was waiting for her in Zanzibar!

> *'I am concerned for your safety. Come soon,* querida. *Meet me at Namba's Café.'*

Annie looked up at El Amir with questions in her eyes, but he shed no light on how he got the letter. Their swim cut short, he told her he had other matters to attend to in

Africa. However, he offered his plane to take her to Zanzibar if she wished. *Should I go?* Unlike the farewell with Sarah, the goodbye to El Amir was a more difficult one. The man with the haunting eyes left with hardly a word.

Chapter 8

Left in Zanzibar, Onward to Thailand

This new entry in her journal was a difficult one:

> *Here I am, sitting alone on the deserted deck of Namba's Café on the remote island of Zanzibar! I decided to live in the present and leave Tanzania (and El Amir), but am I making careless choices to venture thousands of miles from home?*

Annie sipped the last of her Bordeaux while watching the brilliant African sunset off the coast. As the day's final light fell upon the painting in her hands, Annie felt that somehow, she had landed in uncharted waters. Ramone and her beloved home port of Marbella seemed worlds away, but only weeks had passed since she left them. Vivid images from Annie's recent journey flooded her mind—warm Portuguese nights, exotic street markets in Morocco, the intoxicating wilderness of East Africa, as well as an equally intoxicating Arab man. Yet her questions about her goals remained. Was she getting further and further removed from finding news of her father?

Then that fateful letter had interrupted her time with El Amir to summon her here to the coast of Zanzibar, where Ramone was to be waiting. Why was he here of all places? *Such timing. Was I in danger? And why was I enticed to go to Ramone at his beckoning, especially to arrive and find out he left me here?* But now as she watched the remnants of the sun's descent, Annie was left with only this painting, a note, and a plane ticket:

> 'Querida, *I waited as long as I could. Urgent business calls me back to Marbella. News came to me that you were traveling with a man of questionable reputation. The only way I could find you was to send my letter to him in hopes he would give it to you. I am leaving a painting I commissioned while waiting for you. Always remember our night of "dancing till dawn." You had quite an effect on me. Until you return, Ramone'*

Once she made the decision to come to Zanzibar, Annie had sent a telegram to Captain Luis. In his return message, he informed her that Don Marco was far from pleased that he had returned to Marbella without her and that she had traveled alone without the safety and shelter of the *Porto Banus*. Luis had assorted letters for her and wanted to ensure she was safe, but she was too far for him to even attempt to get to her.

Looking at the ticket that could take her back the safe route to her Spanish home of Marbella, she tucked it away. There would be a time that was right to go back, but not just yet. Annie had checked, and there were daily flights to Barcelona where the ticket could take her. However, she knew in her heart she was not ready to end this journey. There remained much she sought to learn and understand about the world and herself. But was she ready to do this alone? Experiences awaited. She would see Luis again eventually, but it was a long distance. For now, her return message asked him to send a bag with some of her clothing, as well as the mail he had for her. Mail arrived in Zanzibar with no particular schedule, so she was prepared to wait.

Content to take advantage of this gem of an island, Annie took the opportunity to slow the pace, walk the beach, and write in her journal. When she felt ambitious, she explored the UNESCO World Heritage Site of Stone Town and marveled at the Slave Chambers and Sultan's Palace. The gorgeous views from her flat boasted white-coral sand beaches and crystal-clear sea, which was perfect for lazy afternoon swims.

During a visit to the local fishing village of Fumba, a snorkeling expedition rewarded her with both whale and dolphin sightings! That excursion rounded off with a traditional Zanzibari buffet lunch filled with local delicacies such as slipper lobster steamed with fragrant spices and an array of tropical fruits. Usually content with solitude, she found herself starved for company. She would have considered returning to Tanzania but knew Sarah was preparing for an exhibition back in London. So here she was. Yet for some reason, on this island, she had remained aloof. As Annie's second week began, she took a boat ride over to the historic Prison Island to see its famous giant tortoises and peacocks. Out on the ocean, she wistfully thought of the *Porto Banus* and how Roff and Helene would love provisioning the ship with local specialties at the Fordhani Night Food Market, filled to the brim, choosing from the appetizing rows of grilled food and fresh juices.

When Annie returned in the afternoon, she was greeted with a large parcel from Captain Luis. Excited as a young child, she rummaged through the bag, realizing Helene had chosen just the right clothes and necessities to send. She put the handful of letters aside for the moment and poured a glass of wine from the bottle of South African rosé she had discovered in Stone Town. Once she was comfortably seated on her balcony, Annie reached for the stack of letters.

She loved seeing the stamps that showed where they originated. She would save the two from her mother and her grandparents, but the one from Thailand bore the most beautiful Thai postmark. She opened the padded envelope, and an exquisite stone prayer necklace fell into her hand as she began to read. *What an intriguing invitation.*

The invitation was to join Professor Todd Middleton, her dear friend and mentor from the States, on his own journey of self-discovery through Thailand. He had heard through her mother that Annie was also on a journey and wanted to share some of his insights with her. The professor planned to be in Thailand and the surrounding area for several months and said he would meet her wherever it worked for her. Who would have thought a college professor and counselor would remain such a lasting friend, and she did find him most interesting. It was his sage advice after Jeffrey's death that had eventually led her back to Boothbay and the position with the museum. Annie found his invitation intriguing and impossible to ignore.

Having been land-bound for such a length of time, she found herself with a mental debate as to whether to fly back to Marbella to start her journey at sea or use the ticket Dom had sent to fly to Thailand. This was not an easy decision. Walking along the beach as the moon rose over black glassy waves, she reflected on where she had been and on this new direction in her path. Thankfully, her mother's letter had good news about Sabine. She had come out of the coma. The doctors had prescribed rehabilitation and speech therapy, but the prognosis was good. A deep feeling of relief came over Annie like a huge weight had been lifted from her. She only hoped her cousin would have a full recovery.

The letter from her grandmother expressed their concern for Annie's departure but, in the end, gave her their love and support. They would love her to fly home to see them, but if her direction moved elsewhere, Annie could count on them to provide what was needed. Annie's eyes glistened as she realized the magnitude of their generosity. Looking at the ticket and the professor's invitation, Annie fastened the necklace around her neck and placed the call to exchange her ticket for Bangkok!

During the days before her flight, Annie lost herself reading enchanting stories of Thai culture and its proud people. Known as the "Land of the Free," it had never experienced the confines of foreign occupation. Formerly called Siam and now officially the Kingdom of Thailand, the country was located at the center of the Indochinese Peninsula in Southeast Asia. Writing a new entry, Annie reflected on how this must affect its people:

> *This powerful sense of independence strikes a chord deep within me, and I grow in anticipation as the time in Thailand draws closer.*

After the long and surprisingly crowded flight, Annie found a shuttle heading to Bangkok's port at Samut Prakan, which represented the very heart of the Thai kingdom. She quickly stowed her luggage in her canal-side inn and set out to find the professor. Annie had arranged to meet him in Sanam Luang, the vast oval grounds at the center of the city. With mounting excitement, Annie shook off her weariness and scanned the bustling sea of vendors, fortune-tellers, and hawkers until finally she saw her old friend. She didn't have to go far. The years melted away as Todd greeted her with a warm hug and a bouquet of exquisite Thai orchids. The professor wanted to start their tour here because of this ancient city's sage-like founder, King Rama.

It was he who claimed, "If man has no knowledge of the past, he is nothing but a vessel without a rudder on the high seas." He knew that would appeal to Annie's mariner senses. *Interesting.*

They quickly made their way through the bubbling cauldron of human activity at Bangkok's center into the misty mountains inhabited by vast species of birds and butterflies, and she was grateful to have such a knowledgeable guide. The next several days found Annie amazed by all that was around her—the majestic beauty of the landscape and the exotic everyday culture were just the start. It was the very energy of Thailand that captured Annie's every sense. At one point, she looked out to sea and could imagine the *Porto Banus* making its way into this vibrant harbor. During that moment, she could almost feel her mother and grandparents propelling her forward.

She had only read of the traditional floating markets, but hearing the calls of the vendors as they clamored to maneuver to her side made her wish she could get a trinket from each one. So compelling were the village women with their brightly colored sarongs that they made a unique contrast to the silence and awe of ancient Buddhist temples. The professor had known this land would hold many gifts for Annie and was genuinely happy she had joined him.

After a day of exploring Northern Thailand's Golden Triangle, Annie returned to her quiet inn to change. It seemed impossible that ten days had already passed! The professor was moving on tomorrow and wanted to enjoy a traditional Thai dinner together before leaving. He suggested an open-air restaurant on the water that served the most delectable local cuisine. It was a pleasant evening, not too hot, so they decided to walk. Once at the restaurant, their server seated them at a table with a magnificent view across the bay and the lights of Bangkok.

The meal started with a green papaya salad, followed by *tom yum goong* (spicy shrimp soup). Annie agreed wholeheartedly that both the food and the view made an exceptional combination for their last evening. And when the waiter served the traditional *pad thai* with a tangy orange tea, she thought the medley of flavors on her taste buds would be a most enjoyable entry in her journal. The professor finished his meal with mango sticky rice, but Annie could not eat one more bite. She sipped her tea, and their conversation turned to where each of their paths from here would take them. Chiang Mai was the professor's next stop.

They were enjoying each other's company, so it was natural for him to ask her to join him.

Annie felt compelled to tell the professor where she was in her journey. "Todd, for some reason, I feel a restlessness urging me to move on. But where to? I am tempted to pull out my map and flip a coin! Am I, in fact, at another crossroads?"

The professor thought about it and answered, "Perhaps...I wonder sometimes whether you made the right choice leaving Portland. You know the architectural firm wants you back, right?"

"What? How would you know that?" Annie questioned.

"I was one of your references from college that helped you get the job." He smiled and continued, "They reached out to me to use my influence with you. You did great work there. Your talent was highly recognized."

"They did send me a letter about six months ago asking me to come back. I loved working as an architect, and they allowed me to bring in some structural influences from other periods and cultures, which was very rewarding. But with my father gone I didn't feel I could leave my mother alone in Boothbay for so long."

Softly, he asked, "Do you think Jeffrey's death was part of what made you leave?"

"There was something so unfair about it, Todd. After college, we drifted apart when he joined the army, and I got my new position at the firm. A year or so later, I heard from him that he was home on a short leave. It was during that time we spent together that I learned about the danger he faced daily as a warrant officer. He was afraid, Todd. I saw it in his eyes. But Jeffrey went back in spite of it, not that he had a choice. We wrote after he left until I received the dreaded word that he had been mortally wounded under fire while attempting to rescue one of his platoon mates. The irony is that only two days later I received his last letter so full of hope and dreams of coming back and possibly pursuing a life together. It tore me apart knowing his life had been cut so short."

He gave her hand a squeeze. "Annie, did you love Jeffrey?"

"I will never have the chance to find out. It seemed so wrong for me to be leading this charmed life after the sacrifice he made. I think I felt I didn't deserve it."

"So that's why you gave it all up? It's time, Annie. Do yourself a favor...flip the coin. Follow your destiny."

Back in her room at the inn, Annie was reflecting about the Buddhist concept of life's transience and irony when she saw something had been left by her bed. A glowing dragonfly lantern softly illuminated the room, and she was surprised to find a note under its foot.

The message read:

> 'Annie, I have thought a great deal about your journey, and I think there is someone you should meet. Her name is Mara. She lives in Bali and is an artist like me. You will like her. Enlightenment might just await you in Bali. Go, my friend. Sarah'

She wrote in her journal:

> How interesting...do I dare? Am I taking advantage of Dom's generosity? Somehow this feels right. Has the coin already been tossed? It occurs to me that sometimes the best way forward is to not get in your own way.

Chapter 9

Thailand to Bali

As she contemplated this new crossroad in her journey, Annie wondered about the artist Sarah wanted her to meet. How did Sarah know she was in Thailand? Certainly, her itinerary had been unpredictable. Was it El Amir? She'd had no feeling of being watched since Morocco, so she decided to go with her instincts and called the professor to get his opinion of the note. Todd, increasingly in tune with Annie's determined destinations after this time in Thailand, gave his immediate approval to set her course for Bali, the jewel of Indonesia. Bidding him a fond farewell, Annie booked her flight across the Java Sea, ready for whatever lay ahead.

Once settled on the plane for a long flight, Annie wrote in her journal:

> *When did I learn to trust my instincts to such an extent? Could it be enlightenment is indeed within my reach? Why do I feel such a pull? Was this the motivation that kept my father away so long? The days in Thailand with the professor have had a spiritual impact on me. Somehow this journey has taken off in its own direction. What was to be a sailing journey has turned into so much more. Is it possible that authentic self-moments come into our lives when we have slowed down a bit, reflected a little, and returned to our true*

selves? Perhaps leaving the fast lane once in a while actually fast-forwards you to the life for which you were destined? Hmmm...

Bali had always intrigued her. Annie knew of family friends who had gone there for a holiday and never returned. She remembered Dom's story about Bali-Ubud as one of the most cultured of all the Balinese towns. He referred to it as "a place where traditional Balinese culture is present in every waking moment. At each turn, religious offerings burst with color along the streets, and hypnotic strains of gamelan are an ever-present soundtrack to everyday life." Annie couldn't wait to experience it herself. What better choice than to start there? Sarah had given her no clue where to begin.

Finding a little bungalow overlooking a lovely lotus garden, Annie, at once, felt drawn to this community of artists and musicians. She wandered through small shops, museums, and galleries along Ubud's main street simply to comprehend the impact of its infinite artistic energy. Back at the garden that evening, there was a lovely Balinese wedding celebration. Annie was enchanted, and before she knew it, she was invited to join them! The young couple being celebrated were quite shy, but both reached out to her with welcome. The women of the wedding party were wearing matching golden lace long-sleeve tunics over bright-fuchsia-patterned sarongs, each with their hair adorned with bright flowers. But the bride, with her sparkling innocent eyes, was outlined in the deepest of green, and her crown of white lilies was the highlight. Even the centerpieces were spectacular works of art, each about two feet tall supported on a platter with a grass skirt and stacked with unique layers of colorful fruit, cakes, flowers, and ornamental bamboo shoots. Lack of understanding each other's words was replaced by a universal language of happiness and gratitude. Their generosity was contagious, and Annie deeply wanted to give the lovely couple a meaningful gift. She went back to her room and returned with a treasure she now wanted to share. Approaching the bride, who she had learned was named Kadek, she reached for her hand to give her the beautiful prayer necklace from Thailand that the professor had sent her. Kadek's eyes widened and began to brim over with grateful tears. Annie held her hands over Kadek's, looked into her eyes, and smiled.

One of the elders spoke a little English, and Annie asked, "Why do all the Balinese people seem so happy?"

With expressive gestures, she replied, "Everyone in Bali is family to us. We live with gratitude...for each day and one another. There is a phrase we use, '*Tri Hita Karana*,' to live in harmony with God, humans, and nature. We learn this at a very young age and grow older grateful for this balance in our lives."

Later that evening, she wrote:

> *How grand to have come to this special place! These people are inherently genuine and filled with a deep sense of gratitude for the smallest things. I'm so grateful to personally experience these sentiments. I need to put my curiosity about why I am here aside and learn from this culture. Mara will surface in due time.*

Annie discovered that deep religious convictions, ceremonial dances, and strong family ties were inherent in Balinese culture. As she strolled along Monkey Forest Road, she realized in this place, she felt her own sense of balance and order expanding. Slowly and gently, she shifted into a whole new view of time. On her third day, breathing in the rejuvenating energy of this place, Annie wandered toward the bamboo torches ahead. She loved the traditional performances and had already seen the Barong and Janger dances.

At the clearing, there was about to be a performance of the traditional Kecak Monkey Dance! On a cliff facing the sea, out in the open air, the musical drama began. There was no artificial backdrop, and the only music was the human-voiced orchestra of men wearing distinct Balinese sarongs and elaborate monkey masks. Their *"Keh-Chak"* chants provided a dramatic sound that moved with the drama. Then as the performance came to an end, the only light left was that of the flickering bamboo torches.

Looking around, Annie saw the most strikingly beautiful Balinese woman. She wore a simple white chemise dress with an exquisitely ornate headdress and matching collar. Colorful beads were woven into a traditional Balinese pattern accenting the solid gold, with fuchsia tassels hanging on either side of her face. The perfect finish were the rhinestones accenting her forehead and side of her coal-black eyes. Such care taken to accent her beauty.

The young woman seemed to be watching her and then started to make a hesitant approach.

Annie's interest was surely piqued. "Pardon me, but I thought you might be here."

"Are you Mara?" Annie questioned with surprise.

With a laugh, the girl explained, "Yes, it was your friend from Africa, the wildlife painter, Sarah. She wanted you to come to my country and asked that I find you. I am Mara, an artist here in Bali. I studied with Sarah in Australia several years ago. She felt you would be inspired by my homeland. I was hoping you would find the lotus garden. My cousins were watching for you. Has it so far been what you might have hoped?"

Annie thought of her time here, the wedding party, and her growing appreciation for this country and its traditions. "Sarah was right. It has been everything and more," Annie replied. "You knew about the wedding? What a special evening."

"My aunt told me about the prayer necklace. That was very generous of you, and Kadek was particularly touched. I can see you were as well."

They sat down for a cup of fresh coconut water surrounded by the haunting sound of a local gamelan orchestra and immediately felt an easy camaraderie.

On an impulse, Annie asked, "We are in fact quite close to Australia...have you ever wanted to return?"

Mara smiled wistfully and said, "I always regretted not taking the opportunity to paint the undersea life of the Great Barrier Reef. I love to dive, but unfortunately, I had to return to my work in Bali before I could get there. Sarah was able to go back and said it was incredibly beautiful. She loved all the wildlife."

The stroll back to Annie's inn was filled with the easy conversation usually kept for close relationships. How curious to meet two women from totally different backgrounds and discover such an immediate connection. Was it their creative nature that drew Annie to them? For now, it didn't matter. She simply knew in her heart that she had made two lifelong friends in Sarah and Mara. She and Mara said good night and agreed to meet the following afternoon. In her room, Annie reflected that Sabine would like them as well, and hopefully someday she could meet both of them.

The owner of the inn, with his white turban neatly in place, was eagerly waiting for her with a wide grin. "Come, come, Ibu. Sit with me for some tea and cookies. A letter came for you today."

Glancing at the letter, Annie saw the Spanish stamp, and she couldn't hold back her anticipation. Once she was seated cross-legged, the innkeeper served the tea and cookies and handed her the letter. This time, the letter was from Don Marco himself. *Have I taken too much advantage?* It was a long letter, starting with his grave concern about her traveling without a chaperone. With her father still missing, one could never be too careful. He had heard from her mother that the professor had paid a visit and told her of the time in Thailand. (It pleased her that Todd knew that would be so important to her.) Dom went on to tell her he knew of her recent travels, and he was particularly pleased she had gone to Bali-Ubud to learn of the uniqueness of the Balinese spirit. As she got toward the end of the letter, Annie could not have been more shocked! She read the words over and over, trying to absorb them while the innkeeper looked on intently:

> 'My dearest Annie, over an aperitif with a client who works out of the Far East, I mentioned your being in Bali, looking for new experiences. As a remarkable coincidence, he has a rather large yacht (not exactly the Porto Banus but respectable). It happens to be in transit from Singapore to Bali on its way to Sydney, Australia, with a stop at the island of Heron on the way. The yacht is named Majestique, and its captain is Georgio Azar. I believe he is Greek. My friend has invited you to enjoy his hospitality on the voyage. The yacht should be there within the week and be ready to depart two days after that. If the trip interests you, simply have the innkeeper contact Georgio to let him know you will be aboard. Love always, Dom'

Australia? Back at sea? With surprising clarity, it was at that moment that Annie realized she could possibly make Mara's dream come true. Plus, the draw of the sea was impossible to resist. She nodded at the innkeeper and asked him to inquire whether she could bring a friend. He left her to go make the call. Looking at the date on the letter, it looked like *Majestique* should arrive in two days. Once Annie got Georgio's approval for her to bring a friend, she couldn't wait to tell Mara. The reward for her the next afternoon was the look in Mara's eyes when she told her of her idea. Mara was now teaching art and was in between courses, so the timing worked perfectly.

Annie turned the next page of her journal to write:

> *Although I am filled with anticipation to see what Australia holds in store, I am getting farther and farther away from home. Perhaps after this next destination, it is time to find my way back home to Spain. I think I perhaps have some unfinished business with a certain matador, but without his interference, none of this would have unfolded and this has certainly been the grandest of journeys! Settled— one last adventure, and home it will be.*

While Annie waited for Mara to arrange her schedule and pack, she visited a local market to get a few last Balinese culinary treats. Annie stopped at one of the stalls and looked up to meet the wise admiring gaze of an old village woman.

"You look as though you are searching for something," the old woman said.

Annie smiled and said, "I suppose everyone looks for happiness, contentment, and a sense of purpose. Bali has taught me many things."

The woman cryptically replied, "Remember, pretty one, the time to be happy is now." *In the present. Yes, I think I will.*

Chapter 10

Australia—Barrier Reef to Ayers Rock

Annie and Mara met at the port of Tanjung Benoa the morning of their departure. Mara arrived without all her ornamentation, dressed simply in a sarong skirt and simple white top. As they followed the directions to the yacht location, nothing had prepared them for the head-turner ahead! A sleek-profile seventy-foot ocean cruiser sporting a slim hull, generous overhangs, and gentle sheer line was tied up at the very end of the dock. Both girls gasped as they looked at each other in amazement, and under her breath, Annie mumbled, "Respectable, indeed."

There was no doubt the debonair gentleman, who looked like he had stepped from the cover of *Vogue*, was the captain of this fine yacht. Georgio stood tall and lean with slick black hair in his formal white captain's attire. He made such a handsome impression that it took great effort for both girls to suppress a giggle. *What are we getting into?*

But upon closer look, they could tell he was much older than he looked from afar (plus, he had a very prominent wedding band). His confident stance assured them he was an experienced seaman. Georgio welcomed Annie and Mara on board and proceeded with the tour of what they discovered was a highly appointed ocean-worthy vessel with powerful offshore capacity. He planned to make most of the trip by high-speed motor, then hoist the sails as they approached

Australia. While they settled into their cabins, Annie took a few minutes to write:

> *Ahh...I have missed the sea and its rhythm that so soothes my soul. These lessons from Africa, Thailand, and Bali fill me with curiosity about what this next adventure will bring. I am grateful Mara has joined me and amazed how she reminds me of Sabine. Like Sabine, without all the makeup and trimmings, Mara is a natural beauty. It is not just the radiance they both exude...it is deeper. There is a gentleness, a delight in the smallest things, and an overwhelming kindness that seemingly combines their kindred spirits. My only wish is that Sabine could be with us on this vessel as we race toward Australia.*

Long before Annie could see the coast of Komodo, their first stop for fuel, she began to see the occasional bird catching the draft of their yacht. Their forked tails told her they must be frigates. Soon enough, the island of Komodo could be sited off the bow. Georgio explained they would be here for several hours to refuel and get a few fresh provisions. Annie and Mara would be able to see this UNESCO World Heritage Site and the famous Komodo dragons, large monitor lizards that could grow up to ten feet long! There would be two more stops as they reached Australia, first at Darwin on the coast of the Northern Territory, then Thursday Island before they rounded the horn and settled in the Australian barrier reef. Georgio had business inland in Queensland, so the *Majestique* would remain anchored off the resort isle of Heron while he was gone.

Finally at their destination, Heron brought endless delights for Annie and inspiration for Mara. Its perfect white

beaches and crystal-clear water melted into a tropical kalei-
doscope of living coral and brightly colored fish as the two
new friends remained intent on finding the best snorkeling
and diving locations. The lazy sun-soaked days on the reef
gave Annie ample time to reflect upon the fateful path that
led her here.

With almost eerie logic, each step had seemed pre-
planned for her. She now trusted the order of this and let
the wild, beautiful country around her determine her next
move. Beachcombing at dawn, exploring sea caves along
the shore, snorkeling before having lunch on deck...she had
never felt so complete. But had she veered from the course
too far? What about her intentions to learn of her father?
With a firm resolve, Annie determined after this venture she
would steer her course back to Marbella.

The next morning, Annie left Mara painting on a
stretched piece of silk to venture to a neighboring island
for a day of horseback riding. It was a day only a seafarer
could love. A foreboding gray sky loomed overhead, and the
spray of the surf stung her face as Annie rode her strapping
horse. Riding along Rainbow Beach, Annie noticed a set of
untouched turtle tracks. This area was a haven for the large
green turtles who came back to the same beach year after
year to lay their eggs. The tracks led to a pile of sand that
was now a new nest. The nature throughout the reef was
awe-inspiring. Stopping to rest, Annie took out her journal
and began to write. Her thoughts turned to Mara and Sarah
and the impact they both had made to her perspective.

She would have loved to share this experience with
Sabine and was absentmindedly watching terns launch from
the towering cliffs when she heard, "G'day, ma'am, didn't
mean to startle you, but saw you sitting here alone. Is everything okay?"

Feeling a now-familiar sense of destiny, Annie knew
that meeting the very charming Jonathan McNamara, an
outback guide and reef analyst, was no accident. She chuck-

led to herself. *After all, an Australian adventure wouldn't be complete without exploring the "Never Never," would it?*

Laughing at the direction of her thoughts, Annie found conversation with Jonathan intriguing. He had been in this section of the Barrier Reef working in connection with the University of Queensland Research Station, which, according to Jonathan, was the largest island-based research station in the southern hemisphere! Jonathan had come to the island from Gladstone on the mainland and was currently collecting samples for the research station.

He explained to Annie, "I enjoy helping out where I can. The station does world-class research, but it is also a teaching facility for students and tourists."

"I saw the turtle tracks about fifty yards back," Annie commented.

Jonathan nodded. "Yes, I just taped off the nest to give it some protection. Are you staying here on Fraser Island?"

"I am actually on a boat over off Heron Island. I didn't know about the research station. My friend, Mara, and I will have to go take a tour."

"Whoa! *Crikey*, you are on that massive motor sailer? It is bloody gorgeous! Are you someone famous I should know?"

At that, Annie laughed. "My friend and I were lucky to catch a ride on it thanks to my grandfather's friend. Not famous at all, just visiting from Marbella, Spain."

Jonathan raised his eyebrows and whistled. "You are a long way from home, ma'am! You don't sound Spanish. How long are you here?"

"I guess I would say I'm a bit of a blend of Spanish, English, French, and American! Actually, I'm not sure how long we are staying."

They chatted easily, and Annie told him a little about her journey so far. And he told her about his research.

After he heard about her quest, he said, "There is a place I think might have great meaning for you. I'm taking a helicopter back to Gladstone tomorrow, then a biplane back to the outback in Central Australia tomorrow. I'd love to show you the sunset over Ayers Rock in Uluru. It's a very special place. The plane can bring you back when you are ready."

Annie, ever ready for an adventure, answered, "I am traveling with my friend, Mara, from Bali. Might she join us?"

Jonathan's response was, "Of course! Two of you? I'm honored to show you part of my country and will meet you at the helipad tomorrow at 11:00 a.m."

Back at the *Majestique* for a change of clothes, Annie told Captain Georgio of her plan. "What do you know of this man you randomly met while riding? Lass, you may be throwing care to the wind, but I promised to look after you. Let me ask around to see if anyone knows of this McNamara fellow."

"Georgio, he works with the Queensland Research Station right here on Heron Island. If we leave tomorrow at eleven, we should still have time to get the tour of the research station before we go."

"Not so fast, young lady! I will get back to you with my findings." And off the captain went.

Annie and Mara rolled their eyes at each other but wisely stayed quiet. After an hour or two, Georgio came back to report. "It seems your young man has a solid reputation, and I hear Ayers Rock is supposed to be very inspirational."

Mara tentatively asked Annie, "Are you sure you want me to come along? I am perfectly content to continue working on my painting. This whole area is beautiful. We used to come dive here while we were in Byron Bay studying."

Her current painting was one that delighted Annie with memories of their cave explorations. Annie said, "Bring it with you. We have just begun our friendship, and I am not eager to waste a moment of this experience."

Jonathan was waiting for them by the helicopter with his ever-present best friend, Roscoe, his white bulldog. The dog was pure grit and a perfect companion for Jonathan. A big strapping man of well over six feet, he towered over Annie and Mara. But when he smiled that big grin with that unruly shock of light-brown hair, Annie laughed at how he made them feel at ease.

Mara wasn't used to dogs and tentatively asked, "Is he coming with us?"

"Roscoe goes everywhere with me, love. I know at first he can have a somewhat intimidating manner, but once he gets to know you, then you will see his loyal and playful side."

Arriving at the airport in Gladstone, he grinned and asked, "Have you ever been on a biplane? You are about to leave urban towns behind and venture into the inner belly of this country. Are you ready?"

Annie and Mara both said, "YES!"

One look at the open-air biplane and Annie felt she had gone back in time. A handsome combination of green body and tan wings, the plane would seat the four of them (including Roscoe) up front and the pilot behind them. Roscoe looked sheepishly at Mara, eager to sit next to her, but Jonathan buckled him into the seat next to him. Annie and Mara exchanged a look of anticipation, excitement, and absolute fear!

They were next introduced to their pilot, Gregory. He saw their look and tried to put them at ease.

"Think of it as a bit like riding a motorcycle up in the sky! Now suit up!"

Mara asked, "Is it safe?"

"Aye, I have been flying over twenty years. I'll see to your safety!" Gregory answered.

Jonathan reassured Mara they would be fine, and his genuine smile seemed to calm her.

They got on their goggles and helmets. Before they boarded, Gregory took a picture of the four of them ready to fly. In the air, the rush of the wind and the views made for a spectacular ride! Once they arrived at the Ayers Rock

Airport, Uluru, Jonathan took the girls to the Pioneer Lodge. Very rustic and relaxed, the owners greeted their party with enthusiastic Aussie hospitality.

Mara couldn't wait to pull out her canvas and paints. She had never seen anything like this. Still a while before sunset, Jonathan took Annie horseback riding around the area. She could see Ayers Rock in the background and couldn't wait to hear more about it that evening. He said he had a special treat planned for them...an evening called "Sounds of Silence." Riding through the area had what could only be called a mystical effect.

Annie shared with Jonathan, "History has always been a fascination of mine. I feel the energy here in this place. Thank you for bringing us!"

Jonathan grinned. "You're welcome, Annie. Your friend seems quite talented. Hopefully she can capture the essence of this place on her canvas."

Jonathan's excitement about his surprise showed when he and Roscoe arrived to pick up Annie and Mara. He had chosen Ayers Rock at sunset for them to hear the stories of its great spiritual and cultural significance. Outside, an Aboriginal guide was waiting for them.

During their transfer, the guide began, "It is more than just a rock. Named Uluru, it is a living cultural landscape. It is said spirits of Aborigines ancestral beings continue to reside in this sacred place."

Fascinated, Annie continued to listen. "The Anangu people belong to the oldest culture known to man dating back sixty thousand years! There is strong belief their culture has always existed in central Australia and that this landscape was created at the beginning of time by the travels of great ancestral tribes. There's actual evidence found here showing this rock was a place used for traditional ceremonies and rites of passage for over ten thousand years."

They were taken to a remote sand dune. As they walked to the top with the rhythmic humming of an ancient didgeridoo, the oldest wind instrument known, in the background, they were greeted by Uluru, almost black against a darkening sky. They were taken to the highest point and seated at their table with a 360-degree view of the sacred landmark and the surrounding area. The sun began to set, giving a spectacular red glow to this impressive discovery for Annie. She could feel the history and ponder, much like in her own journey, the travels and wanderlust of these ancient people. She knew what she would add to her journal:

> *Is it an inherent restlessness that resides in humans who are aware and amazed by what surrounds them? Were there always individuals in ancient civilizations who wanted to venture out to understand those of other cultures?*

Seeing Annie lost in her musings, Jonathan was pleased. There was a great deal to learn from this country.

Mara took pictures to capture the beauty of the sky over Uluru awash with brilliant colors. She would use them to transfer the scene to her painting. When dinner arrived, they were served a creative selection of dishes, including crocodile, kangaroo, *barramundi* (sea bass), and *quandong* (native peach). Each was paired with the perfect Australian wine. After dinner, as the guide began to tell ancient stories of the constellations above in the star-filled southern sky, Jonathan ordered them a cognac with native wattleseed-infused hot chocolate.

What a night! I feel like I am exploding with the magnitude of this experience. Annie couldn't wait to write about it in her journal.

Jonathan filled the next days with descriptions of the spectacular landscape and wide varieties of wildlife. Mara came with them on occasion but seemed quite happy wandering the area and painting. Horseback riding with Jonathan was filled with energy and excitement, but when he showed her how to wrestle a crocodile, she was overwhelmed! As always, Roscoe was right there by his side with his floppy ears and sturdy build.

Annie's journal told of her growing respect for Jonathan and the outback. Jonathan's easy-going attention had been a welcome respite as he led her through the country the Aussies knew as "the Back of Beyond." Since Annie was not looking for romance, having been distracted by both Ramone and El Amir, she was thrilled by the discoveries each day brought, and Jonathan was a most enjoyable companion. The wilderness of Australia's backcountry would forever be entwined in her memory with Jonathan's rugged, good-natured charm. But her mind continued to turn introspective. She missed how often Jonathan suggested Mara come along with them or watched her painting over her shoulder.

Chapter 11

Back to Marbella

When it was time for them to leave, Jonathan took them back to the small airport. This time they were taking a small commuter plane. Mara and Annie reluctantly said goodbye. Neither of them would forget these past days. Jonathan gave Annie a giant hug and kiss on the cheek. The goodbye with Mara took a little longer.

On the flight, Annie said, "Mara, I am so glad you have been here to share this. Such an experience...all of it. Your friendship means much to me, and I know we will see each other again."

Mara hugged her new friend. "You are a fascinating woman, Annie, on this compelling journey, and your perspective truly inspires me. It has been a privilege to be here and spend time with you. There is no need to wish you fair winds and following seas. Your strength and attitude ensure that."

> *I have made two more true friends. Both Jonathan and Mara are in my circle, and I pledge to keep them close. I feel so blessed. Is this the gratitude I am searching for?*

Georgio was anxiously waiting for them. The extra time they had spent in the outback took away the time they had planned in Sydney. The *Majestique* was overdue in Sydney, so they made haste to get there. Mara's flight to Bali was first.

Looking at her captain and crew, Annie knew it was time for her to leave as well. She thanked them all for allowing her to travel with them and making both Annie and Mara feel so at home on board. As she stepped onshore for a final stroll before her drive to the airport, a messenger holding a single red rose approached her. "This came for you."

She instantly recognized the handwriting on the note. It was Ramone's. *How does he continually find me?*

> *'It is time, querida. Come home to Marbella. You've been away far too long, and I want to see you again. Ramone'*

Annie folded the note, smelled the rose, and looked out at the sea. It beckoned her, as always, but which port held her answers? When it was finally made, Annie's decision to return to Marbella brought with it a renewed exhilaration. At the beginning and now at the end, this journey found Annie solo; but along the way, the friends she was making certainly did not allow her to feel alone. Annie looked at the plane ticket Ramone had left for her in Zanzibar. Suddenly she was anxious to get back to Andalusia. She could almost hear her grandfather saying, "Use the ticket, Annie. Come home to Marbella."

Her recent experiences had covered continents and multiple cultures. The encounters along this journey began with an irresistible Spanish matador, moved on to a mysterious Moroccan, then to her new artist friends Sarah and Mara, and finally to her time with a dapper and insightful outback guide.

> *Did this combination of incredible events bring some universal understanding? Such a complex question with such a significant meaning. Perhaps not, but when a woman knows what she truly possesses, her life can*

never be ordinary. The landscape of her days
becomes sweeping and fluid.

And with sudden excitement, Annie could not wait to reunite with her matador! A quick pen of a note:

> *'Ramone, at long last, I am returning*
> *to Marbella. You are right—it is time.*
> *Grandfather has called on me to help at the*
> *villa while Tomás is abroad. So I am finally*
> *using your ticket. We've much to catch up on.*
> *You know where to find me. Annie'*

The long flight gave Annie plenty of time to reflect on where she had started and how far she had come. In her heart, she knew her journey wasn't over, but she had taken far too much advantage of Dom and Gennie's generosity. And it was time for her to give back. Thinking about a reunion with her grandparents made her smile, but with her father still missing and her mother home in Maine alone, there remained obstacles to overcome. Surely she needed to get back to the task of learning her father's whereabouts.

Annie's arrival at the villa was filled with joy at not only seeing her grandparents but also the intriguing prospect of renewing things with a certain matador. She smelled the roses before she saw them and smiled. Attached was a note:

> *'Annie, I have rearranged my schedule to*
> *take advantage of the time when you are not*
> *working at the villa. Meet me at the open-air*
> *restaurant by the port. They have a special*
> *menu tonight, and then there is dancing at the*
> *club next door. Yours, Ramone'*

As Annie readied for the evening, she thoughtfully chose the long red dress. This brilliant shade of red had become

synonymous to Annie's perception of Ramone and his con-
tinuous choice of long-stem red roses. It was a color that
also gave great pleasure to her, and she was happy to recip-
rocate. And when she saw his gaze at the dress she had chosen, she knew it had been no mistake. Over a meal of delicious table-side paella with delicacies fresh from the sea and
a bottle of bubbling prosecco, Annie and Ramone caught up
on the last several months. It was strange to realize they had
known each other much longer than merely for that simple
date after the bullfight that became a "night to remember."

It didn't take long for the two of them to settle into a
compatible rhythm and find the connection they had on that
first night. On her off-hours, they took time to take strolls
through the white villages along the southern coast, stop for
tapas and coffees at sidewalk cafés, and spend lazy hours on
private beaches.

Romance was in the air, but Annie's heart was holding
back. Zanzibar remained a mystery to her, and she admitted
she was not pleased he had left her there alone.

"Ramone, how is it you always seem to know how to
find me when I am away? And why do you never talk about
your family? And Zanzibar? What business keeps urgently
needing your attention if it is not your schedule as a matador?" Annie asked.

"Ahh, *querida*, so many questions! Can you not just
enjoy our time together? You will find your answers soon
enough."

The next day after she finished at the villa, Annie wandered down to the beach. Why was she feeling restless again
so soon? Was it this mystery and unanswered questions that
surrounded Ramone? Seemingly out of nowhere, a young
boy found her and delivered a single red rose with a note
asking her to join Ramone for tapas that afternoon, followed
by a renowned performance of flamenco. With a smile,
Annie thanked the young man and told him she would be
there. As she walked pensively along the shoreline, she won-

dered what could be causing this melancholy. Was it her mom home alone in Maine or the question of her father's whereabouts? She missed them both terribly. Or was it the continuing unknown about Sabine? She felt she had come to terms with the accident but still worried about her. Or was it those haunting golden eyes that tempted her dreams in her sleeping hours? Her journey had held so many memorable moments that affected her deeply. *What is missing?*

Before her rendezvous with Ramone that afternoon, she took her grandfather aside.

"Dom, you and Gennie have been so amazing to me! I cannot begin to thank you enough for my time here and on the incredible journey I experienced. How could I not be ready to settle in one place?"

Dom took her hand and smiled knowingly. "The young matador is not enough to keep you homebound. Is that it?"

Annie thought for a moment. "I don't think it's that, but I know so little about him. What do you know of his background?"

"Unfortunately, I know what most people know...that Ramone Sanchez is revered throughout most of Spain for his legendary bullfighting skills. His younger brother is also a well-known bullfighter. I do not think his father was a *torero*, but I heard his uncle and grandfather were also legendary," Dom answered.

Annie hesitantly broached the subject, "Dom, I know I traveled halfway around the globe because of your generosity, but I felt so alive during that journey."

"Ahh, and you know the captain is due back with *Porto Banus* soon," Dom said.

Suddenly ashamed, Annie blurted out, "No, no, I am so sorry! It would be far too presumptuous of me to think I could go away so soon! You have already been generous beyond words."

Before Dom could answer, Tomás came bounding in the door. "I am finally back and have great news! Where is

Gennie? I need you all here. We should have a toast!"

Annie went to get Gennie, catching some of Tomás's excitement.

When they were all settled in the library, Tomás began, "As you know, I have been traveling in Europe to visit Dom's properties, and one of my destinations was Ireland. I met this girl, Meghan, last summer on holiday in Capri. She is from the Dingle Peninsula on the west coast of Ireland. It seemed a good idea on this trip to detour and visit her. We had corresponded about Dingle, and Meghan very much impressed me. So I thought I would explore it a little. I spent a week there, then she accompanied me to Scotland, showing me around a bit. By the end of the trip, I knew we were meant to be together, and I proposed. She said yes! And guess what! I already checked with Aunt Celeste, and the wedding will be in Maine next spring."

Gennie piped in with a smile, "Well, it is about time, *mon petit-fils*." Laughter and congratulations overtook the room, and champagne was flowing.

Tomás pulled Annie aside. "But there is one thing more, cousin...Meghan heard there is a Scottish colonel who might have some knowledge of your father."

Shaken to the core, Annie asked, "Did you speak with him?"

"No," Tomás replied, "unfortunately, the colonel now frequents the exclusive Royal and Ancient Golf Club of St. Andrews, and we did not have the authority to gain access to the club or even the golf course."

Looking back at Dom, Annie asked, "Can you make arrangements for me to get me in?"

Equally interested in the news, Dom thoughtfully replied, "Let me talk to a few people and see what I can do."

When Annie met Ramone that afternoon, she was more distracted than ever. Ramone studied her face as they ate.

"Your beauty rivals the rose, sweet one, yet there seems to be sadness in your eyes."

Annie's eyes welled up, and Ramone gently wiped away a tear. Annie told him about Tomás's engagement but also that there might be someone who could shed some insight about her father's whereabouts. Unfortunately, she didn't know if she could reach him.

Suddenly a little tense, Ramone asked, "*Querida*, tell me what this place is where you cannot go to."

When Annie sadly replied, "The St. Andrews Golf Club," Ramone gently laughed.

"But I can take you there, *querida*. My uncle has an old membership they still honor. After the weekend's *corrida de toros*, I shall take you!"

Excitedly Annie said with amazement, "YES!"

Chapter 12

Marbella to Scotland

Annie enjoyed the lavish spectacle of bullfighting only when Ramone was center ring. Looking wildly attractive, he spotted her almost immediately and acknowledged her with a subtle nod of his head. As always, he remained focused on the highly ritualized fight at hand. The bull charged into the ring, and Ramone began to test him for his ferocity with waves of his magenta-and-gold cape. Following was a series of passes to observe the quirks and behavior of the bull. Ramone had described this part, but only now in watching did she understand the dance. From there, the goal was to get the bull hurt and angry, thereby making the final matador fight so dangerous. After an intense battle won, Ramone left the ring with a tip of his hat and toss of a rose to Annie.

To Annie, Ramone's fierce fighting skills were in total contrast to the gentleness he showed her. Yet his confidence was ever-present, and she marveled at that. Telling her grandparents she was going to Scotland got Dom telling some of his old stories again of "Scottish music, swirling kilts, and colorful folk dancing."

Tomás heard Dom's story and sat down to join them. "Annie, I really want you to meet Meghan and come to our wedding. We discussed having it there in Ireland or here at the villa in Marbella. But we both love the idea of getting married in Maine! That way, Aunt Celeste can be at the wedding. Besides, Dom and Gennie are long overdue for a trip back to the States. Promise you'll try to look up Meghan while you are in the region." Annie assured him she would.

Packing had become second nature to Annie. But her blood had become accustomed to the warm tropical climate of Andalusia and her recent travels, so dressing for chillier weather sent her shopping for a few heavier wraps and boots. A quick note to Celeste gave Annie pause, not wanting to get her mother's hopes up about news of her father. She tactfully skirted around the purpose of the trip—simply a rare opportunity to see Scotland and one of the most exclusive golf clubs in the world!

The morning Ramone was to pick her up, Annie received a note from him, mysteriously saying:

> *'Dearest Annie, my business calls, but I will find a way to make it to Scotland to meet you. I will miss traveling with you but will see you soon. Ramone'*

Why does he keep doing this? A driver pulled up to gather her luggage. Settled into the back seat for the ride to Malaga, she saw another note on the seat:

> *'Please do not be disappointed, querida. I thought of a way to make it up to you and have arranged a much-coveted opportunity to play a round of golf at St. Andrews!'*

He knew she was an avid golfer and that this would surely tempt her. She composed her next journal entry:

> *So here I am traveling toward this unpredictable man who can kill bulls. I must admit, rational thinking has quite left me...especially if there is a chance I can find out about my father. All I can think of is, why not? There must be a hundred reasons why not, yet I*

can't think of one! After all, living without an agenda is part of the lesson, n'est-ce pas? I plan to find out what I can about my father… hopefully this matador is good with his word. But if not, I will find my own way to reach the colonel.

The train ride to Madrid was always a delight to Annie with the rolling countryside. She couldn't fathom how many olive trees she saw along the way and could understand why a bowl of Spanish olives was included in every tapa's serving. Her flight from Madrid was uneventful, but landing in Edinburgh, Annie's anticipation of her meeting Ramone here in this foreign place grew. He, as promised, was waiting for her to gather her baggage.

Dashingly handsome with his coal-black hair and deep-set brown eyes, Ramone swept Annie off to an Edinburgh street festival. The streets were a veritable carnival, and Annie couldn't help but think of Dom's stories about this place. She enjoyed the assembly of bands and bagpipes gathered from throughout the British Isles…a perfect afternoon with a lone piper finale. Annie had no clue how Ramone had made it there before her or that he had already arranged separate rooms in a small lodge, but she decided to simply accept it. There was much about this man that eluded her.

Annie awoke to a perfect golden day. Sporting her new cooler-weather golf attire, she was ready when Ramone knocked on her door. Her excitement mounted—not only the chance to play such a legendary course but also the opportunity to meet a friend of her father's! As they teed up on the first hole, Annie could tell Ramone was assessing her ability before showing his own skill. Fortunately, her father was an excellent golfer and had taught Annie at a young age, so she was pleased to hold her own. She sensed Ramone was still holding back a bit and raised her eyebrows in a somewhat flirtatious challenge. *Why does this man always seem to be watching me and biding his time? There is something off. I'm flattered, of course, but I'm not sure I embrace such scrutiny.*

At the turn, Ramone went into the clubhouse to quickly speak with the manager and returned, saying, "Colonel MacGregor will join us for a late lunch when we finish."

Annie replied with her heart unexpectedly racing, "That is perfect. Let's hurry."

When, at last, they entered the distinguished dining room, a charming chap with a natty look and tweed jacket walked up to join them. Thankfully, Ramone started the conversation at a comfortable pace, and Annie could tell the colonel was impressed with his bullfighting reputation. "I thought you looked very familiar." The colonel then shifted his attention to Annie, asking about her time in Spain.

Finally, he sat back with a smile and said, "Lassie, you are the spitting image of your father, but of course you know that."

"Yes, I've heard that." Annie nodded. She knew her father had been a British diplomat assigned to North Africa and had an exceptional reputation, but she knew little about the years he served with British Special Forces while he was away.

The colonel spoke fondly of her father and shared tales of their golfing experiences and "sharing a few pints." As she listened, Annie once again felt that sense of destiny or instinct that she was learning to trust. And it was clear this was not over for her and that the colonel was not sharing all he knew. After Scotland, Annie planned to move on to England. She wanted to explore her British heritage, see her paternal grandparents, and perhaps learn more about her elusive father. Although Ramone observed, he remained strangely silent on the subject.

After they all said their goodbyes, Annie was determined to enjoy the rest of her time in Scotland and the attention of her handsome companion. Ramone took her to the high rock fortress that was Edinburgh Castle. She was fascinated by not only its architecture but also its dark and colorful history that held most of the chronology of Scotland itself. Home of royal murders and births, it had been infamous since early medieval times.

Exiting the tour of the castle, Annie and Ramone strolled toward a festival taking place on the grounds. Annie delighted in the celebration of music, dance, and military pageantry. There had to have been a thousand musicians, pipers, singers, and dancers performing on the esplanade! And as the event came to an end, a spotlight shined on a single piper, high on the castle ramparts, playing a haunting lament. As Ramone pulled Annie close, a mass chorus of "Auld Lang Syne" began. Fireworks flared overhead, followed by a military flyover to close the remarkable show.

Annie looked at Ramone with pure amazement and said, "How could an evening like this be more perfect? I will remember it always."

Ramone kissed her hand and replied, "I will as well, *querida*. But I have one more surprise."

He led her to a small pub to share a plate of *haggis* (savory meat pudding), mashed potatoes, and turnips. Oh, and a little taste of local whiskey!

"*Querida*, I saw the look on your face while the colonel was speaking about your father. It is good you plan to go to his home in Yorkshire. I understand this journey is one you need to do alone to get some closure, so I will reluctantly return to Marbella tomorrow. There is much I need to prepare for the upcoming Caballos en Plaza de Toros in Ronda. Perhaps you will be back by then?"

Annie was beginning to have feelings for this man who always seemed to read her so well. As she held both his hands across the table and leaned in to kiss him, a lone singer stepped up on-stage and began the most beautiful and emotional rendition of "Caledonia" Annie had ever heard. The singer was perhaps somewhat plain-looking on the outside, but the amazing voice that came out of this woman brought tears to Annie's eyes as she listened to verse after beautiful verse.

Ramone kissed away her tears and said, "I do not want to be a stranger, *querida*. You have not ended your journey yet, and I am prepared to be patient. I wrote this for you. Keep it close as you travel." He handed her a handwritten note that said:

> *'Sailing maiden, thornless rose. Adventurous heart the sea best knows. The same love that draws me to you lets me set you free. Your journey's end waits next to me.'*

She held the note to her heart and allowed herself a moment of romantic indulgence. But Ramone was right. Their time had not yet come. She got a copy of the "Caledonia" song to put in her journal. As they walked to their lodging and kissed good night, their lips lingered.

Just another moment. She certainly knew of his discipline in the ring but was surprised indeed of how strong it was at her door.

As she closed the door behind her and took a deep breath to clear her mind, Annie reflected on the earlier lunch and what Colonel MacGregor had shared of her father. Granted, most of the colonel's jovial conversation had been outrageous military anecdotes and hearsay, but he knew much more than her. And he had mentioned an old friend of her father's living in London, Ernest Wilbanks, a noted jazz saxophonist. That was where she would begin.

The morning Annie was to say goodbye to Ramone, a package arrived at her door, crudely wrapped in brown paper with her name written in large scrawling print. Annie waited to open it at breakfast with Ramone. When she did, Annie found an old leather-bound portfolio filled to overflowing with equally old papers.

A note from the colonel was attached and read:

> *'I had to sleep on it, lassie, but I'm assured now, you should be havin' this. It belongs to your father, and I'm thinking he would agree it's time you knew about him. You will find your father's friend at the Dolphin Brasserie on Chichester Street in London, but please be careful.'*

Ramone read the note and saw Annie's excitement. Finally, he said, "*Querida*, do you not think there might be a reason your father hasn't contacted you? Will you at least promise me to ask Captain Luis to bring the *Porto Banus* to meet you there? I would feel better if he was close by."

Annie assured Ramone. But she also pledged to herself, remembering the times in Portugal and Morocco when she felt someone was watching her, that she would stay alert.

As promised, Annie sent a message to Captain Luis, copying her grandfather, that she would appreciate him bringing the *Porto Banus* to whatever port was close to London.

As she was about to leave, she got a note:

> *'Received. Will be in the port of Southampton by mid next week.'*

That resolved, Annie booked her train ride to London and said goodbye to a town that had truly touched her...the people, the history, and its soul. Edinburgh had secured a very special place in her heart.

Chapter 13

London, England

When Annie was in Tanzania, Sarah had mentioned she could find Annie a place to stay if she ever found herself in London. Knowing Sarah had an international phone, Annie took a chance and called to tell her she was on the way to London.

Sarah picked up and, when hearing the news, said, "Oh, what great timing. I am in London now, gathering my paintings for an art show. Hate these things, but it's got to be done, right?"

Smiling, Annie said, "I can't believe you will be there. I have some things I need to do, but I want to see you!"

"Come stay with me. I insist. I have plenty of room, and we need to catch up," Sarah implored.

Feeling that fate had stepped in yet again, she answered, "Of course, tell me the address. I'll be there."

Annie didn't arrive in London until early evening. She knew if she went to the flat first, she would get caught up reuniting with Sarah. She had to do this while she had the courage. The smell of old leather and smoke met Annie as she entered the English pub. Glancing around, she hoped she had made the right decision to come here alone. Guessing the sax player on stage was Ernest, she enjoyed the set, then went up to introduce herself.

Friendly but with the reserve of a typical Londoner, Ernest was reluctant to discuss her father. With some cajoling, he talked but then added a warning, "Careful, luv, or you may find out more than you want to know."

It was clear after the brief conversation that Ernest was all about getting back to his sax. Annie, puzzled by the conversation, left to find her friend's apartment. What she missed was his piercing stare as she walked out the door.

Upon arriving at the flat, the two friends hugged, thrilled at being together again! Both were talking at once, each wanting to know what had been going on in the other's life.

Annie finally got a chance to ask, "Sarah, why are you here? I am so excited to see you!"

Sarah began, "I'm here for an art show at a rather well-known gallery. It's at the end of the week. It is a busy process to prepare! By the way, I want to thank you for taking Mara with you to Australia. She said the two of you had the most amazing experiences. Plus, she told me of a certain outback guide. Do tell!"

Annie laughed freely. Her banter with Sarah came so easy. "Mara is now a lifelong friend like you, and it is me who should thank you for bringing us together. You were right: Bali was magical! As for Jonathan, he is such a man's man with a jovial nature and kind heart, full of interesting history about the outback and Australia. The marine research he does is quite fascinating. You would like him. I truly enjoyed my time with them both."

Annie paused for a moment and casually asked, "So have you seen El Amir recently? You two seem to be so close."

Annie wasn't prepared for her answer. "Well, as a matter of fact, he is due here in two days to meet me." Sarah smiled as she answered.

El Amir coming here? Annie threw in a question, "Do you two have business together? I never asked, but are you two in a relationship?"

This time it was Sarah that laughed. "A relationship? Hardly. He had eyes for no one else but you when we were all together. He is the most significant sponsor of my work. El Amir was a patron of the London gallery where I worked during summers as a teenager. He thought I showed signs of talent and encouraged me to apply for a scholarship in Australia with Kenneth Patrick. Of course, I said yes, and it was there in Australia where I met Mara."

Contemplating the idea that so many destinies could be intertwined, Annie demurely asked, "Did he ever mention me after we parted?"

Sarah could read Annie's question behind the question. "El Amir says very little regarding personal matters. I know he did not want you to leave, my friend, but he has not mentioned you further."

Annie accepted that and went on to tell Sarah about the unbelievable time in Scotland and the meeting with the colonel, which resulted in her being here in London to meet the jazz musician.

"I'm hoping to learn more of my father's whereabouts."

Sarah thought for a moment. "You're not speaking of the sax player at the Dolphin Brasserie, are you?"

"Yes, as a matter of fact, I am. Why?" Annie asked.

Sarah said, "El Amir has mentioned him before. I think they've had some sort of dealings. Maybe he could help you get more information?"

Annie's thoughts were swirling. *Why would El Amir know this jazz player?*

But for now, it was time to focus on her hostess. "Sarah, did you bring your artwork here from Tanzania? What happens to prepare for an art show?"

Sarah replied, "Each painting has to be impeccably framed, and that costs money. The art gallery hosting the show makes many demands on the artist, and they do not help with the framing. I was encouraged to include other artistic media, and I hurried to include a bronze statue. While in Africa, I made a molding of a bucking male zebra out of wax and brought it here to be cast in bronze. It should be ready in a few days in time for the show. Normally, I would use a French bronze-casting process, but there was no time to get to Paris before the exhibition. If it were up to me and I didn't need the money, I would skip all this. It is definitely El Amir who runs a tight ship in this partnership!"

Happy to be back in Sarah's company, Annie offered to help with the art show however she could and finally retired for the night. Settled into her room, she tried to make some semblance of the people, the places, and the lessons encountered these last months. In her journal, she wrote:

> *For now, understanding is elusive. Faith and hope prevail to propel me to the next part of my journey. However, knowing that El Amir arrives shortly certainly put my cool reserve to the test.*

Sarah genuinely seemed thrilled to have Annie semi-supervising as she immediately acknowledged this part was not her forte. In fact, Sarah appeared to be running around in circles, stressing over how to make everything perfect.

Annie, with a wisdom that usually came from Dom, took Sarah and lightly shook both shoulders.

"Hey, stop. Don't you understand when life seems overwhelming and you're taking yourself and circumstances far too seriously, you need to stop for a minute? Now...find a reason to laugh. Laughter is a great stress-breaker and doesn't always have to be spontaneous. But perhaps when you force it into the moment, you've created your very own gift. So what shall we laugh about? Let's wager whether El Amir will come decked out in full Moroccan attire, or will he succumb to western influences while here?"

"Oh, he will probably come as a stodgy old benefactor." At that, the two of them laughed, and Sarah noticeably relaxed.

When El Amir finally did arrive, Annie was over in a far corner measuring a canvas and testing various color mats for the frame Sarah had selected. When she did turn around, she was certainly not expecting the dapper, slick-haired businessman who was talking to Sarah. Their eyes finally met, and there was a pause while each of them assessed who might make the first move.

But then Sarah bounded back toward Annie and whispered, "Told ya! Stodgy."

That was not the word she was thinking of, and she smiled. At that, El Amir strode toward her. They greeted each other formally.

El Amir finally loosened his demeanor a bit and said, "Annie, your timing is impeccable. Sarah is ready to display her art to the world but lacks the confidence to have the public scrutinize her work. I am sure you can help her. What brings you to London?"

"Actually," Annie replied, "there was some news about my father that brought me here to search for some clue as to his safety and whereabouts." Remembering Sarah said El Amir might know the musician, she added, "I went to visit Ernest Wilbanks, a jazz musician at the Dolphin Brasserie. Sarah said you might know him."

Before they could continue, Sarah bounded in with so many questions (with a wink at Annie) that El Amir turned his full attention to her. Annie went back to her framing. Later they would determine where the framed pieces would go.

There were glances caught between the two of them, and Annie truthfully wondered which of them was doing the gazing. She couldn't say she was surprised that there was a note on her door when she went back to the flat:

> 'Annie, meet me for breakfast, and do not go
> back to the Brasserie alone. There are many
> things there that lie below the surface. Come
> tomorrow. El Amir'

Chapter 14

Breakfast with El Amir

Ernest's cautionary warning kept circling her mind. Was there, indeed, a reason her father was keeping them in the dark? Annie pulled out the leather portfolio for the hundredth time. It was filled with handwritten papers that looked more like memories and unimportant documents. Why hadn't she thought to ask why the colonel had it? The other notes and materials in the portfolio did nothing to enlighten her father's mysterious military career or his current whereabouts. Had her father given it to the colonel for some reason?

A feeling of incompletion settled over her. Then turning it over, she noticed a crease in the leather on the back. There appeared to be a false backing. Annie studied it and eventually was able to pry it open. Two old papers, folded multiple times, were behind the leather. She pulled the first one out. It was a pen-and-ink sketch of a compass, and next to it, an etching of what eerily looked like a rendering of the *Porto Banus*!

Recognizing her father's writing, beside the drawing were the words: *My safety is in question.* Then there was a section smudged beyond recognition, but on the other side, she could barely make out *My darling daughter Annie.*

Annie was more confused than ever. That was certainly enough to have her attention; but it was the second paper, an old faded photograph, that made her heart skip a beat. It was unmistakably her father, younger and ever-dashing in his dress uniform, but he was not alone. She recognized the colonel and thought she could identify a younger version of Ernest. But the dark military-clad figure in the background looked strangely familiar. Annie let out a gasp! *Ramone?*

Rationally, she knew that was impossible. Ramone was far too young to be included in this older photo, yet the striking resemblance was undeniable. What did El Amir want to speak with her about, and why shouldn't she go back to the Brasserie alone? There were so many questions! Annie knew sleep would be elusive but she closed her eyes, trying to breathe deeply, thinking of her lessons in Africa, Thailand, Bali, and Australia. She thought about how grounded Jonathan McNamara was and wished for a moment he was there to reason with her. Hopefully, El Amir would help unravel which path to pursue, but what was his role in all of this? Trust was something Annie typically gave freely. However, she wisely decided to ensure this time her trust was justified.

After a few fitful hours of sleep, Annie reached for her second cup of tea and mentally tried to prepare herself for what the day would bring. Dressed conservatively in a long khaki skirt and blue chambray shirt, Annie instinctively added a scarf at the neck for a bit of color. Intrigue was not part of Annie's plan, but the question she could not escape was about her father's safety. Pulling out her journal, she made a quick entry:

> *I never thought to question whether he was safe, just where he was and when he would be home. This new realization about his potential jeopardy has shifted my perception and sense of urgency.*

Entering the café in St. John's Square, the aromas coming from freshly baked croissants with pumpkin and hazelnut and doughnuts infused with pistachio custard assailed

Annie's senses. For a moment, she was distracted from the man staring at her from the corner table. But as if by magnetic pull, her glance found him. He didn't look as formal as he had in the studio. The casual headdress was back on, and a slight smile warmed his eyes. *What was it about this man that so mesmerized her?*

He rose when Annie approached the table to help with her chair and said, "Good morning, I am glad you decided to come."

Seated, Annie ordered a clementine coffee and watched as El Amir sipped his saffron Bellini. She lowered her eyes and said, "I have many questions."

El Amir responded, "I will tell you what I know, but there are parts of the story that are unknown to me and my sources." Once the food was served, he began, "Your father's reputation as a diplomatic and military icon is widespread. He was assigned to North Africa for several years, and it was during that time he worked side by side with people I know. They respected him, but there were times your father would disappear for days or weeks. There were many whispers about him. Usually, just before he would be gone, several other military men would arrive to meet with him. My people took note of his absences. Then suddenly your father packed up and left North Africa without a word. The news got to us that he might have gone underground while moving his family out of Spain. I have to assume that was you and your mother."

Annie silently nodded, then said, "Yes, but he didn't stay with us. I remember the vivid stories he told me about his time in North Africa. He seemed to love it there. But after such a short time, he was gone again."

"Over the years, he came back to North Africa several times. Was he often gone after he took you to the States?" El Amir asked.

"Yes, many times, but this time he has been gone for over two years! Something doesn't seem right," Annie replied.

"There was a rumor," El Amir continued. "A mole was buried deep within his group. My sources do not know your father's whereabouts, but they do know of some of his associates. It is for this reason I want you to use caution in going to the Brasserie."

Then quietly El Amir reached his hand across the table, barely touching hers and defying tradition. "Tell me, Annie. What do you honestly know of this Spanish matador that pursues you?"

Looking up at him in surprise, she asked, "How do you know about him?"

His eyes studied her while he gently asked, "So this man has your heart?"

All at once, Annie needed air and to escape this scrutiny. "I—I have to go. Sarah is waiting for me. Thank you for breakfast."

"The pleasure was mine, Annie. I will see you at the gallery later. In the meantime, stay aware of your surroundings."

Raw nerves, edgy pacing...that was how Annie found Sarah when she entered the studio behind the gallery. Ironically, those same emotions echoed in her own restless soul. The meeting with El Amir was unsettling and disturbing, with her list of ever-growing questions rotating through her mind. She tried to shake it off. For now, the focus needed to be on Sarah and a successful exhibition. Only hours away, it was time to move Sarah's artwork to the gallery to hang in their predesignated spots.

Annie gave Sarah a good shake and said, "You've got this! The paintings you create are a gift to those fortunate enough to see them. Allow the willingness to expose yourself and your work to open you to the viewer's appreciation."

Annie went over to her bag and pulled out a stone she usually kept with her. As she put it in Sarah's hand, Annie gently said with a wisdom that surprised herself, "This stone is amethyst, referred to as the 'metamorphosis stone'...an ancient healer of mind, body, and soul. I found it in Bali. This gallery thinks enough of your talent to showcase it. Let this stone help you find a sense of clarity and feeling of renewal as you take this leap of faith. Enjoy this moment and allow the course of your life to take a step toward its destiny."

The gallery was bustling with activity as paintings were hung and preparations completed. However, Annie immediately felt a tingle along her spine and glanced up as El Amir finally made his appearance. Dressed formally again, his austere demeanor enhanced Annie's state of uneasy apprehension. Yet she was determined to see her friend through her evening. Annie and Sarah went back to the flat to change while El Amir attended to final details. Annie chose a long strapless sheath in a brilliant shade of aquamarine and a stunning necklace of matching glass bobbles. Her hair was swept back and sleek, and the look was finished with high strappy heels. When they arrived back at the gallery, and El Amir saw her, his eyes told her she had chosen wisely.

Annie was so proud of her friend. Through all her nerves, Sarah somehow found the serenity and inner strength to graciously accept the continual flow of compliments, and almost her entire collection sold during the show.

As the evening began to wind down, Sarah found Annie and said, "Thank you for being here and sharing this with me. You are such a dear friend!" Sarah reached for a rolled canvas behind the desk. "I held this painting back and would love for you to have it with my gratitude for all you did."

Annie studied the small painting of the two zebras interacting on an African plain, then sighed, "It is beautiful, Sarah!"

Sarah continued, "Look closely. Although their stripes may be different on the outside, their inner nature is entwined with each other. That is like us, Annie. You may leave tomorrow, but know that I will never be far from your side." With a huge hug and misty eyes, the friends said good night.

El Amir had kept his distance most of the evening, but now that Annie was retrieving her wrap to leave, he was at her side.

"Annie, Sarah said you were leaving."

"Yes," Annie quietly replied, "when I was at the Brasserie, Ernest mentioned my father had returned home to Yorkshire to spend a good deal of his time near his parents. I have called my grandparents and a few old family friends there to tell them I plan to visit. I want to explore the area to get a sense of my father."

El Amir's piercing eyes burned into her as he said, "Would you like me to accompany you?"

Annie hesitated for a moment before replying, "There are too many unanswered questions and complications surrounding my life right now. I need time to sort through what is happening around me."

El Amir nodded. "You know my feelings for you are deep and filled with passion. You have awakened a tenderness in me I can't explain. I see in your eyes you have feelings for me as well. With my culture, it is complicated. There are traditions that must be obeyed. But know, visions of the natural beauty you so easily exude are permanently etched in my mind. Take the time you need, but be diligent in the paths that you choose, Annie."

For a moment, Annie didn't realize her breath was on hold. It was the gasp she finally let loose that betrayed her calm when she realized temptation was staring at her.

Chapter 15

Yorkshire, England to Dingle, Ireland

It would be easy for Annie to get caught up in the turbulence of what she had learned, but she knew getting back to the sea would soothe her like nothing else. Captain Luis and the *Porto Banus* were not due in the English Sound until next week. Now seemed the perfect time to take the train to York to visit her paternal grandparents to see if her father's childhood home held any clues about his disappearance.

Alex had been born in York, but Ernest mentioned her father returned often while he was assigned to North Africa. So arriving at the train station, Annie took a cab to the rambling Yorkshire estate with a mission. In the spontaneous way Annie had about her, knowing the beautiful horses her grandparents groomed, she wrote:

> *At the very least, if nothing turns up on my father, I will see my grandparents and get in some excellent riding!*

Annie forgot how long it had been since her last visit. Being back, she was reminded of how much she enjoyed the Yorkshire moors and the refined trappings of gentry life, the source of many childhood memories. Tears of joy fell when Annie reunited with Henry and Trudy, or Papa and Nana to her. Somehow, she found comfort with them, considering her new quest. Just the sight of her grandfather, an older version of her father, gave her such pleasure. She could pause for a moment to breathe in this refuge. The research and questions could wait. Annie let herself melt into days of morning rides and afternoon teas. When her grandmother served high tea on her cheery rose-covered china, it made Annie smile at the memories it evoked when she and Sabine would visit.

After several days, Annie interspersed her research with side trips to York's historical sights. York's Minster, the most beautiful Gothic church in England, brought out the architect in her, and she studied it for hours. Later, she strolled through the Shambles, York's colorful and beautifully preserved medieval quarter. Her love of history and architecture made this area very absorbing. However, there was a moment in the quarter when Annie's consciousness went on full alert. Looking around, she saw no one, but a sense of apprehension stayed with her. Changing her direction toward the ancient library, she thought she might find a clue there. But unfortunately, old town records and library archives turned up little of interest about her father or his military career. Returning heavyhearted to her grandparents' village on the moors, Annie was determined to speak further with them about her questions.

That evening, sitting in the library in front of a blazing fire and sipping a mug of ginger beer, Annie asked about her father's career. She handed Henry the photograph, pointing at the man who looked so much like Ramone. "Papa, do you happen to know this man standing behind my dad?"

"Oh, that chap is Salvador." exclaimed Henry upon seeing the photo. "He was your father's closest mate when they were in school." When asked if Salvador had a son, he scratched his head, glancing at Trudy, and said, "I don't recall a son. Salvador wasn't married the last time we saw him." Continuing, he said, "The boys were in boarding school together in Madrid, then the military, but eventually were given separate assignments. Alex was quiet about what he did. The only time Trudy and I saw him truly anxious was during his visit before he moved you and your mum to that small town in the States, but he was happier once he had you both settled over there. Your father loves you both very much."

Trudy added, "He always called us to let us know when he left on another of his 'missions.' Alex never hesitated to confront danger, especially when he felt he had a noble cause. That was a trait he had since he was a boy. About six months ago, we did receive a telegram assuring us of your father's safety but insisting we stay quiet about it. Shortly after, we heard from your mum that she had received the same cryptic message."

"What?" Annie exclaimed. "I didn't know anything about a telegram." Thinking back, that was about the time her mother encouraged her to go to Marbella. *Why wouldn't my mom have told me? I don't understand.*

Supposedly on a search for inner peace and balance, Annie was more confused than ever. As she studied her father's portfolio yet again, the documents she held did nothing to enlighten her father's mysterious and illustrious military career or his current whereabouts. Was he safe? The idea of a "mole" and the fact her father could be in danger gave her a purpose...to ensure her father's safety and bring him home. Who were these messages from that both her grandparents and mother received? As she looked at the photograph once more, Annie wrote:

> *Is it possible that Ramone is the son of this man, Salvador? The resemblance is haunting.*

Annie knew her time in England would end soon, and she spent her final day there riding and wandering the Yorkshire countryside with friends. Perhaps she was storing energy for the personal quest she knew lay ahead. Instinctively, she knew there was a connection between her elusive father, Salvador, and Ramone.

Annie received word Captain Luis and the *Porto Banus* were waiting for her in Southampton Bay. She sent word to the captain to have Roff pick her up at the station. Although it was hard to leave Papa and Nana, Annie felt strengthened and revitalized by a deep feeling of family and kinship when she bade them a bittersweet goodbye.

On the train, as Annie gazed out the window at the rolling English countryside, two things occurred to her while writing in her journal:

> *I have not fulfilled my promise to Tomás to meet Meghan, about to be his bride, and I am surprised that I have not heard from Ramone since that morning in Edinburgh. That seems strange.*

Despite the cloud of mystery, she gravitated back to Ramone's alluring presence. However, this would not stop her from confronting him with her new findings. For now, a promise was a promise. Southampton was not so far from Dingle Bay on Ireland's rugged west coast, and a little more time at sea might be a soothing distraction.

Once on board the *Porto Banus*, Annie sent a quick note to Meghan that she would soon be in the area for a few days and hoped to meet her.

Captain Luis maneuvered his vessel into the spectacular Dingle Bay while Annie marveled at the dozens of shades of green in the landscape, along with the colorful fishing boats that surrounded the harbor. Once they finished docking, Annie noticed a tall freckle-faced redhead walking toward them. She excitedly rushed off the ship to greet her, and it did not take long to realize she had just met another true friend. Meghan was classic Irish in her long tank dress in bold geometric earth tones. Tomás had chosen well.

Although a delightful and naturally beautiful woman, Meghan's lifelong passion was quite academic. While the two women walked along the pathway toward town in a light mist, Meghan told her of her work. As an Irish historian and founder of a Gaelic League, her work's purpose was to maintain the revival of the ancient Gaelic language and preserve all that is uniquely Irish.

Meghan's Ireland was the one Annie wanted to know, where warm, gregarious people still speak original Gaelic and pull the most out of life there. A land of romantic fairytale castles, sloping green farmlands, dramatic mountains, and quiet plains—Meghan's hometown of Dingle was called a "Gaeltacht," a cultural preserve where Old Irish was spoken and traditional dress, music, and lifestyles were nationally protected. There would be stories here she would be able to share with Dom.

Ireland's landscape was perfect for cycling, so Annie and Meghan bicycled along the coast, savoring the scenic wonders and enjoying the old dignity and hospitable ways of the Gaeltachts. They stopped in Kilrush, a bustling little market town that prospered as a seaport some two hundred years before. It resonated with Irish spirit, and Annie found its seabound setting impossibly magical.

Not able to resist, Annie asked, "How could you leave this place? Your home has such beauty and history."

Meghan shared with a twinkle in her eye, "Well, I suppose your cousin has quite swept me off my feet! When we met originally in Capri, there was a spark between us almost immediately. Tomás came to visit me here in Dingle to see what my work is about, then I agreed to be his guide on a tour of Scotland while he paid a visit to a couple of Dom's properties. That is where I learned of the colonel and that he had been connected to your father somehow. Tomás told me about your journey and its many facets. He shared what happened with Sabine but also about Alex's long absence." Looking intently at Annie, she continued, "He's concerned as well, you know. When Tomás told me how Alex left North Africa to move you to the States, something about it rang a bell with me. Several years ago, I was in Scotland. The father of a friend of mine was talking about the colonel and his time in North Africa right about the same time as Alex. Although Scottish, he was working with the British military."

Captivated that this intelligent woman could have put all that together, Annie went to retrieve her father's portfolio. As she handed it to Meghan, she said, "It was Colonel MacGregor who gave me this."

Meghan found the sketch and commented, "This looks like Don Marco's *Porto Banus*! These all look very old. Doesn't it make you wonder how the colonel got these?"

"Of course! Maybe his safety in question was from a prior time, but I have this strange feeling something is not right with him now. I know he would have contacted us."

Annie and Meghan continued the discussion of various possible scenarios. When Annie showed her the photo and told her about the resemblance of this man named Salvador to Ramone, Meghan's curiosity was piqued.

"This is quite intriguing."

Later that evening, the conversation moved back to Meghan and Tomás. "His proposal shocked me, but I was delighted to be engaged to this man! He is amazing, and it feels right. After the engagement, I had the chance to go to Marbella and meet Dom and Gennie. Tomás showed me the carriage house on the villa property where he lives. It appears we love each other's homes as much as we love each other, so we have decided to live between the two cities. Of course, Tomás will still have to travel to supervise Dom's properties."

Annie had to ask, "Then what made you decide to have the wedding in Maine?"

Smiling, Meghan reflected, "Tomás has told me of his summers there and particularly Wiscasset that he claims is the prettiest village in Maine. I have seen pictures, and it looks rustic and beautiful. I am so thrilled to be part of your lovely family. I do hope you will be able to make it to the wedding."

Annie had quickly developed a deep affection for this young woman and instinctively knew she would be a good wife to Tomás.

Without hesitation, she answered, "Of course I will!" Wistfully, she added, "I just hope my dad will be there too."

Chapter 16

Intrigue Deepens—Dingle to Paris

M eghan was to leave for Dublin the next day, then off to Andalusia to meet Tomás.

She hopefully said to Annie, "Perhaps if you sail back to Marbella, I will still be there when you arrive."

Their last night before she left, they went to a lively Irish pub, enjoying folk music and learning Gaelic toasts. Annie was struck by these proud people whose kind faces seemed like a gnarled reflection of the land. Upon returning alone to the guesthouse on her last night in Ireland, fate was yet again about to intervene.

The amiable proprietor, usually nodding off behind the desk, was nowhere to be found. Annie got her key off the row of hooks on the wall and walked toward her room. A feeling of foreboding hovered over her. Perhaps it was the light out along the corridor. But the quiet, in contrast to the lively noise of the pub, resonated in her mind to the point she could have heard a pin drop.

Forcing herself to ignore her pounding heart, Annie headed for her door; but as she put the key in the lock, a man stepped out from the shadows of the corner and ominously said, "I hear you've been asking about me."

Standing in front of her, blocking the door, stood the man from the photograph! Clearly in his late fifties or early sixties with scruffy dark hair and a beard, what was most noticeable about this man was the scar on his face that crossed his forehead and down one cheek. With his dark-brown leather jacket and dark pants, he easily mingled with the shadows.

Struggling to control her fear, Annie whispered, "You are Salvador, my father's friend? How did you find me?"

Salvador looked at her intently and said, "There are many who know where you are. I am to bring you to your father. Hurry, we must leave right away."

Alarmed, Annie asked, "How do I know you are telling the truth? Did my father send a note for me?"

"There was no time," Salvador said.

Reaching into his pocket, he pulled out a very distinctive ivory pin with a center sword, wings, and a banner that said, "Who Dares Wins." Annie looked at the pin and remembered her father talking about how special it was to him and that he always kept it safe.

"But Captain Luis will be waiting for me," Annie said.

Salvador took the key and opened her door. "We must hurry. Write a message to your captain that you are delayed and that you will meet him back at home port. Pack a few things. We need to go now!"

Mentally praying she was making the right decision, Annie packed her bag obediently. But as she wrote the note to Luis, with Salvador looking over her shoulder, instead of telling him to meet at home port, she wrote *Malaga*, not *Marbella*. She knew that would be a clue to Luis and Salvador did not pick up on it. Annie closed her eyes for a second, took a deep breath, and closed the door behind her. Salvador took her bag, and they walked around the corner to his jeep.

"Where are we going? Is my father waiting for us?" Annie asked.

"We have a short drive to Cork where we catch a freighter to Paris," Salvador replied. "He wants you safe. Enough questions now."

Ironically, Annie had always dreamed of going to Paris. Her visits to Sabine and her family were concentrated in

Bordeaux in the western part of France, and although she had been to the South of France several times, Paris had so far not been a destination of hers. Forcing a positive outlook, she hoped she would not only see her father but also be able to explore this glamorous city. Annie settled into a quiet reverie, especially since Salvador was broodingly silent and any conversation was nonexistent.

The freighter they boarded looked like an old air force plane. She noticed Salvador had watched the rearview mirror during the entire ride to Cork and even now kept glancing behind him. Annie thought about boarding that plane in Portland so many months ago on the way to Madrid and then to Marbella. Her journey had taken her to so many exotic places. She drew strength from the different cultures she had experienced and the friends she had made along the way. With a determination that amazed herself, no matter the direction this path took, she would get through it.

Once they landed in France, Annie said, "I am not stepping outside this plane until you tell me where we are going!" Staring at Salvador, she saw little or no resemblance to her handsome matador, who was so hopelessly romantic. There was no way they could be related.

Salvador reluctantly began, "There is a boarding house in the northern section of Paris. It is on the site of a legendary jazz club, Aero Bleu, and there are still remnants of the old café in the bar on the ground floor. I am taking you there to rest for a few hours. We need to be ready tomorrow morning."

Seeking to learn more, Annie said, "Tell me about this place. Where do we go tomorrow?"

When they entered the bar, with only a few seedy customers present, the bartender shoved two keys across the bar to Salvador.

Keys in hand, he grabbed a bag of cheese and bread and a brochure off the rack, then handed them to Annie, "It is late. Get some rest."

Once she was in her room, Annie turned to secure the door and found it already locked from the outside. *That's to keep me safe, right?* To keep her wits about her and subdue the pounding in her chest, Annie nibbled on the cheese and studied the brochure. In bold letters, the outside read, Aero Bleu—Paris Jazz Club. The story told of the club's notoriety in the late fifties for its all-night jam sessions and eclectic mix of celebrities, high-level military personnel, and dignitaries. Why bring her to such a place, shrouded in mystery with such a history? Was this a place her father frequented while in the service? There was something about the name that triggered a memory. Pulling out her father's weathered portfolio, Annie shuffled through the papers. There it was...a telegram. Addressed to her father in care of Aero Bleu Café, Paris, France. The rest, unfortunately, was too timeworn to read.

Not surprisingly, sleep was elusive. Annie's mind drifted from memories of her father, laughing with her and her mother, to dark mysterious eyes to perfect red roses. She must have nodded off because she was startled awake by a loud knock and a woman's voice yelling, "Breakfast downstairs—ten minutes!"

Annie dressed quickly and found the door unlocked. In the daylight, she could study her surroundings better. Some of the former splendor showed in the quality of the wood and the pewter hardware throughout. But it was in the hallway that Annie suddenly stopped, her attention riveted to the large photo on the wall—the same as in her father's portfolio with a deteriorating wood frame. Alongside it, there were many such photos of patrons of the club. One by one, the images told a story of martinis, glamour, and intrigue, complete with an explanation of how Max Morgan, the elusive owner, vanished mysteriously in the late 1950s.

The only other picture of her father was one with just him and Salvador at the beer tap. Both men were laughing, and Salvador had one arm slung over her father's shoulder.

Annie tried to find this jovial young man in the man who had brought her to this place but could not. The years had not been kind to Salvador, and Annie wondered what had happened to turn him into such a crusty shell of a man. Looking back at the photo, here was the resemblance to Ramone. Annie rubbed her temple. *So many questions!*

The dining area was surprisingly full. The waitress led her to a table in the corner where she was seated alone. Sipping strong coffee and savoring the smell of fresh croissants, eggs, and sausage, Annie sighed with a memory of how amazing the French were with their food, even in the humblest of places. As she began to eat, she fully expected Salvador to appear but did a double take when she saw Ernest Wilbanks stroll through the door!

Ernest walked over and sat down. "Hello, luv! Surprised to see me?" After he ordered a coffee, Ernest reminded her of his warning back at the Brasserie, "You just couldn't leave it alone, could ya, girl?"

Annie reasoned, "Salvador said he was taking me to my father."

"Well," Ernest said, "we expect to see Alex soon enough. Your father should know by now you are with us."

The dark way that Ernest said that had every instinct of danger on alert in Annie, both for herself and her father. *What have I done?*

Ernest paid the check and told Annie to grab her bag but remained close to her, walking to the room. Annie swallowed deeply, not knowing where to turn when something caught her eye. She took her things to repack her bag, and there buried in the corner was a perfect stemless red rose with a tiny handwritten note that said:

'Stay strong, querida!'

Annie closed her eyes as she wondered, *is he here, my matador? What is happening?*

Chapter 17

Somewhere in Paris

"Where are we going now?" Annie demanded, glaring at Ernest.

He distractedly said, "We can't stay at any place too long. Salvador already checked the new location. Sorry, luv, but I must blindfold you. What you don't know won't hurt you."

Just hearing those words and the thought of a blindfold made Annie realize how serious this was. How had she been able to travel so freely before? Sounding a little more than desperate, Annie asked, "Where is my father?"

To that, Ernest replied, "Don't worry, luv. He will show up soon. He has information we need."

Blindfolded, Annie could only recognize that Salvador was now in the room by hearing his voice. "Quiet, Ernest. You always did talk too much. The girl will get Alex here, and we will take it from there."

But the next question had Annie's mind reeling. Ernest asked, "Wasn't that son of yours supposed to get her to Sevilla? We would have been right next to Cadiz and been able to take her by boat."

Annie searched her memory for that first night, "the night to remember," she had spent with Ramone.

He talked about Sevilla and asked her to go, but she felt no sense of urgency or pressure. Could he, in some way, be involved in all this? She thought of Zanzibar and how he was called away. Yet he had led her to the colonel in Edinburgh, and that last night was one of the most romantic she could ever remember. The colonel, in turn, got her to Ernest. How deep did this plot go? *Who's out there to watch out for my father?*

With the blindfold finally removed, she was in what looked like a warehouse. There was a cot over in the corner and a tiny restroom. It did not seem that she was ever to be alone again. For her sense of survival, Annie took her small suitcase over to the cot and opened it, revealing the rose and the note. Careful to keep it hidden, she felt a small glimmer of hope. Ernest and Salvador continued their banter over a game of poker and what appeared to be some strong whiskey. Annie decided this was as good a time as she could think of to pray...for herself and her father.

Salvador stepped outside to take the call they had been expecting. Returning, he told Ernest, "There's been a change of plans. Alex has landed in Paris, presumably in search of the girl. He was picked up by Kung Li's guys as he got off the plane. They took him to the chateau. We are to bring the girl there to speed up the interrogation."

Ernest came over to Annie. "Get your things, luv. You're going to see your father."

Protest screamed in Annie's mind, along with an awareness that the consequences of her actions could end badly. She thought of her mother and Dom and Gennie, all probably worried about her. For now, her wits needed to remain sharp to not make the situation worse.

Blindfold back in place, Annie strained to hear anything that might be a clue as to where they were going. After a time, they pulled up to what must have been a gate. There was a dialogue with the guard, and the gate creaked opened. When they pulled up to the door, Ernest removed Annie's blindfold. She saw an elaborate chateau with an ornate garden and small vineyard.

"Let's go!" Salvador said.

The front door opened, and an Asian butler showed them the way to the library. An older Asian man, balding and with glasses, came over to Annie with a smile. "I am Kung Li from Hong Kong. Welcome to my home."

As she reached out her hand to shake his, she saw her father over in the corner, gagged and hands tied in a chair. Seeing Annie, Alex tried to speak and get up but could do neither with his restraints.

Annie screamed, "Dad! Let him go!"

Kung Li calmly said, "There now...Annie, is it? Your father has some critical information to share with us." Looking at his prisoner, he added, "Don't you, Alex?" To Annie, he said, "Have a seat and mind your tongue."

To Ernest and Salvador, he sternly said, "Good work, men."

Annie could feel the tension in the stare between her father and Salvador.

Kung Li looked at Annie. "Your father has been quite busy the last couple of years. China is no longer willing to tolerate British dominance in Hong Kong. There are only two years before the scheduled handover from Britain, and we want to ensure Hong Kong ceases to bow to Britain as soon as possible. Your father is part of an undercover move- ment to deter our goals, and we need the details." With that, there was a knock on the door. Kung Li smiled. "Ah, we have another guest."

Annie glanced over at the door. Her heart skipped a few beats. There, looking as handsome as always in full Moroccan garb, was El Amir! A slight nod was the only sign of recognition he gave her. Annie watched her father, but what she noticed was his surprised expression. Annie's mind was racing in so many directions with the shock of him here. Instinctively, however, she felt the need to stay silent.

Kung Li introduced El Amir to Salvador and Ernest. El Amir nodded toward Alex and asked, "Is this the Brit?"

Confirming that it was with a nod, Kung Li went on to

explain to Annie, "It appears we have not been the only ones looking for your father. His time in North Africa stirred up some unpleasantness that caused the local tribes to want retaliation." Then to Alex, he ominously added, "El Amir assures me he uses the most authentic 'persuasion' methods. I have instructed him concerning the information regarding the various vulnerabilities within Hong Kong's economy that we need from you, and we have the girl as insurance."

Looking intently at El Amir, Kung Li added, "We know you had the girl in Tanzania and had the opportunity to use her to pull Alex out of Hong Kong yet you let her go. I will keep her until you get us the necessary information."

Annie's eyes were wide with alarm.

El Amir smoothly replied, "That is impossible. I managed to gain her trust and learn more. To effectively get what we both need, the girl needs to remain a pawn. I assure you," he said, looking directly at Kung Li. "As long as we get the compliance we both seek, the girl will remain unharmed." At that point, Alex was straining against his restraints in protest.

Kung Li replied, "I understand, but I can't let you leave the chateau with them both."

Annie saw Ernest glare over at her father. What happened to make these men so angry, and where was the El Amir she knew and trusted?

Ernest stepped up toward Kung Li and said, "What if I tag along with them, sir, just to be sure we get the result we need with no excessive violence to either of them."

Salvador exchanged a look with Ernest, then said to Kung Li, "I will go too if you'd like."

El Amir quietly said, "That will work for me as long as they don't interfere with the questioning I must do."

Kung Li looked at Salvador and Ernest. "You two know what we have to do. Undermining Hong Kong's economic stability is paramount to our mission." Back to El Amir, he asked, "How long should this take?"

El Amir's comment was "My methods have proven rapid results. You can expect a report within forty-eight hours or less."

Annie looked at her father with a knot of fear bubbling up within her. El Amir motioned for Salvador and Ernest to bring Alex. He came over to get Annie and picked up her bag.

Looking at her sternly, he said, "Do not say a word or utter a sound, or your father will not be the only one gagged. Come now."

Annie wanted to scream at the top of her lungs. *How could you do this?* But fear overshadowed her anger.

The five of them left the chateau with a final warning from Kung Li to El Amir: "Do your job and do it well...the sooner the better."

El Amir's driver opened the doors to a large black sedan. Annie tried to sit next to her father, but Ernest and Salvador flanked him on both sides, leaving Annie to sit next to El Amir. She resisted the tug of electricity she always felt when he was near, but the slight whiff of his cologne fueled her anger that this man could be such a traitor.

The sedan drove by the lit-up Eiffel Tower, and Annie couldn't help but think how insane it was to be in such a beautiful city under such conditions. They rode up the private elevator to the penthouse suite. Annie noticed the driver stayed close to El Amir's side.

She pleaded, "Could you at least let me hug him?" Tears welled up in Annie's eyes as she stepped forward to embrace this man she loved so dearly. Her tears were not lost on her father, and his eyes became misty, staring at his beloved daughter. She clung to him, not knowing what to expect next when some movement in the room caught her attention. El Amir's driver had moved over toward the door, and Ernest was pulling something from his pocket.

Salvador must have sensed it too. He tried to draw his gun. In a matter of seconds, El Amir pushed Annie to the ground. The driver grabbed Salvador and held him while Ernest got him cuffed and gagged. Dizzy with what just happened, Annie stared in disbelief as El Amir removed her father's gag and cuffs, then shook his hand and gave him a hug.

Just as surreal, her father slapped El Amir on the back and said, "Son, you are a sight for sore eyes." Looking at Ernest, he grinned. "Buddy, you're amazing. Good to see you both."

But looking over at his totally shocked and confused daughter still on the floor, Alex came over and gently helped her up. "Sweetheart, let me give you a real hug. I've missed you so much, baby girl!"

In the corner, Salvador was pulling at the cuffs and growling in his recognition of the trap that had been set for him.

El Amir saw that Annie was still dazed and said, "Perhaps we should clear some of this up, Alex. The girl seems thoroughly rattled."

Ernest laughed as El Amir began, "Annie, the part about your father being stationed in North Africa is true. There was a colonial uprising, and your father was on a British mission working with local militia to subdue the militants. A battle ensued, and your father was key to saving the life of one of the local men on the assignment. That man was my father. I was a young man and my father would often speak of Alex's bravery. I had the privilege to meet him several years ago in London. Sadly, my father died of natural causes last year, but he never forgot your father and made sure I remembered the debt we owed him. It was my honor to be of service and honor that debt."

Annie, totally baffled, sat on the couch while he continued, "I learned your father was missing when you were in Morocco and thought it wise to keep you close. In London, prior to Sarah's exhibition, I heard about Ernest at the jazz club and that he might know more about your father's whereabouts. It was during our conversations that I learned there had been a mole in the platoon and that the traitor was Salvador. Ernest was undercover trying to gain his trust. Alex did not know this was the plan until he saw Ernest and me. Annie, we hated to put you through that, but it had to look authentic."

Now it was Alex's turn to look confused. "How did you know all of this was happening? Excellent timing, but my getting out of Hong Kong was very hush-hush. I heard Annie was asking questions about me from the colonel and was trying to get to her. I am still unsure how Kung Li's thugs knew my flight." Looking at Salvador, he felt he knew the answer.

El Amir explained, "For my part, it was the matador. He knew of his father's plot to capture Annie and came to me to ask for help. Salvador was the one who let Kung Li know your flight. I was skeptical at first. Between Ramone and Ernest, however, I knew enough to use my influences to make this charade happen."

There was a knock on the door, and in walked Ramone. He shook hands with Alex, El Amir, and Ernest, then walked up to Annie and said, "*Querida*, I was never far from you. My father pointed you out at the bullfight on that first day we met. I was to court you and gain your trust. When you didn't join me in Sevilla, my father was furious. They knew you were in Portugal and that you went to Tanzania with El Amir. I was to get you to Zanzibar, but knowing their plan, I couldn't do it. I thought you would use the ticket to fly home to the safety of Don Marco. When I heard you had moved on to the other countries, I admit I was relieved you were away from their grip. The plan was to kidnap you to bring your father out in the open. Thankfully, when Luis told Don Marco of your cryptic message in your note, he sought me out to see what I could learn. He remembered Colonel MacGregor and that I helped connect you with him. I am so grateful he did."

Annie sat on the sofa, staring back and forth between

Ramone and El Amir. To Ramone, she asked, "I was a job for you?" And to both, she said, "You worked together?"

While Annie sorted through all this, Ramone stepped over in front of his father. "Papa, you were not always like this. When I was a boy, you were always there for me. It was only when I began this weekly dance I do with the bulls that things changed. I was left with your brother's encouragement and support, not yours, that gave me the strength to accomplish those goals. What happened to make you so bitter? Once I met Annie and spent time with her, I wasn't prepared for what I would feel, and there was nothing that would allow me to hurt her."

Hoping to shed a little light, Alex looked at Ramone and reminisced, "Your father and I went to boarding school together. He often spent the summer up in York when we were boys, and we formed a fast friendship. Salvador was my closest mate for many years. It felt like we would do anything for the other. When I joined the British military out of school, I encouraged Salvador to enlist so we could carry on together. Frequently we participated in the same missions. It's true, we had a wild side and spent many hours in Paris at Aero Bleu. But then I got assigned to North Africa, and Salvador to Hong Kong. So we separated. Getting married and having children settled both of us down for a while. But shortly before I moved Celeste and Annie to Maine, Salvador and I had a falling out."

Going over to Salvador, Alex removed his gag only to get spit in the face. Wiping his face, Alex gritted his teeth and said to Salvador, "I tried to find you when they moved me to Hong Kong. You seemingly disappeared." Looking at the others, he continued, "Salvador was deep undercover in Kung Li's circle of Chinese thugs by the time I got there. When he heard I was in Hong Kong, he showed up acting as my friend and tried to lure me to Kung Li. I caught wind of the trap and luckily escaped."

Back to Salvador, Alex tensely said, "That's when you

turned on me, you coward! You shot me and left me for dead. Do you hear me? YOU LEFT YOUR SUPPOSED BEST FRIEND FOR DEAD!"

Salvador snickered. "You should have died that night, but you wouldn't stay dead, would you? When we found out about your rescue, Kung Li was furious with me. It became personal to rectify the situation, and I assured him I would find a way to get you back. You always were the righteous one. This is not over."

Alex answered, "Such a pathetic thing to see a powerful friendship wrecked. And, Salvador, it is over. My recovery took many months undercover with my family unaware of what happened to me. You will be reckoned with...the British government has declared you a wanted man."

To Ernest, he said, "You must take him to the consulate tonight."

El Amir looked over at Annie with sympathy and saw pure exhaustion. "Annie, there is plenty of room here for you and your father to stay the night. Get some rest. We will sort everything else out in the morning."

Her father regained his composure, embraced her, and said good night, then went to make a private phone call to her mother to let her know they were together and safe. Annie walked to the door at the end of the hall and took one last look at both Ramone and El Amir. Shaking her head in utter confusion, she retired for the evening.

Chapter 18

Paris, France—Beyond the Drama

Lack of sleep and mental exhaustion took over. Annie fell into a deep sleep laced with passing visions of her father's laugh, red roses, and golden eyes. She finally awoke and, while she dressed, braced herself for whatever was coming next. Her joy was beyond words to see her father on the balcony sipping his coffee and reading a newspaper. She bent over to give him a giant hug and laughed when her stomach churned with hunger and excitement at the abundance of delicacies on the room-service cart.

As she sat down to fix a plate, she glanced around. "Is El Amir gone?"

Alex explained, "The two of us stayed up last night planning what was to be said to Kung Li. El Amir and Ernest have gone to give him the report. The conflict between Britain and China is real, even with the turnover still two years away. I was there to monitor the situation and ensure Britain's influence would remain until the turnover of Hong Kong to Beijing. After I was shot, the military tucked me away anonymously at a base hospital. I only returned to active duty four months ago."

Annie hated to think of her father wounded and hospitalized without their knowing about it. So much time had been swallowed up in the secrecy of his British military maneuverings, but now it was hard to believe he might be free to be part of Annie's life again.

"I was positioned near Kowloon, absolutely one of the world's greatest harbors. My role in the negotiations with China was extremely delicate. We knew of Kung Li's group, and danger surrounded us. They were looking for me. The best I could do was get Ernest to send Celeste and my parents word I was safe for the time being. Annie, after this is all settled, I need to take you there. Hong Kong literally spreads out into the surrounding blue sea with its ever-increasing population and high-rises. There's a symbiotic relationship this amazing area has between the sea and its cultural diversity and infinite vitality. It is absolutely absorbing." He studied her for a moment, this daughter of his who had his heart, then said, "I think, perhaps, you get your restless spirit from me, Annie. It is not about seeking danger. Rather, it is a compulsion to experience the more obscure and intimate parts of different cultures that stand out and fascinate. Don't you agree?"

Annie answered, "Yes, and it was some of the lessons I learned along my recent journey that gave me the strength to get through the last few days. And to think, both of those men who were strangers such a short time ago, would go to such lengths to ensure our safety. It's hard to imagine."

Alex reached for her hand, "It appears, my love, you have two admirers in these remarkable young men."

Annie lowered her eyes and said, "They are both incredible...but unique to themselves. You said where El Amir was. Where did Ramone go?"

"He went with Ernest last night to take Salvador to the consulate, perhaps to put closure on it," Alex mused. "The consulate will extradite his father back to England to determine his fate. But before they left, Ramone scribbled out this note and asked me to give it to you."

'Querida, *I knew this moment was coming, and I could not be part of what my father plotted. The man you felt occasionally watching you was sent by me. The meeting with the colonel was scheduled to help you sort through what was happening beneath the surface. It was that lovely last night in Edinburgh, standing at the door saying good night, when I knew I could never take advantage of you. Now knowing El Amir's obligation to your father, I am happy I reached out to him to help. He has an interesting way about him. I can see he has feelings for you as well as I do. I return to Spain tomorrow to let my mother and brother know what happened to Papa. Come back to me soon. Ramone'*

Watching his daughter while she read, Alex noticed a single tear. He reached over to wipe it away. Annie wasn't accustomed to letting romance problems muddle her emotions and claim her peace of mind. Were her feelings for Ramone stronger than she realized?

Then with an uncanny sense of timing, El Amir walked back in. Shaking hands with her father, with a brief glance at Annie, El Amir told Alex about the visit with Kung Li.

"Everything seemed to go as planned. From there, we dropped Ernest at the airport to return to London." He looked at his watch. "The authorities should be paying a visit to Kung Li any moment."

Turning his attention to Annie, El Amir smiled that smile that started in those golden eyes. "Fate has brought us here to Paris. Your father is safe now. I thought a couple of days sightseeing might lift your spirit, so I took the liberty to invite Sarah to join us. She agreed and will be here this afternoon. Will you stay?"

Annie looked inquisitively at her father, daring to allow a bit of excitement rise about seeing this city known both as the "City of Lights" and the "City of Love."

Her father, reading her mind so clearly, said, "Annie,

stay and enjoy this city that has so much to offer! Now that I'm out of Hong Kong, I must still be discreet. I want to make a quick stop in York to see my parents, then get to Maine and your mother as soon as possible."

El Amir left the two of them to catch up while he made plans for the next few days. Annie told her father about her visit in York with his parents. Suddenly she remembered the journal and went to get it.

Giving it to her father, she asked, "Why did Colonel MacGregor have this portfolio? Was he working with Salvador?"

Alex held it in his hands, turning it over thoughtfully. "This was from many years ago. We were all working together and such friends. Peter MacGregor was with me in North Africa. You and your mother were still in Marbella... you were very young. I received word that a rebel group had discovered you were there. There was no chance for me to leave yet, so MacGregor offered to covertly escape and get to you. I gave him the journal so your mother would know he came from me. He was to persuade Don Marco to help get you and your mother on the *Porto Banus* and to safety. The plan was for me to meet you in Cadiz to take you to America. I had forgotten about the journal."

Annie tentatively asked, overwhelmed by the impact of all that happened, "Will you have to go away again?"

Alex held his daughter tight and replied, "Sweetheart, it is time for me to come home." After a few moments, he smiled and said, "Now tell me about your journey so far."

She enjoyed sharing stories of Africa and Thailand (her father remembered the professor).

When she mentioned Mara from Bali, and then Jonathan from Australia, her father raised his eyebrows, "Another one?"

Annie laughed and settled into an easy conversation with her father; she was delighted the years apart melted away so quickly. She told him about Tomás's engagement to Meghan and that the wedding would be in Maine in a few months.

"I plan to go back for the wedding. It will be good to be home. In the meantime, I want to get back to Marbella for a while and sail the *Porto Banus* at least once more."

The way Alex was taken at the airport in Paris meant bringing no belongings, and Annie was delighted to shop with her father for a few things in this beautiful city. While they set out to "hunt and gather" as her father put it, El Amir finished the details of their sightseeing tour and left to meet Sarah at the airport.

Annie's father...packed, clean-shaven, and ready...said to Annie, "In all your travels, sweetheart, be true to yourself. If you learn to live fully in the time and place at hand, your life will become an adventure of can't-miss sights and opportunities. These people you have met along the way are in your life for a reason. See them again with fresh eyes and let your awareness of their purpose in this journey of yours make you appreciate them even more. You are in France. This is your heritage too. The French have a lot to teach us about connecting to life and living each moment as a sensory experience. Their language sounds like poetry. Their food is prepared and enjoyed with uncompromised passion. Their dedication to art and fashion is unparalleled. Breathe it in, Annie, and enrich your soul with what you learn."

El Amir arrived with Sarah just as Alex was to leave for the train station. Introductions complete, the girls instantly started catching up on all the events of the last week and a half since London. Alex hugged Annie goodbye, happy they would reconnect in Maine soon, and agreed to El Amir's offer of a ride to the train station.

Riding along, Alex looked over at El Amir and said, "You have done well, son. Your father would be proud. You got me out of a dangerous situation, and I have been able to reconnect with my family. For that, I will always be grateful. Take care of my daughter. She can be headstrong at times, but in her heart and soul lies great tenderness and vulnerability."

El Amir reflected for a few minutes, trying to put into words the assurance Annie's father wanted to hear. "I had, of course, heard she was arriving in Casablanca. Knowing Annie was your daughter and traveling alone, I sought nothing more than to keep watch from afar." With a chuckle, he continued, "The first night she was there, I saw her 'experiencing' her meal and was pleased to see how she delighted in the smallest of things. Annie is most beautiful, but you know that. When I surprised her for dinner in Marrakech, I learned more about her soul that you speak of. It kept occurring to me how much she is like Sarah, and I wanted to be sure they would meet. I know the matador cares for her and that it must have been difficult for him to come to me for help. I have much respect for him for that. Custom is very clear in my country about boundaries that cannot be crossed. I respect both my country and your daughter, so I will leave you knowing she is my priority whenever she is in my care."

With newfound respect for this young man and the honor he displayed, Alex said, "Then I leave her in your care...take heed that you keep those boundaries in check."

Chapter 19

Time to Play Tourist in Paris

Back at the penthouse, El Amir found Annie and Sarah busy talking about all the places they would like to see. Sarah looked up at him approvingly. "You did well, my friend."

Annie chimed in, looking at Sarah, "Well, he was pretty scary yesterday!"

The idea of recreating this exotic combination of personalities on a short journey filled Annie with anticipation but, when she looked at the small bag she brought from Ireland, regretted her lack of appropriate attire. This morning had been all about getting necessities for her father. Now she hesitantly asked if there might be time to pick up a few fashions for herself.

Pouring a glass of champagne for the three of them, El Amir smiled and said, "I think I am going to enjoy spoiling you ladies!" Making a toast to their time together in France, he outlined the plan. "Since shopping is on our agenda, let's do a little walking. We will easily have a view of the Eiffel Tower as we leave the hotel and wander over the Seine River via the Pont de Grenelle. From there, it is a short walk to Rue de Passy. I think you might find a few things there you will like in some of its many boutiques." Continuing, he added, "Tonight, I am treating you to a celebration dinner at L'Oiseau Blanc. The view from its rooftop location is unsurpassed, and the food excellent. Tomorrow we shall be tourists and see the sites, then cruise down the Seine. The next day, what about a wine tour? How does that sound?"

Both ladies gave an enthusiastic "YES!" and Annie felt the tension that had been lodged in her the last few days slowly begin to dissolve.

Annie and Sarah lost all trace of sophistication on their shopping spree, giggling and acting like teenage girls, while El Amir, more than amused, sipped on champagne and enjoyed watching them move from one outfit to the next. His mood, seated on the velvet sofa, subtly shifted when Annie came out wearing a long black chiffon gown. Subtle ruffles hung from the armholes, leaving bare shoulders; a dramatically low-cut neckline; and a side slit up to her thigh—a dangerous combination that left little to the imagination. The familiar burning eyes stopped Annie mid laugh as she contemplated the reaction of this man. With a twinkle in her eye, she taunted a little with sensual turns and dips, pleased with the strength of El Amir's attraction.

Looking in the mirror, Annie said, "I love this dress. It will be perfect."

Sarah came out in time to see the exchange and said with a smile, "Oh yes, you have to have that dress."

Not so sure he was pleased with the direction the afternoon was taking, El Amir told the women to make their selections so they could have the boutique pack them up and deliver them to the hotel. Obediently wrapping up, Annie and Sarah dressed and came out to El Amir paying the bill.

Annie looked at him and gave him her warmest smile. "You really are spoiling us!"

El Amir merely muttered as he escorted them out the door.

Walking along the streets in Paris, the blend of old and new in every direction was invigorating. Once back at the hotel, however, El Amir said he had some business to attend while the ladies rested prior to their late dinner in the Peninsula Paris rooftop bar, L'Oiseau Blanc. Once he was gone, they sat out on the balcony, enjoying the view and waiting for the packages to arrive.

"Annie, you were shamelessly taunting that man...you should be ashamed! If you are not careful, you will fall into the image Arab men hold about oversexed Western women," Sarah lectured.

Properly chagrined, Annie said, "Oh, Sarah, you're right! And after all he did for my father and me. It just felt for the first time he might have the same attraction for me that I do for him. One thing is for certain—things are never ordinary around that man."

Sarah had to agree with that.

Reflecting on Sarah's comment, Annie decided to forego the black dress by choosing a more subtle emerald green sheath with a high neck and three-quarter sleeves. It was one of Annie's favorite colors to wear because it showed off her hazel eyes that leaned more to the green side. El Amir was dressed more formally again to escort them to dinner. The restaurant was a delight and showcased the best of French cuisine and delicious local wine. Annie particularly liked the biplane hanging outside the window that paid tribute to the early attempts of a trans-Atlantic crossing. It reminded her of the ride with Jonathan and Mara in Australia. El Amir was noticeably quiet, and again, she felt a pang of guilt for teasing him.

Back at the penthouse, Sarah yawned and said good night, thanking their host for such a fabulous afternoon and evening.

He was on the verge of retiring as well when Annie asked, "Have a nightcap with me?"

He nodded and ordered two Camparis.

Sitting on the balcony in silence for a while, Annie finally said, "I owe you an apology for today at the boutique."

After what seemed like an eternity, El Amir replied, "There is no denying the attraction we feel toward each other." His eyes penetrated deep into her. "However, I made a promise to your father, and I have an obligation to my cul-ture. If we were to lie together, we would have to be engaged to be married, and Annie, you are far from that place yet in your journey."

"Am I not allowed to touch you?" Annie timidly asked. "One kiss?"

El Amir looked away. When he looked back, there was sadness in those beautiful eyes. "We both know there could not be one kiss. I must hold to the honor that I have. You have a matador who adores you. He is also a man of deep conviction. When I marry, tradition insists it be with another Arab woman. But you tempt me beyond my endurance. Stay friends with me, Annie. Don't make it more difficult."

Closing her door after saying good night, Annie thought about both men with their code of honor that kept them so strong. How ironic they had come into her life and the impact they already had on her. She had to admit, she had strong feelings for them both, but she would not let them challenge her clearheaded plans for the future. *What I need is a little shift in perception.* Determined to make the next two days memorable with these incredible friends, Annie set her mind adrift and slept soundly.

Refreshed and eager to see Paris, Annie dressed quickly to join Sarah and El Amir on the balcony for café au lait and decadent strawberry crepes. When El Amir tentatively glanced her way, Annie gave him her most genuine smile, looking at him with fresh eyes, and was pleased to see him noticeably relax. She thought about her latest journal entry:

> *This is one of those true-self moments that occasionally happens when we have honestly reflected a little and returned to ourselves. The friendships I am developing on this journey make a solid foundation for the life I was destined to find.*

Sarah had seen the tension the night before and was proud of both her friends for getting past it. Excitedly she asked, "What are we doing today?"

El Amir picked up their schedule. "Our driver will be here shortly. We have a behind-the-scenes tour of Musée d'Orsay this morning. It has quite an interesting history. The museum is in the center of Paris on the banks of the Seine, opposite the Tuileries Gardens, which we will also see, and is on the site of the former Orsay railway station built in 1900. So the building itself is considered the first work of art. Unlike the Louvre, this smaller museum features artistic collections from the specific period between 1848 to 1914."

"After a walk through the gardens, we have a tour by boat along the Seine, which will take us by the Eiffel Tower and give us a perspective from the water. From there, I thought it was important to explore some culinary special-ties since French heritage certainly cannot be summed up in a list of monuments to visit. We will do a wine and food tour where we visit some of the non-tourist neighborhoods and a noteworthy open market. It will be a full day before heading our separate ways. How does that sound?"

Annie and Sarah both gave an enthusiastic thumbs-up, and El Amir smiled at how close the two friends had become.

Not surprising, when they arrived at the museum, Sarah wandered off, obsessed with comparing the techniques of these many artists who came before her to her own style of painting. She commented that she had been here with her father before visiting the exhibition of an artist who inspired her. There was so much to see and learn during their tour. Annie was particularly fascinated by the architectural draw-ings, the architect and historian in her on full sensory over-load! She never ceased to admire the exceptional accom-plishments made architecturally in countries throughout history.

Tuileries Gardens was in full bloom with an abundance of exotic fragrances. Annie recalled that Queen Catherine de Medici had built the Palais des Tuileries in 1564 on this very spot, but it was Andre Le Notre, the famous gardener of King

Louis XIV, who re-landscaped the gardens a hundred years later to give them their current French formal garden style—such history and so many lives touched by this beauty.

It was out on the open boat meandering along the Seine River when Annie realized how deeply she missed her connection with the sea. She would be back in Marbella soon, but perhaps there was still time before the wedding to possibly squeeze in one more adventure.

The highlight of the day exceeded both Sarah's and Annie's imaginations! They began a walking tour along out-of-the-way neighborhoods to get the "flavor" of the local French culture. Their guide, Pierre, was a charming young Frenchman who told them from the start they were in for a special treat. He knew many of the locals, and they often stopped to be introduced. Inevitably, that usually resulted in the offer of some specialty of theirs to the three friendly visitors. One older gentleman waved them inside his small home, then pulled out a loaf of bread, some fresh camembert cheese, and a small carafe of wine produced from his own vineyard. His pride showed when he gave them a tour of his small block of vines, and Annie thought in this humble surrounding that she had never tasted a better pairing.

As they walked by a jovial woman who spoke no English, Pierre gave a friendly salutation that resulted in another invitation inside. To everyone's delight, the woman told Pierre she would like to share her specialty, *foie gras*. Pierre explained her process of making the renowned goose liver pâté dated back to antiquity. Annie found her mouth watering in anticipation when she saw the woman pull out the delicacy and a basketful of brioches, then accent the plate with a bit of onion spread and fig jam. Served with a small cup of local wine from a jug, the guests were all appreciative of the flavors and her generosity. Pierre assured them this was a common practice.

When Pierre led them into an enormous open market

filled with everything imaginable, he told them they were each to pick out a gift for their hostess, who was preparing a special meal for them and a few others. Intrigued with how the last two visits could be topped, Annie picked out a large bouquet of colorful flowers. El Amir had Pierre help him pick out several bottles of local wine. Sarah found a beautiful piece of black-and-white earthenware and a sheet of parchment with some black-and-white charcoal, thinking she would sketch out a drawing of her zebras to go with the pot. Pierre smiled in appreciation for what they had chosen, and they walked to the home of their hostess.

Graciela warmly greeted them at her door and led them into a dining area filled with three round tables, each set for six. Their hostess spoke broken English and graciously accepted their gifts but was fascinated when Sarah sat down at the table and began her drawing. Other guests drifted in, and the three tables quickly filled. At their table, an Australian couple traveling on holiday occupied the other two seats. On the remote chance, Annie asked them if they knew Jonathan McNamara from the outback.

The husband said, "Not personally, but I have read about his tours. If I recall, he is also on the marine research team. He is highly respected."

They all fell into an easy conversation while Graciela went back to the kitchen and her two daughters remained to fill the guests' wineglasses. They were served the most delicious version of soupe à l'oignon any of them had ever tasted. Sarah was busily working on her sketch until her first spoonful of soup when all thoughts of anything but this savory soup vanished! The home-cooked meal continued to amaze them with individual cheese soufflés cooked to perfection, followed by a classic *coq au vin* with Lyonnaise potatoes. The wine was delicious, and the conversation lively.

As everyone anticipated dessert and after-dinner coffee, Sarah took a few moments to finish her sketch. The lights dimmed and Graciela, along with her daughters, brought out three large platters of crêpes Suzette flavored with oranges from their backyard garden. Together in harmony, they created a tableside performance by pouring the flavored liquor over the crepes and lighting a *flambé*. The applause from all the guests showed their appreciation.

As the feast came to an end and everyone was thanking Graciela and her daughters, Sarah gave her the sketch of a mother and two young zebras pointing to her family. Touched, Graciela promised she would put it in a place of honor. Annie watched the interaction and appreciated Sarah's gesture and the talent she so freely gave. All three friends agreed that Pierre had provided the perfect tour, and they were all happily full and satiated after a most memorable meal.

On the walk back, Annie took time to think about the experience in France and its culture. *Was it possible my time in this city that started so harshly only three days ago could end on such a high note?*

As they got to the hotel and said good night to Pierre, everyone agreed to retire early to get their packing done and be ready to travel the next day.

Chapter 20

Back to Home Port—Marbella, Spain

Sarah and El Amir were returning to London by train to complete the details of several paintings collectors had commissioned from Sarah at the exhibit. Once completed, she planned to go back to Tanzania, and El Amir to Morocco. Annie was taking El Amir's plane to Spain, back to Marbella.

When it was time to say goodbye, both ladies were surprised when El Amir gave each of them a hug. Annie held him for a moment and whispered, "You will always have a special place in my heart."

He thoughtfully answered, "As you will in mine. That place is yours forever. But now it is time to give the matador a chance. Explore the uncharted, Annie."

She replied, "I don't know if I'm there yet, or even if I want that distraction. You have done so much for Sarah, myself, and my father. Thank you, my dear friend."

"There is no reason to hasten your journey, Annie. Slow it down if necessary. Even stop completely to give yourself time to see all the different avenues available to you. My experience has taught me that a journey taken in haste usually involves wrong turns and missed destinations. Take the time to imagine a life map, then proceed on your journey toward your goals."

El Amir's words inspired her to move forward.

When Annie next turned to Sarah, she knew tears would readily come with leaving her friend. But instead, Sarah leaned in and, with a giggle, whispered, "Wear the black dress for your matador, Annie. Torture him mercilessly. I do hope to meet him someday. Don't worry, my friend. We will find a way to meet again soon."

At that, she reached into her pocket, took the amethyst Annie had given her before the gallery exhibition, and handed it back to Annie. "You shared this with me when I needed it most. Take it with you for now and let it help you in your quest for clarity."

With a lump in her throat, Annie gave Sarah one last hug and promised to keep in touch. The comradery of Sarah's gracious heart and El Amir's dark charm rejuvenated Annie and lifted her spirit. The three friends parted, and Annie resolved to remember their time together and make the most of the next stage of her journey.

Annie's decision to return home to Marbella brought with it a renewed exhilaration. It had been far too long since she had walked the shoreline with her grandfather and absorbed the Andalusian culture. There were still several months before she would return to Maine for Tomás and Meghan's wedding. As she thought about her upcoming trip to the States, her heart soared at the thought of reuniting with her mother and father in Maine, erasing any doubts or indecision about going. Annie smiled inwardly. She was willing to consider a little distraction and wondered if a certain matador would know she had returned. It had to have been difficult for his family to learn about Salvador's plots and incarceration. She thought better of contacting Ramone and instead decided it wiser to leave further contact to him.

By the time Annie arrived at the villa, Tomás and Meghan had already returned to Ireland to look at apartments. Their goal of living half the year in Ireland and the other half in Spain was a lofty one, and she admired them doing this for each other. Annie regretted missing the additional time with Meghan, but considering all that happened since their visit in Ireland, there had been no alternative. She would see them again soon.

Running into the arms of Gennie and Dom, Annie felt as though she had indeed come home. Everyone talked at once about the kidnapping, her father's release, Ramone's role in exposing his father, and El Amir doing this for her father because of his own father's wish. *So* much had happened to catch up on. And that didn't even touch Scotland and England.

When they finally paused to take a breath, Gennie went to the kitchen to prepare a platter of tapas, including Annie's favorite *tortilla de patatas*. She loved how the Spanish would make an omelet with eggs, potatoes, and onions that was delicious any time of the day, hot or cold. Making a mental note to herself, she resolved that some serious exercise was needed to compensate for the culinary delicacies she had recently been enjoying.

At ease on the patio and happy to be back, Annie noticed Dom went to get several letters that had come for her while she was gone. One was from her mother, another from Mara in Bali, and the last from Ramone. Turning that letter over in her hand, thinking something was missing, Annie realized there was no rose. How many notes had reached her from this matador, but there was always a red rose. Surprised at her disappointment, Annie looked up to see Gennie walk in with a vase full of a dozen long-stem red roses, and she was even more surprised at the delight those roses brought. Fragrant as always, each rose was perfect.

Attached was a small card that read:

> 'Welcome home, querida! Read my letter and
> my invitation. Come with me.'

Putting Ramone's letter aside, Annie reached for her mother's letter.

> 'Dearest Annie, ahhh...mi hija linda, you had
> me so worried! When I heard you had been

*taken, I knew I could not bear to lose both you
and your father. He told me what happened
and about your two young men who ensured
his safety and yours. Alex is with Henry and
Trudy for another day or two, but I expect
him to be here by the end of the week. He says
he has recovered from his wound. You do plan
to come home for the wedding? Why don't you
extend your stay so we might have a proper
reunion with the three of us? As always, you
are missed. Love, Mother.'*

Mara's letter thanked her for the time in Australia. She
told recent stories of her painting in Bali, especially one evening while she was teaching a silk-painting class to a group
of Greek tourists. There was a man in the class who caught
on quite well. She was impressed with the talent she saw in
him. When he came up after the class to ask her to join him
for a coffee, she had said yes. Over coffee, the man described
the Greek islands to her with beautiful details about the
sponge divers, as well as the brilliant white buildings contrasted with the blue sea and cherry-red bougainvillea.
Mara's enthusiasm was catching.

Annie mused, *Greek isles? Hmmm...is there time for
one more journey before returning to Maine?*

Lastly, she opened Ramone's letter. As she did, she
thought about this man who had defied his own father to
keep her safe. How hard must it have been to return to tell
his mother and brother what happened.

*'Querida, I am sorry I left Paris without a
proper goodbye. I have thought often about
your last words asking if you were a job to
me. I tried to be a good son. Honestly, I did not
know how far Papa would go to get what he
needed from your father. Hearing what your*

father said to him made me wonder how Papa could have stooped so low. It is a long story that should be told in person. Please have dinner with me and let me explain. Fondly, Ramone'

Closing her eyes, Annie could feel that "weather vane in her soul" Dom had described so many months before. She was at another crossroad in her journey and somehow felt the path she chose might be an important one. Captain Luis might offer some insight; plus, she wanted to thank him for understanding the clue that led to their rescue. The undeniable urge to see him and set foot on the *Porto Banus* again found her out the door in moments and on a walk to the port. Bustling with activity, Marbella's jet-setter port was one of a kind along the Mediterranean. On the far dock, she could see the *Porto Banus*, and her pace quickened.

Roff was busy washing the bow and waved when he saw her. "Hola! We've missed you, Annie! Come aboard. Are you here to see the captain?"

Annie grinned. "Ahoy, Roff, yes, is Luis here?"

Hearing the exchange, Captain Luis surfaced. "Welcome back, lass! You had us worried. Come sit and fill me in." They settled midship in the lounge area.

Helene brought a bottle of prosecco and two glasses. "Good to see you, Annie."

Annie felt so comfortable on board and realized how much she missed the three of them and her time at sea. She noted that Roff and Helene were both close by to hear the tale of what had happened, so she obliged.

It was Luis who observed, "What you're saying, lass, is that both the matador and the Arab you met in Morocco had a part in freeing your father and bringing you to safety? Well, well. We do owe them our deepest gratitude."

That seemed to satisfy Roff and Helene, and they went to complete their chores.

Luis looked at Annie and saw the question in her eyes. "What is it, girl? Tell me."

Annie began, "You know we go to Maine for the wedding in a few months."

"Aye, that I do." Luis nodded.

"Do you remember Mara who went to Australia with me on the *Majestique*? She mentioned the possibility of our meeting in Greece for another adventure. And then there is Ramone. My feelings are so mixed about him. He seems sincere, but I'm not sure I want entanglement right now. Is there time to get to Greece and back before leaving for Maine? I feel so confused about what to do next."

Taking a few sips of his wine, the captain patted her hand. "Annie, do you remember my teaching you to sail when you were a little girl?" When she nodded, he went on, "Well, learning to sail, you cannot change the current of the water, nor do you have any effect on the wind. But you learn to hoist your sail—turn it this way and that—to utilize those greater forces that surround you. By understanding them, you become one with them, and in doing so, you become better able to find your own direction. Your instinct is strong. Use it and you will know what path to take. And to answer your question, yes, we can get to the Greek islands and back before your trip back to the States...with the assurance of Don Marco's approval."

The captain's analogy made Annie realize how much she missed sailing and the rhythm of the sea. Annie left him, saying, "I will speak with Dom today."

Chapter 21

Marbella—Time for Ramone

On her walk back to the villa, thinking about her conversation with Captain Luis, Annie determined how she would answer each letter. The letter to her mother would be easy. She looked forward to reconnecting with her parents and her American home. After all, it was those connections that created the grounding that put perspective into all her world travels. She would stay in Maine until her relentless, restless spirit propelled her back to Marbella and the sea.

Mara's letter depended on her conversation with Dom. It was the response to Ramone that gave her pause. The time in Scotland had brought the two of them close, but after everything that happened in Paris, Annie questioned whether she knew him at all. Thoughtful, she made a quick entry in her journal:

> *Is it my independence or fear of the unknown with this man that makes me hesitate? Am I conflicted with thoughts of El Amir? Any future relationship with him is impossible. Could it be true that sometimes the best things in life come from a willingness to change, to risk the unknown, to do the very things you might have feared most? At the very least, I owe Ramone my gratitude and the chance to answer some lingering questions.*

She would agree to lunch tomorrow, rather than dinner, and see where it goes. At the villa, Annie found Don Marco out in the gardens.

He saw her and asked, "Did you find Luis?"

"Yes, and he shared some of his wisdom as always," she answered. Continuing, Annie questioned, "Dom, the letter from Mara, the Balinese painter I told you about, spoke of the beauty of the Greek islands. Have you been there? What makes them unique?"

Delighted when he began one of his tales, Annie smiled as she listened. He spoke of daring Greek sponge divers and mermaids of the Aegean, the book of Revelation written in Patmos, the dazzling nightlife in Mykonos, and the serene beauty of Santorini. As Dom continued, a familiar yearning stirred in Annie.

When he finally paused in his story, Annie wistfully asked, "Would it be possible to take the *Porto Banus* there for a visit before our trip to Maine? I would like to ask Mara to join me."

Dom replied, "Of course, my dear, you must see a few of the islands, but rest assured you will want to go back when you have more time. Your grandmother and I will be quite busy arranging caretaking for the villa during our time away at the wedding since Tomás will also be away. I admit, we are both anxiously waiting for our visit and to see Celeste. It has been far too long since we have been together with our precious daughter, and we plan to convince her to come back home to Marbella more often."

Annie couldn't agree more. Guiltily, Annie said, "Oh, Dom, do you need me here at the villa? I am so sorry I didn't think of it sooner."

Dom patted her hand. "We'll be fine. Tomás will be here to help. Meghan might even visit."

His words seemed to satisfy her that they would be all right in her absence. With her mother's letter and Mara's invitation to meet her in Greece completed, Annie turned her attention to the note to Ramone. Trying not to over-think, she started writing:

> *'Dear Ramone, it is good to be back in Marbella, and I agree we have much to discuss. Would it be possible for you to come by the villa tomorrow? Perhaps we could go for a walk along the shore? Annie'*

Note sent, Annie wandered from the garden to the private beach that bordered the villa. In times of indecision, Annie seemed always to turn to the sea. Her comfort, her answers, her future always seemed to reside there. During her swim, she let the anticipation of being back on the *Porto Banus* sailing through open water fill her. The lure of the Greek islands now beckoned, having come to life through Dom's stories, and seeing them through a painter like Mara's eyes would be most enchanting.

The next day, writing in her journal in the garden, Annie reflected on the sentiment at the top of today's page, "Begin each day with a grateful heart."

She had much to be thankful for—the list was long. Then why the restlessness and wanderlust that pushed her to always venture out? It would be several days before she received confirmation about the trip from Mara, and Annie determined she would take El Amir's advice he gave her as they left Paris to "slow it down, even stop completely" to give herself time to see all the avenues available.

It was at that point in her writing when Ramone strode down the hill to the garden. Annie looked up and saw a completely different man from the tensely serious one in that Paris hotel. He was casually dressed in a white turtleneck and jeans, with those hypnotic brown eyes, dark wavy hair, day-old beard, and a smile as genuine as she remembered from Scotland. *This* was the matador Annie wanted to see. Such relief washed over her, and she stood up to hug him hello. He literally swept her off her feet and held on so tight she could hardly breathe. And the kiss that followed left no misunderstanding about how hard it had been for him to leave her at that door in Edinburgh.

Ramone leaned back, not letting go of her, and said, "Let me look at you, *querida*. The blush has returned to your cheeks, and for that, I am most thankful. Leaving you in such confusion in Paris put a weight on my heart that I prayed time would heal. We have much to talk about...shall we walk?"

Walking hand in hand along the shore, Annie appreciated the time to breathe him in without the complications of the story he planned to tell her. As if he sensed her hesitancy to get started, Ramone pulled her close for a tender kiss and kept his arm around her while they walked.

Slowly he began, "It wasn't supposed to be me."

Annie watched him, trying to understand what he was saying.

He continued, "My father asked my brother, Antonio, to court you. After all, he is younger and quite handsome, also a matador." At Annie's surprised expression, he added, "We come from many generations of bullfighters. Our father did not accept the calling. But my uncle, brother, and I did. We did not understand Papa's decision to go into the military instead. There were parts of his military career we knew, but many we did not. The day you and I met, before the *corrida de toros* began, my father directed our attention to your grandfather's box with the explanation that he needed the blonde woman in the box to come to Sevilla.

"From the moment I saw you, *querida*, you took my breath away. It was at that moment I decided it would be me who would court you. Antonio was to fight after me. I remember nodding at you as I began the traditional corrida. The bull gave me a hard fight that day. I wanted you to notice me. It honored me when you caught my rose. As I left the ring, my brother laughed and slapped me on the back, saying, 'It looks like you are the one to get the girl after all.' My brother and I are very close, and I knew he would respect my intention. But my father did not feel the same way. At the time, I didn't understand why."

Pausing in his story to gauge her reaction, Ramone squeezed her hand. Annie felt an irresistible urge to tease this serious man and said, "So, if I am to understand, you have a very handsome brother who is also a matador? Hmmm..." She couldn't keep her straight face when she saw the crestfallen look that came over him and laughed out loud. Chagrined, she gently added, "I saw other matadors that day, Ramone, but you were the one who stole the show for me."

There was more to say, but for now they seemed to take comfort in each other's responses. Hand in hand, they settled into a leisurely walk with no special destination in mind. The boardwalk was up ahead, but Ramone and Annie weren't ready for people and the interruptions that would surely come from his fans. They saw a beachfront café, and Ramone requested a table out on the terrace.

Annie commented, "Such a beautiful view. Whether on board the *Porto Banus* or ashore, I never tire of gazing across the water." Ramone watched her as she continued, "I am not sure why I find such solace with the sea. Perhaps it is the rhythm of the waves. Or possibly the wind and mist from the spray of the sea against my face. In those moments, it feels like an isolated island in time...past and future demands no longer exist. There's only the present. Does that make any sense?"

Their coffee came, and Ramone quietly asked, "With your love of the sea and endless curiosity about other cultures, do you think it possible to ever settle in one port?"

"I did try in Maine, working in Portland, then back home in Boothbay. With my father away so long, I hated the thought of leaving my mother. I had a great job at an architectural firm in Portland. After a few years, I quit to return home and took a position at the Maritime Museum in Boothbay, which was not nearly as challenging. It was an odd time for me. With my father gone, my mother convinced me to stay at the house rather than get an apartment. Even though I joined a sailing club and met some new friends, I felt stuck. It was the sailing in Boothbay that kept me somewhat centered. My cousin Sabine could see it and tried to help me move forward. When the accident happened and she was hurt, that small comfort of sailing was disrupted and was no longer enough. I was lost. My mother was the first to recognize it and pushed me to change my course. I am not sure what I would have done if I had remained there."

Sensing Annie opening up to him, Ramone wisely left the subject of his father and brother alone for the time being. "How is Sabine?" he asked.

Annie tried to shield the sadness in her eyes and said, "I check on her often. She had a brain injury during the accident that caused her to fall into a coma. For a long while, the doctors kept her in the coma to give her body a chance to heal. When she finally woke up, her speech was impaired. With speech therapy and rehabilitation, there is now hope for a full recovery. I don't think I can stop my restless journey until she gets through this."

Ramone nodded his understanding and responded, "In my profession with the danger it holds, I see people get their lives cut short or changed drastically more often than I'd like."

Annie thought about this and asked, "I would like to know more about the bullfighting and the hold it has on you and your family."

Warming to his topic, Ramone began, "In the Mediterranean, sacrificing bulls is a practice dating back to prehistoric times. You mentioned you will be traveling to Greece soon. There, killing the minotaur was symbolic of a bullfight. Here in Spain, the first formal bullring emerged in Ronda back in the late eighteenth century. As it gained popularity, the bullfight, or *corrida*, began to follow a distinct sequence of events. It was a ritual, actually...a ceremony carried out in carefully prearranged steps that requires a sacrifice, a sacrifice to the death.

"The history of bullfighting in my family was my inspiration. As a young teenager, I attended a bullfighting festival in Granada with my grandfather and my brother. My uncle was in the ring, and I couldn't take my eyes off the fierce fighting bull. It has been said, 'A true matador has a tenuous relationship between the fear of death and the willingness to risk it.' The bull personifies death. It is also said by physically overcoming death in the arena, a man seeks immortality. There is some truth to that. Antonio and I both attended the school for bullfighting in Almeria. There we learned the technique and spirit of bullfighting, but it was my grandfather and uncle who inspired us to find our individual character as a matador. The feeling is unlike any other to fight the fiercest of bulls and leave the ring a victor."

Annie was captivated by his description. Was there some parallel between them when past and future ceased to exist and only the present remained? Naturally, that must take over in the ring when his full concentration meant life or death.

Thoughtfully, she asked, "Why do you suppose your father chose Antonio to be the one to convince me to go to Sevilla?"

"Antonio was always closer to Papa," he answered. "I was the rebellious one. It was always a disappointment to me that he did not follow the family tradition. For that reason, I found myself closer to my uncle over the years. When Papa saw I was pursuing you instead of Antonio, the anger in his eyes was clear. It was then I realized the rage I saw in him was new. Over the last couple of years, his personality changed. My mother noticed that he was drinking more and often disheveled. The scar on his face was new. She shared her concern with me. I hate what might have happened to both you and your father if we hadn't foiled his plans. It hurt terribly to hear he had shot your father. I did ask you to Sevilla as he wanted. As much as I wanted to see you again, I was relieved you didn't come. Again, I couldn't fulfill the plan in Zanzibar."

Conversation flowed smoothly over the next several hours. Ramone asked about her time in Paris after he left. Leaving out a couple of unnecessary details, she enthusiastically shared stories about the friendship the three of them have, the unforgettable art and food, and the general ambiance of Paris. She also told him about the upcoming trip to Greece and her hope that her friend, Mara, would join her.

He nodded and commented, "The Greek islands are a special place to me. There was a time in my youth I wanted to be a sponge diver. I admired the Greek tradition of free diving with no equipment. I got to the island of Kalymnos one summer, ready to learn. After a week, what I learned was how hard it is. I gained a true admiration for the men who do this on a regular basis."

On the walk back to the villa as the sun was setting, Ramone told Annie about a festive party the following night. Most of his fellow bullfighters would be there, including his brother. There would be music and flamenco.

"Would you accompany me, *querida*?"

Chapter 22

Annie and Ramone—A New Beginning

Annie had of course accepted. Naturally curious about meeting Ramone's brother, she thought again how fate had intervened. Her introspection drifted toward the two men who had so ironically worked together to help her and her father. Both men were fiercely dark, handsome, and enmeshed in their own cultures. There was no denying the attraction she felt toward El Amir, but he convinced her in Paris a relationship between the two of them was not possible. Ramone was both brave and confident but also a hopeless romantic. He had pursued her since the day they met, and she had to admit, it surprised her how easy conversation was with him. However, even though Annie's heart told her Ramone's affections were sincere, she was struggling to learn the value of thinking things through and acting with clear intention.

Just as she planned to keep levelheaded and "act with intention," Annie smiled to herself as she went over to her suitcase and pulled out the black chiffon dress. *Tonight should be interesting.* She continued her mischievous thoughts along that line, *Tame equals safe. Where's the fun in that?*

Annie took care in her preparations for the evening. Her hair, swept back on one side featuring a single-pearl earring, fell in waves on the other alongside her face. She tried various necklaces, but clearly the best for this neckline was none. Finishing the look, she chose ruby-red lips, black strappy heels, and a black single-button wrap. Finally, she walked downstairs to test the look on her grandparents. They both stood up to embrace her.

Dom was first to speak, "Stunning, my dear! There will be no man in the room able to take his eyes off you in that dress."

And Gennie added with a wink, "*Chérie*, your French heritage is coming out tonight. Take care that you do not venture too far beyond your sense of comfort."

Annie hugged her and asked, "I won't. Did I go too far with this dress?"

Gennie glanced toward the door as she said, "Looks like you will find out soon enough. Your young man has arrived."

A quick moment of nerves and hesitation almost had Annie running back to the shelter of her room until she saw the look on Ramone's face.

In Spanish custom, he went to shake Dom's hand, softly saying, "And I thought facing a bull took strength!"

Dom grinned mercilessly. "Take care of her, son," Dom replied.

Ramone then hugged Gennie and came over to Annie, reaching for her hands. He approvingly noticed there was no place for the rose corsage that lay waiting in the car. While Ramone was helping her with her wrap, Annie took the chance to observe him in his formal dark-gray suit, obviously custom-cut, showing off his lean and very well-built body. A bright-white shirt with charcoal-and-crimson-striped tie was the perfect contrast to his tanned complexion and dark hair. Dashingly handsome, she thought as they left.

In the car, Ramone tossed the rose corsage aside, softly saying, "*Querida*, there is no flower that could compete with your beauty tonight...you steal my breath."

Nerves still slightly rattled by her grandmother's words, she said, "I bought this dress in Paris. Do you think it too much for tonight's party?"

Frowning slightly, Ramone said with a jealousy he was

not used to, "Did he see you in it?"

Catching her mistake too late, she assured him, "Only when Sarah and I were trying on clothes at the boutique. You are the first I have worn it for."

"*Querida*, I plan to be the last."

Well, Annie thought, raising her eyebrow, *this might be the most interesting adventure yet...*

At the entrance to the party, even before she took off her wrap, Annie could feel the curious stares, probably wondering who this new blonde was on Ramone's arm. They checked her cloak, and he tucked her arm into his. Her matador was staying close, and she felt a warm, unfamiliar contentment. He guided them through the ballroom, casually introducing her to friends and acquaintances along the way. They finally stopped when he saw his brother, Antonio, standing next to a dazzling brunette with hair back in a tight bun and dressed in traditional flamenco attire. Antonio was dressed flashier than most with a red ruffle-front shirt garnishing his dark suit. Ramone was correct. His brother was dangerously handsome, and the flamenco dancer was doing everything in her power to hold his attention.

Antonio seemed unaware of her ploy and was genuinely pleased to see his brother. But Annie knew the moment he looked her way, feeling both his intensity, as well as scrutiny.

Ignoring the girl next to him, he strode right up to Annie and boldly said, "You must be Annie. Are you aware it should be me next to you?"

Ramone gave him a slight shove and said, "Thankfully it worked out the way it did, or she might not be with us tonight."

Immediately contrite, Antonio apologized, "You are right, brother, of course! Who knew what tempted our father to plan such dire actions?" Looking at Annie, he continued, "And thank you for sharing her with us tonight."

At that, he smiled, and the dimples deepened, showing his rascal side. They were introduced to the dancer and told she would be performing later. The brothers lapsed into a relaxed conversation about an upcoming festival where both would be fighting, giving Annie a chance to look around the room at an intriguing cast of characters. The evening went well through dinner and the show.

When the dancing began, Antonio got up to approach Annie; but Ramone stepped in, saying, "Tonight she dances only with me."

Reminiscent of their first night together, Annie and Ramone danced to song after song with thoughts of only each other. When he held her close and they swayed to the slower music, there was no mistaking the effect her dress had on him. She found herself curious about further intimacy with this man of undeniable machismo.

When the musicians took a break, Ramone guided Annie down the hallway to a terrace that led to the garden. As they approached the shadowed corner where the garden began, Annie shivered. Ramone quickly removed his jacket. Putting it around her, the back of his fingers connected with her open neckline. Watching her intently, he slowly moved them along the border of her skin and fabric over the inner swell of her breast. Ramone caught her gasp with a deep lingering kiss while he continued to explore the soft ivory skin that was exposed to him. Then as if reaching for something on the ground, he wrapped his hand around her ankle and made his way up her leg, following the slit of her dress to her thigh.

Kissing her again, he murmured, "I have wanted you from that first night, *querida*. Tonight, in that dress, my hunger becomes impatient."

Under the privacy of his jacket, Ramone gently placed the palm of his hand at her neck. As he lowered his hand, his fingertips broke the border of the neckline, searching for more of what was so tempting.

Finding it impossible to concentrate on anything but this strong athlete's gentle manner in his kisses and touch,

Annie leaned in closer to the flame she saw in him. There was more kissing and more dancing, but a spell had been cast over them both. Toward the end of the evening, Antonio approached them to say good night. The look from his brother stopped him midstep. Antonio merely tipped his head with a subtle salute, smiled, and turned to leave.

Ramone was quiet while driving Annie back to the villa, so she allowed herself a few moments to absorb what had happened between them that evening.

At the door, Ramone huskily said, "Be clear, *querida*. This is not over. I will not bring you back to your grandparents ravaged in that beautiful dress. There is a waterfall by the mountain not far from here. Let me show it to you tomorrow. Fix a picnic? I'll bring the wine."

Annie finally found her voice and smiled. "That will be lovely. I know exactly what I'll bring." With that settled, she reached her arms around the neck of this impossibly sexy matador for one final kiss. This time, closing the door behind her, she smiled in anticipation of doing a little more of her own exploration.

Chapter 23

Love Blossoms

Annie's excitement for the new day was contagious. Her grandfather was reading the paper on the poolside patio when Annie came over and gave him a big kiss on the cheek.

He said with a chuckle, "Someone is feeling good this morning."

She laughed, then went off to find Gennie. Perfect! She was in the kitchen. "Gennie, can we make some of those *tortillas de patatas*? I need to make a picnic."

Gennie, always ready for any excuse to cook, heartily agreed. "Let's add some Manchego cheese, Iberico ham, chorizo, cured olives, and grilled crostini. That should satisfy your matador's appetite."

Annie didn't miss the innocent reminder of her matador's "hunger."

Dom came into the kitchen to let Annie know there was a call from Mara. As soon as she answered the call, her enthusiasm was equally met by Mara's.

"I can't believe you want to share the Greek islands with me! It will be delightful to travel together again. Can the *Porto Banus* pick me up in Rhodes? I could fly there to meet you."

Annie said, "That will be perfect! We can concentrate on the islands close by since I do have to be back in time to get to Tomás and Meghan's wedding. There is so much to catch up on. I can't wait to see you."

Annie sent word to Captain Luis that the Greece trip was a "go" and asked him to coordinate the timing with a stop in Rhodes to pick up Mara. On an impulse, Annie called Sarah to see if it would be possible for her to join them. She knew it was doubtful since Sarah was working on her newly commissioned pieces.

As expected, she regretfully declined. "Next time, for sure."

Luis responded that if they left on Saturday, it would take a little over a week and a half to get there. That gave her four days for a little Marbella distraction and to be ready for her next journey.

Now was the time to change her focus to her date with Ramone. Annie decided on her blue-and-white-print bikini with her white cutoff shorts and cobalt-blue button-down shirt. She toyed with ways to wear the shirt and decided to leave it unbuttoned and tie the tales at the waist. *Tennis shoes or sandals?* Picking up the tennis shoes, she threw the sandals and some other things in a "just in case" bag. She wanted to be ready for whatever came her way. As she walked down the stairs to get the picnic basket, it occurred to her she had just dressed in the colors of her upcoming trip to the Aegean! Would she ever tire of the discovery of new places and cultures that taught her so much, not only about the people she met along the way but especially herself? In her excitement about the day, she pondered, *Where did Ramone fit into this journey?*

Distracted by these thoughts, Annie did not hear the knock on the door, so Gennie let Ramone inside with a warm welcome and hug. Annie turned around to see a man in complete contrast to the formal matador in his gilded suit and slicked-back hair. Wearing a black-and-white t-shirt, knee-length board shorts, and sandals, he could be any ordinary guy until you saw his face. The warm smile, captivating eyes, dark wavy hair with a bit of facial hair—ah yes.

Realizing she was staring at him, Annie shook herself out of it and grabbed her bag and picnic basket, saying, "Ready!"

Ramone hadn't missed the look on her face and smiled to himself. Seeing her long legs and bikini top under that shirt assured him this would be a day to remember. Ramone was driving his red Fiat convertible. The day was sunny and warm, perfect for a picnic. They tossed their bags in the trunk and headed north. Andalusia was unique with its temperate climate primarily because of the mountain ridge that protected it from northern Spain. As they got closer to the first line of hills, there were olive-tree orchards everywhere.

Annie asked, "Do you think there might be a market in the area? I would love to take some local olive oil back to Gennie and my mother too since I will see her soon."

Ramone thought a minute and replied, "Yes, of course, there is a small village not far from here. I think I remember a small local market there." He told her about the local wine he brought, and she laughed about Gennie creating a feast.

The village was charming. Annie was delighted to stop there. They quickly found the market and got caught up trying samples of various olive products. While Annie chose her olive oil, Ramone wandered about the merchants.

As they left, she noticed he had a bag. "What did you buy?"

Ramone smiled at her and innocently replied, "The lady made me try this *crema de aceite de oliva*. It is a version of the cream that was used in times of the ancient Egyptians to preserve beauty. I thought we might try it."

Full well knowing his intentions, Annie blushed but recovered quickly. "Anything in the name of beauty, right?"

When they finally arrived, other than a rough path, there was no indication of anything but wilderness. Ramone put the top up and secured the car. They gathered their things (cream included, Annie noticed) and began the walk up the path. Wild orchids gave a vibrant color to the terrain they passed. Ramone led the way, and Annie had to admit she did not mind the rear view of her matador. After about a twenty-minute hike, they reached an opening. She could hear the waterfall before she could see it. Walking through to the open area, Annie noticed a crystal-clear pond based at the bottom of the most beautiful waterfall she had ever seen! Reaching up over one hundred feet and at least twenty-five feet wide, the mist of the fall created prism-like rainbows throughout the air over the water.

Annie stared in disbelief. "This is magical! I have never seen anything like it. Thank you for bringing me here."

Ramone smiled at her excitement. "I thought you might find it as special as I do."

Feeling like there was no one else in the world but them, they spread out the blanket on a flat grassy area.

"How cold is the water?" Annie asked on her way to touch it.

He answered, "Cool but refreshing. Would you care to swim?"

About that time, she noticed the flat area cut into the rock behind the waterfall, and the urge to explore took over.

Ramone came over to her, kissed her neck, and whispered, "Behind the waterfall, *querida*?"

Annie gave him a flirtatious nod, and he kissed her again, on the mouth this time. He released the knot of her shirt, and it fell down her arms to the grass. Ramone kissed more deeply, feeling Annie's response and made slow work of unzipping her shorts.

Annie pulled away, laughing. "Come on!"

She started toward the waterfall, then turned around. His t-shirt and board shorts were gone, leaving a small Speedo that did not leave much to the imagination. Smiling at him, she walked back toward him for another kiss. It was then Annie saw all the scars marring his perfect body. A look of sadness swept over her. She gently touched each one, followed by what she hoped was a healing kiss...his shoulder, his chest, his stomach, his thighs. Yet he still went back to fight again and again.

Ramone gently held her shoulders and lifted her to him for a lengthy sensual kiss, then said, "I do not show these often, *querida*. Does it make me ugly in your eyes?"

Annie looked closely at him. "No, but it gives me pain that you suffered each of these. Let me find the cream."

Thoughts of "behind the waterfall" vanished for now. All Annie wanted was to touch this amazing man and make his scars go away. She had not expected this, to be the one to touch first. But opening the cream and rubbing it into his body, Annie knew this was right. She did not want to taunt him but instead to make him feel safe and beautiful. Ramone's eyes were closed and breathing heavy, struggling to keep a rein on his composure. She made a move to turn him over and tried to swallow a small gasp when she saw the wide scar on his back. Rubbing the cream into his back, then his legs, Annie moved back up to kiss his back. So ironic that she felt a need to protect this man of steel who so boldly faced such fierce creatures fight after fight.

Rolling to his side, Ramone reached for her to lie next to him and simply held her. He had never seen such compassion in any woman he had been with, and he tightened his hold. Now it was his turn to explore this ivory beauty in his arms. Annie had a combination of strength and softness to her body that resonated "all woman" to him. The swimsuit left little to the imagination, yet he needed the barrier gone—now! She saw the raw need in his eyes as he loosened the ties of her top revealing rounded curves and sensuous peaks. His hands couldn't get enough, but his lips demanded their priority. Kissing, sucking, tugging, Annie's moans drove him on. Beneath the swimsuit bottom, Ramone's hand wandered, pleased with skin so incredibly soft yet covering firm muscles. His mouth went back to hers as he found her core and felt her molten heat. She arched in his arms, and he hastily removed the obstruction, then his own.

Annie was passionately returning his kisses, but when she glanced down, she had a moment of concern with his size.

Ramone must have felt the hesitation, "What is it, *querida*?"

"How will this work? I am so small, and you!"

Ramone laughed softly and reassured her, "You will be ready for me. Trust me always to be gentle with you."

Even in the daylight, Ramone made Annie feel beautiful. He could not get enough of her, and the responses she gave him humbled him to take his time. When his hand and fingers found her core again, Annie's hands held tight to his shoulders, then shuddered with a small scream. All it did was make her want more, and she wiggled to get closer to him. She wanted to touch him. When she did, she took pleasure in his moans. He rolled her on her back and entered her slowly with small gentle thrusts that were driving them both to the brink. She reached behind him and pulled hard, feeling the whole of him enter inside her. Gulping for air, she held tight as he began the age-old rhythmic dance. Pacing themselves and each other, their climax shattered any expectation they might have had about each other, and their screams pierced the sound of the waterfall.

Neither could move. Lying there, content, time ceased to exist. When Annie started to nod off, Ramone adjusted and cradled her. As she drifted, she knew she had never experienced anything like this man.

Chapter 24

Romance Takes Over

The bonding experience during the afternoon at the water-fall was more than just physical for Annie and Ramone. They swam, made love again behind the waterfall, talked, and laughed, then finally got to the picnic. Annie marveled at how lighthearted and funny Ramone could be rather than his more normal serious side. The longer he was with her, the more Ramone's spirit lifted. She made him laugh, but most of all, he had seen a tenderness in her that melted his heart. They talked about the Greece trip, as well as her trip to Maine for the wedding. Realizing how little time they had to spend together, both felt a tug of need.

Ramone suggested, "Perhaps I could join you for a long weekend in Greece."

"Would you do that?" Annie questioned. He assured her he would check his schedule and try.

Still in the convertible back at the villa, one final kiss led to a dozen, and Ramone was not convinced they could avoid coupling right there in an open car! Someone had to be strong, so he gently pushed her to arm's length.

"What are you doing to me, *querida*?"

Annie wasn't quite sure she could answer that question since she felt the same. They finally said good night after agreeing to meet for a late breakfast the next morning. She walked into the villa by the hall mirror and was glad her grandparents were out. The glow on her face was not just from lack of sunscreen!

Annie poured a glass of wine and decided on a hot bubble bath. She soaked and sipped, thinking of her upcoming time at sea, which typically provided such a sense of peace. *When romance comes along, it does seem to take over, doesn't it?* At that, she put on her comfiest pajamas, grabbed her journal, and went down to the library to write about this newest development.

Pen in hand, feet tucked under her, she began to write. She tried to describe how she felt seeing Ramone's scars for the first time. It was more than sadness she felt for those harsh reminders of how dangerous his profession is. Apprehension? If they were to form a serious relationship, how would she feel each time he entered the ring, knowing the result might be serious injury or, God forbid, a fatal wound. *How do these bullfighters' families deal with the constant worry?*

She paused and forced herself to continue. There was no question she was seriously attracted to El Amir and wondered where a relationship with him would have gone if they had gotten together that night in Paris. Annie took the liberty on paper to privately compare the two men who had produced such an effect on her. The similarities were many. Both were dark-complected with wavy brown hair. Both had amazing eyes that communicated their feelings. Both were honorable men. Both were men of means. Both were from cultures different from her own where strong, macho men were the norm. *So what are the differences?* Annie stopped to ponder, then wrote:

> *Generous versus romantic? El Amir did not hesitate to lend me his plane, support Sarah's talent, and spoil us in Paris. On the other hand, Ramone chose red roses to accompany his notes, had a painting commissioned to commemorate their night together, shared that deeply emotional rendition of Caledonia*

with me, and was a giving and sexy lover. Hmmm, putting the choice on the scale, I think romance wins out.

Chuckling at herself for even thinking along these lines, she put the journal down when she heard Dom and Gennie come in. Gennie naturally asked how Ramone had liked the picnic, and Annie said it was perfect. She told them a little about this hidden waterfall by the mountain ridge and how beautiful it was.

Then she pulled out the olive oil for Gennie and told her, "When we went through all the olive orchards, we found a market that sold this oil made right there locally. We tried it, and it's delicious."

Gennie smiled and thanked her, giving Annie a giant hug. And with another closer look of speculation, her French grandmother gave her a knowing final embrace good night.

Back in her room, she looked in the mirror to see if she was wearing a neon sign. What she saw was a woman deeply flushed, looking quite pleased. *Ugh, I must stop mooning over this man!* But she could hardly get the thought out of her head before she recalled the feel of his hands and lips over her body and the full length of him inside her. There would be little sleep tonight, she acknowledged with a shrug and a smile.

Annie woke up early, suddenly missing her early morning walks in Maine. In this contemplative state of mind, she needed the solitude of a walk to sort through the emotions she was feeling. The urge to run from this new relationship was overwhelming. Could she indeed force herself to ignore it? Just three days until she left—she could either spend them brooding and alone or with a handsome and loving man. In all fairness, the choice was not a hard one, but she would not let her choice challenge her clearheaded future plans.

Her resolve in place, Annie was ready to enjoy the next three days thoroughly. When Ramone arrived, Annie let her instincts take over. The days were filled with exploration of the nearby countryside, water sports, and long walks. In the meantime, the evenings out gave Annie time to dress up a bit and shine in the Marbella nightlife.

Interspersed throughout were opportunities for more intimate pleasures and many hours spent in Ramone's small flat in the old town near the square. The sparsely decorated apartment found its personality with its colorful fabrics and pillows indicating a woman's touch.

Ramone, sensing her question, shrugged. "My mother. She insists a matador needs color, and it was easier to agree."

But he was not thinking of décor. Just looking at Annie aroused him, and his hunger for her was insatiable. What pleasantly surprised him was her desire equally matched his. Their exploration of each other moved from sensual to overtly erotic and back again with ease. Somehow, they had found the other's rhythm to know when to slow down and when to speed up. However, Ramone's kisses the last night seemed more intense.

Breathless, Annie asked, "What is it? What's wrong?"

"I will miss you, *querida*," Ramone whispered into her ear. "I will find a way to join you when you get to Karpathos."

The awareness of her departure the next morning hung over them. Annie had to pack. They agreed Ramone would help with her luggage and take her to the port. Packing usually held excitement for Annie as she planned a new adventure. This time, leaving was bittersweet, yet a deep knowledge seemed to slowly permeate Annie's soul. Her journey was not yet completed. The balance she craved seemed to always remain an adventure away. After Greece, her journey would take her back home to her parents and Maine. It was not yet time to let a darkly handsome man become sole captain of her heart.

Both caught up in thought, the ride to the port was a quiet one. Once there, Ramone passed her bags to Roff and came aboard to meet Captain Luis.

Shaking hands, Luis said, "Ah, you're the matador everyone raves over. I have seen you fight. You have great skill! We all want to thank you for your help in keeping Annie and her father safe."

Ramone got the royal tour, and then sensing their desire for privacy, the captain set about, readying the ship to depart. Annie showed Ramone her cabin, and he gently closed the door behind him for a more private farewell.

Holding her, locking eyes, he said, "These last days have touched me deeply, *querida*. I will count the days until I see you again, and when I fight, I will feel you watching me."

The upcoming reminder of the danger he encountered regularly prompted her to squeeze him tighter and say, "Be careful."

Chapter 25

Marbella to Rhodes, Greece

Upon Ramone's departure, Roff untied the lines. The wind caught Annie's hair as they made their way out of Marbella and into the Mediterranean. Just the reunion with Captain Luis and her beloved *Porto Banus* gave Annie a warm welcome-home feeling. Her soul, as always, stirred at the prospect of a new adventure. But had she left a piece of her heart there on the dock? Did her matador have more serious plans in mind? She thought ahead to his joining her in Greece and predicted another most intriguing adventure. In her journal, she wrote:

> *Perhaps it is not farther wanderings that will*
> *supply my answers.*

For now, however, she settled into the rhythm of life at sea. Dom's lively tales of the islands of Greece encouraged her forward, as did the upcoming time she would spend with Mara.

Several days into the voyage, when they were through the pass between Tunisia and Sicily, Luis pointed out the island of Malta. Such a beautiful area. Annie made a note to herself that a visit here might hold interest for her someday. Indeed, it would be easier for Sarah to join her here. *Hmmm...*

The vast expanse of sea between Malta and Crete gave Annie many hours to write in her journal and read about island life in Greece. She was to meet Mara in Rhodes, the largest of the Dodecanese islands, where this trip would focus. In its central location, where the Mediterranean met the Aegean Sea, Rhodes was strategic in both early and classical antiquity. The more she read, the more excited Annie became to share this island with Mara.

Her anticipation grew as the *Porto Banus* entered Mandraki Port and passed by the ancient Old Town walls. Mara had arrived earlier that morning, and she came aboard once the captain and the crew docked and secured the lines. Delighted to be together again, they planned their tour of the island over the delicious Greek salad Helene prepared.

The medieval Old Town, the Acropolis of Lindos, the ancient cities of Kamiros and Lalysos, the Valley of Butterflies...Annie and Mara were excited about this island's rich history and couldn't wait to get started. They had much to see in a short amount of time.

Rhodes boasted a landscape of eye-catching, generous natural beauty that included vast sandy beaches, emerald waters, castles, and ancient civilizations. But what captured Annie's admiration most was its beautiful mosaic of cultures. Byzantines, Romans, Greeks, Venetians, and Turks had all left their mark to remember them. Walking through the Old Town, every stone told a story, a history of over 2,400 years. Ancient statues, marble crests, fountains, the Street of the Knights...these people had evolved from a rich heritage left behind by past civilizations.

During their second day, while looking for a traditional taverna, they walked by a woman baking bread in an outdoor wood-burning oven. This way of baking had survived hundreds of years. She offered Annie and Mara a slice with fresh butter, and it was so tasty they had to buy two loaves to take back on board. The woman was friendly and warm, and they could tell how pleased she was they liked her bread. She pointed to a taverna down the road, and the girls set off to get some Greek specialties.

Their waiter spoke a little English and introduced himself as Estevan. Annie asked for an assortment of local delicacies; and he came back with a tray filled with moussaka, stuffed eggplant, cumin-scented meatballs, pilaf with ultrafresh mussels, and shrimp in tomato sauce. A tableside tossed Greek salad and cup of ouzo finished the feast.

While they were eating, Estevan told them of the mighty statue of Colossus, depicting the sun god Helios, which stood an impressive 157 feet tall! Finished in 280 BC, it became one of the Seven Wonders of the Ancient World. The statue supposedly straddled the entry to the port and stood guarding the harbor for 54 years before a devastating earthquake hit, and the statue of Colossus cracked at the knees, tumbling it to the ground. For 800 years, it lay where it fell, and people came from all over to see it—until an Ottoman ruler stormed Rhodes, capturing the island for his own. He had the statue melted down and sold to a Jewish merchant, who carried it off on nine hundred camels.

The architect in Annie was inspired at every turn. The stories, legends, history, and culture of Rhodes would stay with them, but their time here had ended. They made a pact to come back. The next day, they set sail for Kalymnos.

Chapter 26

Islands of Kalymnos and Kos, Greece

With Captain Luis at the helm, the *Porto Banus* left the harbor and headed out to sea. Annie and Mara sat comfortably up at the bow, finally with time to catch up on the events since they last saw each other. Annie filled her in on what happened with her father, Sarah's show at the London gallery, the odd twist with El Amir, and that she was seeing Ramone.

Mara could not believe how much had happened in such a short time! A little more shyly, she told Annie, "Do you remember in Australia when we said goodbye to Jonathan? He pulled me aside and said he would like to see me again. Not too long after I got home from our trip to Australia, I received a letter from him, and we have been corresponding."

That got Annie's attention. "Really? What does he have to say?"

Mara continued, "Just that he had enjoyed meeting us and was thinking of a trip to Bali someday...his last letter asked if he could come visit me."

"Why didn't you tell me? Hopefully you said yes." Annie smiled.

Mara blushed and said, "I hadn't gotten his letter asking to visit yet. When I did, I was shocked, of course. There was nothing between us on our trip other than a few glances and smiles. He spent most of the time with you. But, Annie, Jonathan arrives in two weeks."

Annie thought back. "Ah, yes, I do remember. He often

tried to include you, and I did see him admire your painting skills. You told Jonathan you'd see him, right?"

Mara looked down at her hands. "Yes, the path is never the way you think it will be, is it? I am trying not to make too much of it."

Annie put her arm around Mara and said, "I completely agree. It's impossible to foresee every twist and turn. Certainly, I have just recently seen that firsthand. I suppose you have to be willing to navigate each turn as you arrive at it. Jonathan is a good man. Give him a chance."

"And your matador? Has he captured your heart?" Mara asked.

"Perhaps," Annie answered. "I worry about the risks that he takes. When I saw his scars, I couldn't bear the thought of another one. Yet fight after fight, he returns to defeat the bull. I am not sure I can be that brave."

Annie and Mara were still talking when the captain rounded the rocky landscape of Kalymnos, and the *Porto Banus* entered lovely Pothia Harbor. A sculptured mermaid, reminiscent of Don Marco's stories, sat steadfastly on the breakfront to comfort departing sponge divers, as well as greet their arrival. Annie, remembering his tales and what Ramone shared about his experience with sponge diving, told Mara there were over five thousand different species of sponge varying in color, size, and quality! Some were smooth and velvety; others were rough and hard. They agreed to collect an assortment to bring home as gifts.

Annie had chosen Kalymnos for a reason. Aside from Ramone's memories, it seemed that the barren soil of the island, together with the superb beauty of the depths of the Mediterranean, had played a significant role in molding the character of the Kalymnian people. Her grandfather said these people exude a diversity that combined marked bluntness with a certain nobility of the soul, which ironically mimicked the nature of the sponges they sought. What Annie did not realize was that they were arriving in time for the annual Kalymnos Climbing Festival!

Annie and Mara were fascinated by the dazzling contrasts of pure-white houses set above the bluest sea, along with the dramatic coastline of coves and cliffs, all against a dark mountainous backdrop. Mara immediately reached for a canvas to portray the unique landscape.

But ashore, all the talk was about the sports climbing. Annie was captivated by the swarthy natives, exotic Turkish influences, and the fiercely independent spirit of the people. Mara...with canvas, brushes, and paint in hand...followed Annie to where the climbing was taking place.

Just a few minutes' walk from the port, Annie and Mara looked closer at the rocky landscape. Many of the rock faces had a unique quality for sport climbing. They learned the island was filled with well-equipped sport-climbing routes, from easy to extremely hard ones for the experts. Aside from the skill required, part of the lure was the breathtaking views of the endless blue of the Aegean Sea.

As they got to what appeared to be the center of activity, there was a group of people wearing helmets clustered around climbing lines attached to a tall slab of rock. Beginners were waiting their turn to try their skill. But as Annie looked closer at the surrounding cliffs and mountains, she saw what looked like specks but, in reality, were climbers in the most scary and intimidating positions she could imagine. One climber was at least 250 feet high and completely inverted, defying the simple law of gravity. Another was traversing a wild overhang suspended far up and out to sea. Another was somehow maneuvering between stalactites.

Mesmerized, Annie and Mara kept finding other climbers along the rocks, pointing them out as they saw them. When they sat down to watch, Mara pulled out her paints. What a magical place!

That night, they ventured out to a café on Grigos Bay where many of the climbers would be. Ouzo and wine were abundant, and the two women found a hearty welcome among the men.

All the languages spoken attested to the variety of countries represented, but the strength and build of these climbers were the same. It occurred to Annie that these thrill-seeking individuals who challenged danger were not that different from Ramone. She asked one young man named Georgio what it was that drove the climbers to take such risk.

He answered, "For me, it takes every ounce of focus I have. There cannot be a mistake. When I accomplish a particularly difficult climb, it is an unbelievable high to know I defied injury or death that day." Looking at Annie, he added, "You should try it! I do not climb tomorrow. Let me help you at the beginner rock. Perhaps you will understand the feeling."

About that time, the tables and chairs were shoved to the side, creating a dance floor, and Annie and Mara found themselves in the middle of the *Khassapikos* (or traditional "Butcher's Dance"). They danced and swayed, arms linked, following the age-old steps. Then the opas started as plates smashed.

Laughing and exhausted, Annie yelled over to Georgio, "Perhaps I will try climbing after all."

Mara looked at Annie in disbelief as the plans finalized for the following day.

Not an irresponsible person at heart, Annie struggled whether to tell Luis of her intention. She knew this was something that had come into her path for a reason. If she were to ever understand the danger Ramone put himself in, she needed to feel the adrenaline rush that came with risk. In the end, she decided not to tell Luis and convinced herself it was to not worry him. Mara adamantly refused to climb but said she would be there to support Annie and sketch a picture.

Annie's heart was already pounding when they saw Georgio up ahead. He handed the helmet and climbing gear to her and saw the shiver of fear in Annie. He reminded her he would be holding the rope for her and calling out her instructions.

"You want to make very precise moves to place your

feet correctly. There are handles bolted into the rock placed randomly for your hands." Georgio gave Annie a few more instructions, then told her she was next.

Just when she was sure the fear would debilitate her, Annie drew a stubborn bravery from deep within her. *I will not die today. I can do this and will see it through!* She tuned out all noise but Georgio's voice calling out where to put her foot next.

One move, then the other, she slowly found the next foot-hold or handle to continue to move her up the rock. She surprised herself when she maneuvered a full lateral move and looked down to give a thumbs-up to Georgio and Mara. That one moment of distraction was all it took to begin a slide down the mountain. A feeling of pure panic invaded while she slid for a few moments until Georgio's rope caught her. Taking several deep breaths while she dangled, she realized Georgio was fully supporting her. She quickly reached out to grab the nearest handle and foothold. Annie thought for a moment about these climbers who had no one with a rope to support them and how precariously they moved across the cliffs. The top of the rock looked about ten feet away. *Focus Annie.*

Then she'd be able to rappel down as Georgio had shown her.

Determination replaced the fear, and she finished the climb. Mara ran up to hug her, and the others who were watching called out all sorts of support and congratulations. She had done it! Not perfectly, but she had persevered. Was there a lesson with the climb? Pondering the answer, Annie knew her next journal entry:

> *Challenges are real and many in life. Yet the possibilities available to you are many more and come from all directions. Challenge plus achievement equals fulfillment? Value?*

Thanking Georgio profusely, Annie left with Mara, who couldn't stop raving over her friend's achievement.

The next morning, before the *Porto Banus* set sail for the isle of Kos, Annie and Mara made one last round of the vendors to round out their sponge collection. Kos would be the last stop before Mara took the ferry back to Rhodes for her trip home. Ramone would then join Annie on the island of Karpathos.

After entering the harbor at Kos Town, Annie and Mara wandered the shady tree-lined streets until they found a small Italian-style villa that rented bicycles and boasted the best catch of the Aegean. Securing the bikes, they sat down to share the whole fish served with root vegetables. The hostess told them this fish was so good there was no need for seasoning, and she was right. Serving them a glass of local wine, she told them to ride the bikes to Therma Beach for the local hot springs or to try the windsurfing at Psalidi Beach. And of course, they should not miss the ancient archaeological sites.

The girls both hated the thought of parting company. Mara's last day in Greece was a busy one, filled with visits to the fifteenth-century knight's castle and the Hippocrates plane tree where tradition said Hippocrates used to sit to teach his students around the fifth century BC. The day ended perfectly with a trip to the enticing Turkish quarter, listening to bouzouki music and toasting a successful trip over rich dark Levantine coffee. Later, Annie was helping Mara pack when she received an unexpected telegram—it was from Ramone!

> 'Querida, *I could not wait any longer to see you and have freed up my schedule a day early to meet you in Karpathos. I will await you there, Ramone.'*

Chapter 27

Arrival in Karpathos, Greece

Secretly, Annie liked the idea of being alone with Ramone. When she found out the distance to Karpathos and how long it would take the *Porto Banus* to get there, Annie decided to take the ferry instead when Mara left. Captain Luis would follow. She quickly sent a telegram back, telling Ramone of her decision to arrive by ferry at the main port of Pigadia late tomorrow afternoon and that she had reserved a small flat at the port. She gave him the information about the hotel and realized it was her turn to pack. Annie and Mara talked and laughed until the wee hours about the wondrous islands they had explored, Annie's rock-climbing feat, and their upcoming adventures with Ramone and Jonathan.

Roff helped with their bags the following morning. Their ferries were leaving close to the same time, so the friends walked together to the ferry dock. Both Annie and Mara agreed the hardest part of these long-distance friendships were the goodbyes. Once boarded on her ferry, Annie felt a surge of excitement to be alone with this viral man again. However, she was also intrigued by Karpathos, known as the "Island of Contradictions." One village they planned to visit was Olympos. The oldest and most enchanting village on Karpathos fiercely preserved its ancient dialect and customs, fine folk crafts, and traditional dress, making it a living museum. It sounded so much like Meghan's Irish hometown of Dingle that Annie's curiosity was aroused at what their similarities might be, and she was pleased that she would be able to share her newfound knowledge of this place with Meghan at the wedding.

The hours on the ferry gave Annie time to update her journal. As she started to write, the sketch Mara had drawn of Annie doing the rock climb fell out. Annie thought about the irony of having two close girlfriends who were both such talented painters. *What talent to be able to capture a moment in time and allow it to last forever. Is there such a thing as forever?*

Annie wrote about her conversation with Mara about life's path and the twists and turns it was sure to bring and ended with:

How does that allow anything to last?

Annie went to the top deck as the ferry got closer to Karpathos. The tall mountains, pristine scenery, and turquoise water were breathtaking.

Ahh...a unique island paradise with a purely natural environment combined with an authentic tradition lost in the centuries by most.

Entering the port of Pigadia, Annie saw remnants of the ancient city of Poseidio, named to honor the god of the sea, Poseidon. At the entrance stood parts of the ancient acropolis and the Cyclopean walls that protected it. On the left of the harbor was an impressive building that the woman next to her pointed out and said dated back to the Venetian rule. Annie could see why Ramone had chosen this island.

There he stood, on the dock waiting for her. Hair slick, day-old beard, mirrored sunglasses—Ramone looked as confident and debonair as any celebrity. His shorts and button-down pale-gray shirt looked to be of exceptional quality. Annie had chosen a coral-and-white print pullover knit dress that fit in all the right places. Ramone saw her and immediately took charge. Giving her a sound and thorough kiss hello, he handed a coin to a boy to take her bag up to their terraced room at the top of the hill. They were going by scooter. It did not go unnoticed when Annie had to hike her dress up to straddle the seat behind him. Ramone caressed her thighs wrapped around him and worked his hands up her legs under her dress. Moving to her inner thighs, he gently pulled her open and adjusted tightly against her.

Annie's eyes rolled in pleasure and whispered, "People are staring."

Ramone's answer, "Do not bring inhibitions, *querida*. I will have all of you." At that, he started the engine, and Annie experienced a most sensual ride to the top.

The whitewashed building with the brilliant blue door led to a room with a terrace overlooking the sea and the incredible harbor. There was even a dipping pool. Surrounded by vines and flowers strategically placed, they had total privacy.

"I love it!" Annie exclaimed.

Ramone had exchanged the small room Annie had gotten for this apartment. She noticed everything. The traditional linens on the bed with a hand-stitched coverlet, the earthenware flower boxes, and tiled accents felt like going back in time but with all the modern amenities. Ramone loved to see her so pleased; he had picked this apartment for her.

Looking at the way her dress clung to her, however, he was no longer thinking about the room. Going up behind her as she stared out at sea, he swept her hair to one side to kiss her neck. His hands made their way down her body, pausing at strategic curves and valleys. Annie's eyes were closed, absorbing the feelings when he turned her to him. He slid her dress over her head with the tiny undergarments following close behind.

Seeing her tan lines, Ramone softly murmured, "You

have been kissed by the sun, *querida*. Now it is my turn."

Annie slowly unbuttoned his shirt and let it fall from his arms next his shorts. When they were skin to skin and kissing, Annie gave a fleeting thought as to whether she would be able to leave her inhibitions behind. Ramone swept her up to lay her flat on the bed; sometimes she forgot his strength. His kisses deepened, and his hands found her breasts. When Annie arched her chest in response, Ramone could no longer keep his kisses from moving in that direction. Teasing the tips until they hardened was driving Annie's desire, and her response drove his lips lower, letting his fingers continue to arouse her breasts.

As Ramone found her inner sweet nectar, his hands moved slowly down her body and around to massage her bottom. Between his wet kisses and her moisture, he probed her with his index finger to get her thoroughly wet. That finger made its way from her rear inside her, and his mouth and finger found a rhythm, making her arch and buck in raw need for release. When wave after wave of ecstasy flooded through her, Ramone's control left him, and he moved back up to her. Annie was spent with eyes glazed. But when he entered, her every sense awakened, and she wrapped her legs around him to take his full length and met him thrust after thrust. A climax that shuddered and shook them both with its power left them collapsed in each other's arms. Content to lie there together, they felt no need to move.

Time ceased to exist until the room began to darken. Ramone led Annie to the dipping pool on the terrace as they watched as the sun set over the sea. The connection they had along with the sexual experience made both hold each other closer. When Annie's stomach growled, she apologized with an embarrassed laugh. Ramone got up and wrapped a towel around himself. Retrieving her bag from the front stoop, he then prepared a small picnic he had put together with olives, cheese and bread, and a bottle of local wine. Annie got out of the pool, and Ramone handed her the terry robe that was hanging in the room. They sat at the small table on the terrace, eating and drinking. Ramone lazily asked about her trip before he joined her. She had much to tell. Annie went over to her bag and pulled out the sketch of her rock climb to show him.

Looking shocked, Ramone asked, "You did the rock climb? *Querida*, what if something happened to you? I couldn't bear it."

"But, Ramone, that's exactly how I feel each time you put yourself in danger in the ring."

Annie and Ramone finally decided to venture out. They walked down to the shore and found countless cafés and tavernas right on the water. On the way, two women dressed in traditional black dresses with white cuffs and hemline were carrying large bowls overflowing with fresh baked goods, taking them to one of the local restaurants. This island was not touristy at all, which made the couple feel like they had found a real treasure. They decided on an open-air, waterfront restaurant with a display of fish, shellfish, and octopus on ice at the entrance. They chose a redfish, which was grilled, then served tableside. Annie thought it might have been the best fish she ever tasted.

Chapter 28

Karpathos—Poseidon's Cave and Olympos

Looking forward to the new day, the plans would start with a visit to Poseidon's Cave. The next stop would be Olympos by scooter. There was a debate as to whether to go by boat, but the final decision seemed to offer the most flexibility. Annie told Ramone about Dingle, Ireland, and they were excited to see this most traditional village perched on top of a hill above the small fishing village of Diafani.

Content and happy to finally be able to wake up together, their lovemaking that morning took on a gentler pace with urgency replaced by sensual exploration. Annie loved the feel of Ramone's body and his reaction to her touch and kisses. However, the scars were a constant reminder of how he regularly faced danger. Although she was not ready to use the word love yet, her feelings for him grew deeper each day they were together. The way he kissed and caressed her seemed to effortlessly pull the most intimate responses from her. Annie could not help but think about a future with this man. However, could she commit to a lifestyle in which she never knew if her lover would survive the next fight? She wondered how his mother felt when either he or his brother entered into the ring. At some point, if she and Ramone were to move forward, they would need to have this conversation and tackle this potential obstacle.

For now, walking out on the terrace to the most brilliant day, Annie decided to enjoy the time they had. The *Porto Banus* should arrive late tomorrow. There had been some talk about Ramone sailing back to Spain with her, but she questioned whether it would be awkward having him on board under the nose of Captain Luis.

Freshly showered, Ramone came up behind her and nibbled on the back of her ear. "What a beautiful way to start the day, *querida*. Do you suppose we have indeed found paradise on this island?"

Annie looked at the cobalt-blue sky and emerald green water contrasting with the whitewashed houses and magenta flowers...stunning. Leaning back into him and reaching for his hand, she sighed. "Ahhh, I think we might just have."

They took the scooter down to the harbor and asked directions to Poseidon's Cave. The secret was to look for a relatively hidden stone staircase about a ten-minute walk from the harbor. Stopping for a cup of coffee, Ramone decided on the scrambled eggs with tomatoes and feta, while Annie had the yogurt with honey and walnuts. The food tasted delicious, and they were ready to start their adventure. The decision to walk was an easy one. Just breathing the air on this island gave a sense of purity.

Annie was in rare spirits and bounded ahead on the path, laughing, determined to find the hidden stone staircase. Ramone smiled as he watched her. Hair back in a ponytail, very little makeup, white shorts with a yellow tank top, and a light wrap tied around her shoulders, Ramone thought Annie had the unique combination of girlish innocence and womanly wisdom. He wondered, walking behind her, if she truly knew what she possessed. Annie was making her way into his heart, and Ramone was very aware he would never contain her restless spirit. But could he capture her heart?

"I found it!" Annie called out to him. "The stairs are over here."

His final thought as he caught up to her was to gaze at those long tanned legs. "We need to do something about those tan lines." With a smile, he knew just where to take care of that.

Annie had read about the cave and shared some of its history with Ramone. "Karpathos is an island immersed in an ancient past and mythology. Did you know Homer mentioned this island in the *Iliad*?"

They descended the rocky, uneven stairs and found a monumental cave with multiple caverns and openings. Annie continued, "It is said the cave was either a rock-cut tomb or a sanctuary dedicated to Poseidon or Aphrodite, the Greek goddess of love and beauty." Looking around and through the cave, Annie said, "I think I like the latter explanation. Can you imagine how old this is? Look at the shells embedded in the rock. This cave has to have been underwater at some time in the distant past."

Ramone studied the shells in the rock walls and agreed. "You can tell shepherds used the cave for what might be hundreds of years. Can you imagine how this holy place might have looked in ancient times?"

Ramone took her hand and walked through the cave again, imagining the lives of those who came so many years before. In the back corner, he kissed her, whispering, "Thank you for sharing this with me, *querida*."

Annie softly answered, "It has been unforgettable. Let's get back to the harbor and ride to Olympos. I have read so many things about it and can't wait to see it with you. Did you know it is the most traditional village of all Greece, either on the islands or the mainland?"

The scooter was the perfect transportation with the fresh air and gorgeous day, although Annie felt a blush remembering her first ride from the port. They rode up into the mountains, and the landscape was fascinating. When they rounded the corner and got their first glimpse of the village, the only word Annie could find to describe her impression was striking. Located at the top of a hill, traditional colorful houses cascaded down the two steep slopes, giving them a breathtaking view of the Aegean, and Annie thought it certainly lived up to its "Balcony of the Aegean" reputation. The stone-based windmills and the bell tower of the church mingled into the image gave an unprecedented picture.

They rode into the village and slowly wound through the narrow streets, absorbing the beautiful figures of women wearing their colorful handmade costumes and the genuine smiles and waves from the locals as they passed by. The first stop was the church of Panagia. Dating back to the sixteenth century, Annie and Ramone marveled at its wood-carved temple and painted murals. From there, they wanted to see the ancient Vrykous, with ruins from the fourth century! On foot now, they wandered past a traditional flour mill. Everywhere they went, the hospitality of these village people gave the couple such an appreciation of just how the people of Karpathos seemed to grasp the joys of life while maintaining their long-lasting traditions.

Passing a yard with the most artistic pottery scattered around it, Annie walked over to get a closer look.

Ramone said, "It looks like this might be a shop. Let's go in."

In the yard, they stopped to look at the individual pieces. An older man, dressed in traditional garb, came out to greet them. He spoke a little broken English and welcomed them into his home, where one room was lined with shelves and tables filled with his handmade pottery pieces. Beautifully shaped and decorated, some were glazed, and some natural. Annie found a terra-cotta pitcher painted with beautiful flowers and glazed to allow it to be used. She loved it and had to have it to remember this lovely place. Ramone was looking at another unique piece that almost looked like a basket or bud vase with two side-by-side openings. He was fascinated at the aubergine color mixed with a sun yellow.

Annie came over to show him the pitcher and saw the piece in his hand. They looked at the owner and asked what it was. He gestured with his hands, touching his heart and pointing at the two of them smiling. He finally found the words "marriage vase" that was used in traditional ceremonies when a man and woman married. Both Ramone and Annie laughed and put it down.

But picking it back up, Annie said, "What a perfect gift for Tomás and Meghan."

Pleased with their choices, they paid the man after he painstakingly wrapped each one in brown paper.

He shook hands with Ramone, and Annie came right up to him for a hug.

"What is your name?"

"Alessandro," he said.

Annie replied, "Alessandro, your work is amazing. I am Annie. He is my friend, Ramone."

Ramone put the two packages in his backpack. Before they left, Alessandro told them to find the Drosia Taverna, or shepherd's house, to taste fresh goat meat and local cheeses. The couple thanked him again and set off to find the taverna.

Annie and Ramone walked into welcoming hellos and jovial spirit. The proprietor heard they bought some of Alessandro's pottery and brought them a bottle of local wine from his own vineyard as a gift. They sat down to a feast of roasted goat, crusted bread with *tarama* (fish spread), *gimista* (bell peppers and zucchini filled with rice), and assorted cheeses.

Annie wistfully thought, *I could stay here forever.*

As if Ramone could read her mind, he said reaching for her hand, "This is perfect, *querida*."

Chapter 29

Karpathos—Gypsy Beach

Saddened by leaving Olympos behind but determined to enjoy the rest of the island, they rode the scooter through the mountains along a most scenic route through a dense pinewood forest toward the village of Messochori. Stopping on a whim at the great church of Panagia built on Sacred Rock, the reward was a spectacular view of the Pigadia town and harbor, where their flat was. When Annie stifled a yawn, Ramone turned the scooter toward the village of Affiartis.

He was looking for the unpaved road past the Poseidon Hotel. Once Ramone found it, he maneuvered the scooter down to a staircase leading to a beach. Annie looked out at the Aegean and took a mental picture she could take with her to remember. She wished Sarah or Mara would come here to paint it someday. Ramone told her this was a very little-known beach called Gypsy Beach, where they could swim and have beach time alone.

They went down the stairs and found the perfect place off to the side. Ramone pulled a blanket from his backpack, along with the leftover wine and two cups. "Let's go for a swim!" Ramone suggested.

"I didn't know we were stopping at a beach...I forgot to pack a swimsuit," Annie said, disappointed.

"*Querida*, it is just us. Feel the freedom to swim in the sea in this private place." Ramone stripped down and headed to the water.

Annie sat down for a moment, content, looking at this

fine specimen of a man as he walked away, remembering intimately the feel of each of those bulging muscles. Distracted by her thoughts, she was startled when he called to her to hurry. *Why not?*

As she entered the water, Annie could quickly tell Ramone was feeling frisky. Then out of sight, Ramone swam underwater and grabbed her by the legs. Coming up gasping for air, she determined to swim back to grab him when the realization set in that she was dealing with a solid wall that wasn't going anywhere.

Time to change tactics! Annie smiled and decided to practice her sidestroke, lazily gliding through the water, then her backstroke, giving Ramone a view that would not allow him to stand still.

"*Querida*, you are a temptress! Do not torment me so."

In response, Annie tried what might have to be called a backward breaststroke, drifting her back into him. Entranced with her backside, Ramone pulled her to him. Wrapping her legs around him, he supported her with his hands on her breasts. The water surrounding them added a new dimension to their intimate foreplay. Feeling the freedom of this place, Annie rubbed up against him, delighted in his arousal. Ramone easily supported her with one arm and moved his other hand over her body, not missing an inch. A growing passion and sexual need quickly replaced their playfulness. He slowly moved her up his body, then down until she was straddling him with full penetration. With his fingers and hands busy along with her helping to deepen his thrusts, Annie's desire erupted. How he had such control astounded her. She called out in release mere seconds before he did, and it took every ounce of strength he had to hold them together.

Going to shallower water, Ramone released her for a moment so he could sit and pulled her forward onto his lap to reconnect them. They sat there joined, kissing and holding each other. The sun was lowering in the sky, casting a warm glow over them while they both soaked up this romantic scene. They finally moved to the blanket to catch a few final rays, and Ramone was pleased to see those tan lines fading. This would be yet another day to remember for them both. Packing up the blanket and the empty bottle of wine, they took a last look at the beach they called theirs. Annie had a fleeting thought for her journal:

> *Is it fate to have such an afternoon on a beach with the name Gypsy? Aren't I a gypsy at heart?*

She smiled at the irony.

On the scooter ride back "home," as she now called it, Annie had her arms around Ramone with her head resting on the back of his broad shoulders. Affection between them was growing deeper by the hour. The *Porto Banus* would arrive the next afternoon to take her back to Marbella in time to join Dom and Gennie for the flight to Portland. How is it she wanted to freeze this moment with Ramone?

After a quick shower, Ramone went to pick up a light snack to have on their terrace. Annie showered more slowly, then grabbed her journal to write a little in her favorite lounge chair. Inspiration was abundant with such a view. She knew how hard this unique island would be to leave.

Remembering something Sarah said about living in a tent among the animals and reflecting on the meaning of how she felt, she began to write:

> *It is not necessarily the more glamorous parts of travel that leave the most lasting impressions. The Greek hospitality, along with their sense of history and tradition in this country, and especially this island have made an impact on me that I will not soon forget. And this time with Ramone has me questioning my constant roaming.*

Annie set aside her journal when Ramone came in with his backpack filled—a fresh loaf of bread, cheese, several skewers of souvlaki, a bottle of wine, and a large slice of baklava that he couldn't resist. Annie smiled at how at ease Ramone was with her compared to the serious matador facade he maintained back in Spain. She loved seeing this side of him and wondered how they would be after they left Greece. He arranged the food on the little table, and they thoroughly enjoyed their balcony picnic.

Talking about the next day, Ramone asked, "Do you have any idea what time the *Porto Banus* will arrive?"

"Only that it will be in the afternoon. We don't leave here until the following day," Annie replied.

"Will you feel the need to stay on board tomorrow night, or can you stay another night with me?" Ramone hated the thought of being in this flat without her.

"Have you given any more thought to sailing back with me? It will probably take at least a week and a half." Annie looked at him hopefully.

"I am to fight in Sevilla next week. The only way I could sail with you is if Antonio would replace me in the ring. We have fought for each other before. I will send him a message to check if that would be possible."

There was no international phone service on Karpathos, so Ramone used the local phone to call the manager asking to send a telegram to his brother. He hoped to hear back by early tomorrow.

After such a full day, Annie and Ramone decided to spend their time on the terrace, talking and sipping wine. The leftover baklava was a highlight and, combined with a little French-kissing, made quite a sweet confection! Delighting in the sweetness, Ramone undressed Annie, rubbing the remnants of the baklava over her breasts and down her torso, licking and sucking the taste. Fighting for the last piece, Annie began to do the same to him, smiling at how quickly she could get his erection. When the sweet baklava found his hardness and her kisses and sucking followed, Ramone found control slipping from him. Grabbing her to straddle him, they came together in a sticky and sweaty coupling, both astounded at how powerfully the climax shook them. After, there was laughing and bathing each other in the small terrace pool, which in the natural course of events led to more lovemaking.

Chapter 30

Arkasa and Arkesia, Karpathos

Annie awakened early, feeling restless. Ramone was sleeping soundly, and she didn't want to disturb him. Quietly slipping out of bed, she wrapped a quilt around her and grabbed her journal and a cup of tea. She looked out to sea, constantly inspired by its serenity and beauty. But Annie also knew about rough storms and angry seas. Those thoughts were a reminder of Sabine. She should have been on this journey with Annie.

She began to write:

> *Every choice, every action or lack of action, has consequences. I suppose the thing is to choose the very best consequences for yourself and your world by choosing to do what is required to bring about those consequences. Is there anything I could have done to help Sabine? Did I make a mistake by not visiting her rather than traveling on this journey? I don't think it is best to second-guess myself. I have this moment to decide how to move forward. If I don't have time before the wedding, I am committing to go see her when I get back to Marbella.*

Putting down her journal with her head full of questions. *Did I just write that..."when I get back?" Is that an assumption already? Am I so entwined with this man that I do not see a future without him?*

"Good morning, *querida*. You look so serious," Ramone said, quietly standing at the doorway.

Startled, Annie stammered, "I was thinking about Sabine and wrote a few observations in my journal."

"Do you write of me?" he softly asked.

She looked up and smiled at this handsome man in his naked splendor. "Sometimes. But often I write about the cultures I have experienced and the people I have met along the way...people like Georgio, the rock climber, and Alessandro, the pottery maker. They all play a role in helping find the person in me that I am striving to be."

"I see that. You seem to grow and stretch from each experience you have. Sometimes I question how I fit into your journey. For now, though, I have some not-so-great news. The manager knocked on the door a while ago with a telegram from Antonio. He wanted me to know he did inquire but is not able to fight in my place. In Sevilla, this bull has been raised to be particularly fierce. I was the matador chosen to face him. It is a huge honor. Antonio said they want me there at the beginning of the festival for the opening parade. I can stay today until the *Porto Banus* gets into port, but then I must take the late ferry to Rhodes to get a flight out early in the morning. I'm so sorry, *querida*."

Digesting all he said, Annie put her journal aside. The quilt fell to the floor as she looked up at him with misty eyes. "So this is our last day?"

"Yes, *querida*, our last day in Greece, but certainly not our last day," Ramone said, holding her tight. Then affectionately popping her rear end, he tried to lighten the mood. "Go take a shower. We have some exploring to do!"

While showering, all Annie could think of was a bull raised to be so fierce they only wanted Ramone to fight him. *How can I endure the anxiety knowing the danger he faces in just a few days?* Thinking about her journal and lessons over the last few months, Annie knew there was a choice. Knowing there was but one choice for her, Annie determinedly chose to make this day great and to make every moment she had with Ramone count. The rest could wait until she was back out at sea.

Ramone was happy to see Annie smiling and ready for the day.

"Where to this morning?" Annie asked.

"First, we will head to the coastal village of Arkasa, where we can get a late breakfast. It is about sixteen kilometers from here. There is a temple dating back to the fifth century called the Basilica of St. Anastasia. From what I read, I think you will appreciate its architectural structure. Then perhaps a ride to Cape Paliokastrou, where there are remains of the city of Arkesia and its acropolis. There is a beach we might want to explore, Apella. It's supposedly the best beach in all of Europe. There are hiking trails through the surrounding rocky terrain and pine trees that slope all the way to the sea."

Annie enthusiastically replied, "What a wonderful day you have planned. I can't wait! But truthfully, I can't imagine a better beach than Gypsy Beach."

On the ride to Arkasa, Annie recognized much of the route and felt like the island was growing more familiar during this short time. However, she was fascinated to see what fresh discoveries today would bring. As they approached Arkasa Village, they saw before them an authentically scenic Greek island settlement—picturesque whitewashed adobe houses with narrow cobblestone streets, all reflecting the unique ambiance and tradition of the original Greek island design and architecture that remained through the years. Annie absorbed all of it.

Ramone left the scooter, and taking Annie's hand, they walked from the sea toward the town. When they passed a little outdoor café with a folded street sign outside touting their flavorful gyros of the day, Annie smiled at Ramone.

"How about skipping breakfast and going straight to lunch? I'm starving, and the smells are irresistible."

"Perfect! A lamb gyro with a little tzatziki sounds great." Ramone quickly replied.

They had become so at ease with each other that conversation flowed between them...with one significant exception. Annie refrained from expressing any more about her fear of him fighting. It hung over her, but she tried to tuck it away, at least for now.

"How is it Greek food in any other country never tastes as good as it does here?" she asked.

"Maybe it is the soil and its minerals that feed the plants and the animals. Or perhaps their special blend of spices," he speculated.

After the meal, they walked up to the basilica. Trying to grasp the age, over 1,600 years ago, they both were fascinated by the beauty of the art reflected in the mosaic floors. Annie began to study them closer and realized some of these floors had meticulously been excavated and restored. Comprehending what a difficult task that must have been made her appreciate their beauty that much more. From there, it was an easy hike farther up the hill to see the acropolis at Paliokastrou.

Annie shared, "This trip to Rhodes, Kalymnos, Kos, and now Karpathos has made me appreciate all the generations of those who have come before us. I don't understand why, throughout history with all its civilizations, there was always some group trying to terrorize and conquer another."

Ramone thought about what she said and replied, "It has to be an inherent tendency in human nature that cannot be changed. Strategic location for protection of trade routes, power, greed, religious beliefs? Some leaders just have it stronger than others. But there were also great leaders along the way."

Hand in hand, they walked back to the scooter as Annie thought about their discussion.

Ramone took off toward the southeastern part of the island to Apella Beach. At the top of one of the steep hills, he pulled the scooter over to the side of the road. Off in the distance, they could see the *Porto Banus* making its way toward Karpathos. Annie walked away, trying to cover her tears.

Ramone walked to her, turning her around to kiss her tears. "Do not cry, *querida*. We still have time. It will take them several hours to make their way into the port and finish their docking."

All Annie could do was reach around his neck and hold on to this man who had become so important in her life.

Ramone gently said, "Look at me. These days I have spent with you will stay with me forever. You have captured my heart, and I cannot bear to see you sad."

Forgetting all her good intentions, Annie asked, "Will you promise me you'll be careful? I am sick with worry about this fiercest of bulls you must face."

Ramone held her tight. "For a matador, worry and distraction are the kiss of death. I am well-trained and know what to do, *querida*."

All Annie could say as the tears continued to roll down her cheeks was "But your scars..."

Chapter 31

Apella, then Farewell to Karpathos

U nable to resist her tears, Ramone looked into her eyes. "Would you rather go back to the flat?"

Annie dried her eyes and said, "No, let's go find that beach you want to see." She didn't want to waste a moment.

When they arrived at Apella, they were elated with her decision. The beach was nestled between rock formations on either side with boulders that looked like they'd been randomly tossed into the water. Some rose above the water, and some remained submerged. What was most striking about the crystal-clear water was its two-tone color, moving from a brilliant turquoise by the sand to the deepest shade of cobalt blue Annie had ever seen. Pine trees covered the hill on one side, giving the entire scene a lush feeling. There were some lounge chairs and a few umbrellas, but the beach was not overly crowded.

"Do you want to swim or hike?" Ramone questioned.

Annie realized yesterday's private swim could not be topped, so she answered, "Let's take the trail."

As they climbed the path, the view got even more spectacular if that was possible. This area was not a place to be missed. As she looked down at this unexpected beauty, Annie thought about what she might write in her journal:

> *Where the ocean meets the beach is the earth's best-kept secret of renewal. Here, one is forced against one's mind, against nagging*

problems. Listening to the primal rhythms of the sea, it becomes easier to keep an island quality intact within. I will remember this soulful place and the richness Ramone and I have shared.

She stood close to him, looking out at the sea. Aloud to Ramone, she said, "There is a soulful quality about this island that will always stay with me. The time we have had here together has affected me more than I can say. Thank you for sharing Karpathos with me."

He just wanted to breathe her in, this woman who had breached his heart and soul. "I will count the days until your return to Spain." Kissing her deeply, he huskily said, "Let's go back. I want to hold you once more before we part."

They hiked down the path to the scooter and made their way back to Pigadia. When they passed the harbor, they saw the *Porto Banus* rounding the corner. It would dock soon, and the perfect romantic adventure would end. Ramone would take the ferry tonight.

Annie and Ramone got back to the flat that had become a haven to them. Their final lovemaking had a heavier weight to it. It was as though his thrusts could not get deep enough.

When they were as close together as they could physically get, Ramone murmured in her ear, "We are one, *querida*. You are my woman. Our love is strong. Do not forget that."

With one final thrust, they both came together in an age-old ecstasy shared by the lucky few.

Packed and not so ready, they both took a final look around their little home they had grown to love. The manager brought his cart to gather the bags. Ramone had taken the pitcher and marriage vase from Alessandro's pottery shop to put them in a protective padded bag. It was time. The last ride down to the harbor was quiet. When they got to the *Porto Banus*, Roff was already loading her bag.

Ramone turned to Annie and brushed a stray hair from her face. His hand lingered as he leaned in to kiss her.

Annie kissed him back, then said, "This has been an adventure I won't forget."

With that, Ramone left to take the scooter back to catch his ferry, and Annie boarded the *Porto Banus*.

When Captain Luis saw the tears in her eyes, he worriedly said, "Ah, lass, I have never known you to weep upon boarding this vessel. We will get you out to sea. You'll be fine. There now, Helene will bring you a fresh cup of tea. We will need to provision this evening but will leave at first light tomorrow."

Annie sat at the bow for a while sipping her tea. The allure of one more walk along the shore was enough to have Annie tell Luis she would be back in an hour or two. Annie had to chuckle at herself. The island hadn't changed, but the atmosphere had. She wondered at the powerful presence she felt around Ramone. Without him, it was like the air had changed, thinned out like going to a higher elevation. She walked until she found the taverna, where they had their first dinner and decided to get a table overlooking the boats in the harbor. A Greek salad and glass of wine should be perfect. Annie was no stranger to traveling by herself or eating alone. *It is time for me to reset my compass!*

Back on board, she asked Helene to wake her before they weighed anchor in the morning. There would be a chance to take another look at the island from the sea, and she didn't want to miss that perspective. Annie glanced at her journal and thought about writing, but she was too exhausted with emotion. There would be time enough at sea to write. Sleep, however, was elusive. Thoughts of scooters, beaches, and baklava invaded her dreams in the most unusual ways. Happy to see daylight, Annie was awake and dressed before Helene knocked on her door. Helene told her they planned to leave the island early, then she would prepare and serve a light breakfast once they were under sail.

"In the meantime, the coffee is hot. Would you like a cup?" Helene offered.

Annie smiled and quickly responded, "Absolutely!"

Her cup of coffee in hand, Annie went up on deck to watch them release the dock lines. As they motored out the entrance of the harbor, Annie remembered Ramone waiting for her at the dock, so handsome and eager to see her. It was time to say a silent farewell to Karpathos, but Annie promised herself out loud, "I'll be back."

For now, a new journey lay ahead. Time at sea to uncover her true feelings and consider what future was out there waiting for her. Annie grabbed her journal and wrote:

> *Is there an opportunity to live a life of joy, meaning, and fulfillment even if the conditions aren't perfect? I have learned through these experiences that the power of positive, focused thoughts and effort can go a long way in attracting what you desire.*

It did not take Annie long to get the rhythm of the sea back in her veins. She took the time to take frequent naps; most likely because of all the romantic exercise, she smiled to herself. Several days into the journey, Captain Luis found Annie at the bow with her journal.

"There's a storm brewing, lass. I'll be navigating around the worst of it, but I wanted to prepare you for some possible rough seas ahead."

Annie answered, "Thanks, Luis. I have never been the seasick type. Just in case, do you happen to have any green apples on board? I learned that cure from the fishermen in Maine."

"Why, yes, we should. I will have Helene find them if necessary."

The wind picked up later that afternoon, and a pelting rain followed. The captain found a small anchorage to secure them through the first night, but the weather was not letting up the next day. If they were to continue, the charts showed no island close enough to set anchor, which meant Luis and Roff would have to man the ship overnight without being blown too far off course.

Annie immediately said, "Is there any way I can help or do a shift?"

"Sure, lass, hold the wheel steady while Roff and I trim the sails," Luis answered.

Annie put on her rain gear and went to the wheel. The sea was taking on an angry churn, and the wave height was increasing. She took the wheel while the two men worked on the sails. The recollection of that day in Maine when Sabine's accident landed her into the sea gave Annie a skin-tingling sense of foreboding. Trying to reason, the nausea she felt was surely the recollection of the accident.

Captain Luis came back to the wheel and took over. Looking at Annie, he said, worried, "Are you okay? Maybe you need one of those apples. Find Helene. Roff and I will be fine."

Annie insisted on staying with them. "It is just the reminder of the accident with Sabine that made me squeamish."

The captain looked at Annie with rain spilling off her hood. "You know, lass, you will always be safe with me. You can't go run and hide whenever there is a storm."

"Of course, I know I am safe with you!" Annie replied. "If things are well enough up here on deck, maybe I will go below for a while."

She maneuvered down the stairs carefully to the salon. The swells had gotten larger. By the time she had her rain gear off, she barely made it to the head to throw up. Helene heard her and was right there, helping tie her hair back and trying to comfort her. When Annie felt it was finally over, she looked up to find Helene seated next to her.

Annie looked at her and said, "I don't get seasick, but I

was thinking about the sailing accident in Maine and maybe that combined with the storm..."

Helene offered Annie one of the apples, but there was no way Annie could eat.

"Thank you for staying with me. I am okay now."

In his highly skilled manner, the captain maneuvered around the brunt of the storm and found a small harbor to anchor in for the afternoon so he and Roff could sleep. The storm had blown them off course, but fortunately the storm was now behind them.

Annie's queasiness persisted. When the nausea reared its head again, Helene brought her a cup of green tea and very gently asked, "Annie, I have never known you to be seasick on board. Could this nausea possibly come from something else?"

Suddenly realizing the implication of what Helene meant, Annie shook her head to think. She and Ramone had used precaution each time, right? Then she remembered Gypsy Beach. She had not brought her swimsuit (or anything else). Surely fate would not have stepped in on that one mishap! She struggled to think about when she was due. She mentally figured within the next few days. Surely, even in that remote possibility, it would be too soon to have symptoms.

To Helene, needing a confidant right then, Annie said, "Surely it can't be. We were very careful. I am not even due for a few more days, and we will most likely discover I have the stomach flu or an overreaction to the storm. Helene, please, the captain and Roff cannot know about this. Will you help me?"

Annie's nausea intermittently continued. Helene nursed her with warm tea blended with a lot of lemon, soup, and a bag of peppermints to suck on. When the captain questioned her ailment, Helene jumped in to say Annie had a slight fever and must have caught a bug.

Annie finally went to Luis and asked, "Is there a close

harbor where we can stop for a day or so while I get my land legs? Do we have time?"

The captain knew firsthand this girl had sea legs before practically walking. However, he replied, "We backtracked some during the storm, and Crete is close by. We can stop in Chania, which is the Venice of Crete. You will like it, lass. You've enjoyed your time in Greece. You know, Crete is the birthplace of the first European civilization, the Minoan! If I recall correctly, sometime between 3000 and 1200 BC. We can pick up a few provisions there while you take a short break."

Annie felt a trickle of excitement. "YES! I would love that."

Chapter 32

Island of Crete, Greece

Entering the harbor of Chania, Annie could see the old town district originally built by the Venetians in the fourteenth century. They passed by the old lighthouse on the left. Luis told her there used to be a heavy underwater chain that connected the lighthouse to the Venetian fortress on the right so they could raise it to close the port if under attack. Annie noticed all the colorful houses, but what surprised her were all the people. Having so recently been in more remote islands with few tourists, she thought this harbor might be an exciting place to people watch. Once they docked, Luis pointed out a small harborside inn, where she could stay if she decided not to stay on board.

After the *Porto Banus* docked and they were sitting around the outer salon, the captain shared some of his experiences here.

"Lass, you have said how much you have enjoyed the Greek food, but there is something unique about the Cretan way of cooking. It's healthy and simple but so flavorful and delicious! We will stock up with some good samples while we are here. Your grandmother will be quite pleased with this detour!"

Annie, fascinated, asked, "What is it about their food or their way of cooking?"

Luis laughed and asked, "What do you think the average consumption of olive oil per person is in the States?"

Annie pondered. "I have no idea."

"The average is 0.5 liters a year. In Crete, no lie, it is over 25 liters a year. Cretans eat the largest quantities of fruits and vegetables in the Western world...with no use of hormones! There's very little beef. Cows don't do well in this rocky terrain, so the local cheeses come from sheep and goats. And everything is served with a liberal portion of extra virgin olive oil."

Luis went on, "When we were here last and shopping the market, we heard there are over five hundred types of greens and herbs used raw in the salads, as well as the meat or vegetable pies!"

"That is incredible. Do they drink ouzo like on the other islands?" Annie asked.

"No, here I believe the drink that takes its place is Raki. I'm not sure what is in it, but it does not have the licorice flavor of ouzo."

Annie laughed and said to Luis, "You actually have my mouth watering! Maybe I'll go find a late lunch ashore."

Luis smiled and said, "I'm glad to see you feeling better, lass. I was a little worried about you."

Her response was, "No need to worry...just a touch of stomach flu. It sounds like you brought me to the perfect place to get that out of the way." Inwardly, she hoped that was true.

Annie packed a few toiletries and a couple of clothing changes into her backpack. She reminded herself that as a passionate explorer and devoted mariner, areas that have played a critical role in maritime history held treasures to discover. Waving goodbye, Annie called out to Helene that she might see them in the market.

Ready for an adventure, Annie was surprised that the crowd on the waterfront gave her a feeling of claustrophobia. She was relieved when she reached the inn and inquired about a room for the night. The innkeeper had one room on the top floor that overlooked the harbor from a small open balcony. She took it.

Unfortunately, the nausea had returned probably because of all the people. Maybe at the market, there would be some herbs that would settle her stomach.

Reality check, Annie.

Was it possible she was pregnant with Ramone's child? How could she face him with such news? Their entire life would change. Surely it couldn't be.

After resting for a short while, Annie opened her journal to find the phrase that started her journey.

> *Caught up in the moment, it is impossible to see the designs in motion or the webs being woven...a pause at a fork in the road, choices made, future path rerouting.*

For the first time since the accident with Sabine, Annie was homesick for her mother and the knowing advice she so readily gave. Realizing her father was there too, she desperately needed to talk with them. Checking the time difference, she decided to call. When she heard her mother answer the phone, Annie couldn't keep the quiver out of her voice, "Mom?"

Concerned, Celeste asked, "Annie, sweetheart, are you all right?"

Annie swallowed a sob and answered, "Yes, I'm just homesick and missing our talks. I really need to see you and Dad and can hardly wait for the wedding."

Hearing Celeste's concern, Alex got on the other line. "Honey, where are you?"

"I have just had the most amazing time in Greece. The *Porto Banus* is on its way back to Marbella, but Captain Luis let us stop for a day or two in Crete. We won't be back in Marbella for another week. It's not until the week after that I am supposed to come home for the wedding."

The catch in Annie's voice made Celeste gently ask, "Sweetheart, do you want to come home early? You know we would love to see you."

Annie squeezed her eyes shut for a moment. "I would love to, but I don't see how. I usually love being on board the *Porto Banus*, but I think I might have caught a stomach bug."

Mentally calculating how he could make this happen, Alex said to Annie, "Let me see what I can do, honey. If you came straight home from Crete, is there anything in Marbella you would need for the wedding?"

Thinking it through, Annie felt she had left behind plenty of clothes in Maine, plus what she had with her. "I think the only thing would be my bridesmaid's dress."

Celeste chimed in, "Wait until you hear back from your father. If he can work it out, you can call Dom and Gennie to see if they can bring the dress when they come. Oh! I do have exciting news! Tomás heard from Sabine. She feels she is well enough to come over for the wedding."

Now excited, Annie exclaimed, "Oh my gosh. That is the best news ever!" Tears of joy were running down her face. "Dad, please make it happen. I want to come home."

Alex promised to get back to her later in the day, mindful of the time difference. Annie's spirits lifted, especially hearing the news about Sabine, and she looked forward to seeing how she was for herself. Plus, it was so good to hear her parents' voices. Perhaps she should venture over to the market to see if she could find anything for this darn nausea. After that, she might have an appetite to try some of the great food Luis spoke about.

The innkeeper gave Annie walking directions to the market. She made her way there, avoiding some of the more crowded areas. The market was huge. Anything and everything she could imagine was there, from meats and cheeses to a delectable array of fruits and vegetables, to assorted pasta and pies, to more seafood than she knew existed, to all the local wines and everything in between.

She spotted a booth with fragrant oils and thought that

might be an excellent place to start. Telling the saleswoman about her nausea, Annie was given two oils to try, one peppermint and the other lemongrass. She decided to get both.

While she finished the transaction, Helene found her. "Annie, I've been looking for you. Around the corner, they have ginger root, along with multiple selections of ginger goodies. Ginger was always my best remedy for nausea."

"Great!" Annie replied. "Let's go see what they have."

"I'll show you where it is, but then I need to find Roff and the cart we have filled." Helene laughed. "Ah, here is the counter! See you later."

Annie's eyes grew wide at the selection—ginger lozenges, tea, cookies, candy, gum, and a variety of bags with ground ginger powder. The lady gave her a lozenge to try; and before she knew it, she left the market, smiling with her sack filled with the two oils, the lozenges, a box of tea, and several kinds of cookies. *That should take care of it.*

But just in case, she made sure all was natural with no adverse side effects.

Outside the market, she asked directions to the old town. There was a somewhat hidden steep alleyway next to the Maritime Museum where she should turn. She found it (the street's name was Angelou) and walked up the hill looking in wonder at the examples of Venetian architecture from the sixteenth and seventeenth century. What a beautiful street! Atop the hill, away from the crowds, Annie found an outdoor café that seemed to suit her. Her waiter was attentive but not so much as to invade her thoughtful introspection.

If her father found a way to get her straight home and she did not return to Marbella, was she merely avoiding the potential consequence of seeing Ramone? No, she needed time to think straight and to even find out if the unthinkable had happened. This was certainly not a goal of this journey, but somehow, she convinced herself she would try to stay open to the possibility.

She knew to expect good food, but honestly, she didn't

know what she ate. And the waiter wrapped up the rest of her meal. Eagerly anticipating a call back from her parents, Annie went back down to the harbor and the inn. Right as she was opening the door, the phone rang. Perfect timing, she ran to get it, and it was her father.

"Annie, I think I have worked it out for you. I was able to change your ticket from Madrid to Portland. I've arranged a plane from the airport there in Crete at Heraklion to take you to Madrid. It will be there to pick you up day after tomorrow in the morning. Perhaps Roff can take you. The pilot should have a card with your name, so look for him. You just need to call your grandparents and advise Luis. You will be home soon, honey. It is way past time for us to be together again as a family."

Annie rubbed her eyes. *Am I doing the right thing?* First, a call to her grandparents.

Dom answered on the second ring, "*Buenos dias!*"

Annie quickly told him, "Dom, it's Annie. I have made a very rash decision to go back to the States early before the wedding. I hope it is all right if I let the *Porto Banus* sail home without me. Dad has arranged my flight."

Dom replied, "I think your young man is going to be quite disappointed. Gennie and I received tickets to his fight in Sevilla, and he gave us excellent seats. We are planning to go. Does that mean you will not come back to Marbella before the wedding?"

"Yes," Annie said guiltily, "please do not mention this to Ramone. I will send him a note. The only thing I need is my bridesmaid dress. Would you and Gennie bring it?"

Dom, thinking this through, asked, "Annie, are you okay? You don't sound like yourself. Do you need anything from us?"

"Dom, I'm fine. Did you hear that Sabine will be at the wedding? I am going to try to get her to come in a few days early so we can catch up."

That settled, Annie planned to speak with Captain Luis

early tomorrow. They would most likely leave since their provisions were complete. She would get all her shipboard bags packed up and be ready to depart for the airport at Heraklion the following morning.

Her next step was a letter to Ramone. This was the hard one. She knew he would be hurt. He asked her grandparents to watch him fight! It was clear he was ahead of her in his determination, and seeing him right now would cause too much confusion. The fear of him fighting was getting stronger as her feelings deepened—and if there was a possibility of a child. So she wrote:

> 'My dearest Ramone, our time on Karpathos together was unforgettable, but once out at sea, I felt so homesick to see my parents. I decided to go home and stay for a while before the wedding. My grandparents told me they were coming to see you fight in Sevilla. I know you will excel as always! I will miss you and hope we see each other again very soon. Annie'

Chapter 33

Final Day in Crete

The next morning, Annie planned her day to prepare for tomorrow's flight home. It felt right to her, and she could feel her focus shift, both body and soul. She knew without a doubt she needed to see her cousin, so her next call was to Sabine in France. When she first answered the phone, Annie didn't recognize her voice.

"Sabine, is that you?"

"Annie? *Oui, c'est moi*," she said haltingly.

Tears sprung to Annie's eyes to be finally talking to Sabine. "I've been so worried! Mother said you were well enough to come to the wedding. When do you plan to come? My plans have changed, and I'm going to fly back to Maine tomorrow. Is there any chance you might come early so we can spend time together?"

Sabine mumbled, "Annie, you talk so fast! Yes, I am coming and want to see you so badly. I was planning to come to Spain and fly with Dom and Gennie. If Tomás flies over sooner, I can try to come with him."

Annie tried to grasp the meaning of why Sabine felt she needed to fly with someone. If she didn't sorely need some alone time with her parents, Annie would have gone and gotten her.

To Sabine, she said, "I heard Tomás is coming five or six days early and meeting Meghan in New York City. Why don't you check with him? And I can always meet you."

Sabine answered, "That sounds good. I will speak with

Tomás and let you know. I miss you, Annie. My parents told me you felt responsible for that day. I knew better than to have those earphones in. I can't wait to see you."

Annie could hear Sabine's voice getting tired, so she wrapped it up. "I love you, Sabine. See you soon."

"*Au revoir*, Annie."

Hanging up, Annie made a personal commitment to do anything she could to help Sabine. Next, it was time to go back to the *Porto Banus* and tell Captain Luis her plans. Thanks to the oils and ginger, she supposed, her nausea seemed to be in check. She walked along the waterfront of the Venetian harbor and stopped for a bite to eat at one of the outdoor cafés.

Her waitress told her everything on the menu came from either a nearby farm or village. Annie ordered an herbal tea and found it more flavorful than any tea she ever tasted. The waitress suggested she order the *dakos*. Not exactly sure what she would be served, she was told this was a very typical Cretan dish. They started with rusks, a traditional dried bread, that were baked several times and kept for months. When they were ready to be used, they were moistened in a bit of water and topped with grated tomato, olive oil, feta cheese, and oregano...somewhat like Italian bruschetta but crunchy, light, and bursting with flavor. That and the tea would tide her over nicely.

Helene greeted Annie when she came aboard. She couldn't wait to show her what she'd found.

"Yesterday afternoon, after I saw you, Roff and I went out toward the mountains." Helene showed her to the galley, where Annie took in the most amazing aromas. "We stopped to gather arms full of wild sage, oregano, thyme, and marjoram. They are simply growing wild all over."

Annie took a pinch of each to smell. "These are out of this world! Luis was right about the food here. I just had dakos, and it was the perfect blend of natural flavors."

"Are you feeling any better?" Helene asked.

"Yes," Annie said, "but I have decided to fly home. Things are a little confusing right now, and I'd like to see my parents."

With an understanding look, Helene replied, "Of course, you have been away a long time. The captain is meeting with the harbormaster. He should be back soon."

Annie gratefully looked at Helene and said, "Thank you for understanding. I do not know anything yet, but I appreciate your keeping my situation to yourself. I'll go to my cabin and start packing. I must figure out what I can take on the plane. Here on the yacht, I've been able to bring as many bags as I wanted."

Helene laughed and went to her cabin to retrieve a large suitcase. "Here, you can use this. Maybe that will ensure you come back to us."

That made Annie give her a big hug. "I'll always be back. Marbella beckons me like no other place."

As soon as she said it, a realization occurred to her. *Except Karpathos?*

Captain Luis walked in to see this tender scene. "What's up, lass? Why are you packing?"

"Luis, it is nothing to do with being on board. I always look forward to being at sea with you and the *Porto Banus*. But for some reason, I feel very homesick and need to see my parents. I had so little time with my father, and he has arranged for a plane to pick me up in Heraklion tomorrow. Would it be possible for Roff to take me to the airport?"

Luis responded, "Oh, lass, of course. We will miss you on the way home. However, your grandmother will be quite pleased with all the savory spices we are bringing her."

Going over to her desk, Annie got the pitcher from the Karpathos pottery shop. "I can fit the present for Tomás and Meghan in my bag, but I don't have room for this pitcher. Is it possible for you to take it to Dom and Gennie to hold for me?"

"Yes, along with anything else you might not need for

your trip. We intend to see you back again soon. Annie, your adventures have turned into ours too, and you are family to us."

Tears welling again, Annie gave him a big hug. *Why am I so emotional?*

"Once you have your suitcase packed, leave it here. Roff will bring it when he picks you up tomorrow morning."

All packed and secure, she said her goodbyes to Luis and Helene, arranging the pickup time with Roff. Annie walked back along the waterfront. As her departure to the US approached, Annie acknowledged there were times when only a dose of her American roots could piece her back together. The anticipation of this was all that could ease the pain of leaving Ramone.

His intentions for their future appeared clear. Her response, especially now, however, was not. With no real destination in mind, Annie strolled to one of the narrow alleys and made her way up to the old town. She wandered past the archaeological excavation sites. Chania was developed on the site of an important ancient city named Cydonia, which was the third-largest city established by King Minos of Crete between 3650 and 3000 BC. She had not had time to go to Knossos, but she had heard what engineering skills they had that were later lost for centuries. Hard to imagine that remains still existed from the Minoan civilization so many thousands of years ago.

Annie reflected about what she would add to her journal:

> *Thinking of all the people who have walked this place before is like looking up at the sky and realizing we are but one star among an unfathomable multitude. Very humbling. The past is what it was, and now it is gone. Now is the time and place where the next part of life unfolds. And what will be left behind from our culture generations from now?*

Annie hoped that at home, she might discover some answers and reflect on the various cultures and history of the places her journey had taken her. *Hmmm...living with purpose, adventure, and love. Is it too greedy to ask for it all?*

Chapter 34

Crete to Madrid—Bumpy Road Home

Roff arrived right on time with her suitcase. She tossed her backpack in the back seat and mentally said goodbye to Crete and to Greece. She would never forget any of her time here. Roff explained they planned to set sail as soon as he returned. His estimate was about six days to reach Marbella. It was an easy conversation, and Annie realized how close she had become to Luis and his crew during these months.

Before long, they arrived at the airport in Heraklion. Roff drove up to the small terminal and unloaded her bag by the man carrying the sign with her name. He looked vaguely familiar, but Annie couldn't imagine from where. He told her they would transfer to the private plane, so he loaded her and her bags onto a small vehicle. A final goodbye to Roff, and they were off.

Preparing herself for the long trip ahead, she didn't pay much attention to the plane. But as she began to walk up the steps, a man came out to meet her at the door. Shocked and confused, she was looking at the face of El Amir and realized this was his plane!

"What...? How is this possible?" Annie nervously questioned.

El Amir replied, "Your father called me to ask if my plane could fly you from Crete to Madrid. He sounded concerned, so I decided to come myself to escort you and be sure you are all right. It's the least I could do."

At that moment, a wave of nausea came over Annie, and she rushed to the plane's restroom. He observed. When she was out, he showed her to her seat, and they buckled up to settle in for the ride. Her nerves were not helping her nausea.

His penetrating eyes looked knowingly at her, probing, "You had relations with the matador?"

Unable to lie to this man, she gave him a simple yes.

As if punched in the gut, he sighed and asked, "Are you carrying his child?"

"Amir, don't do this...please. I honestly don't know." She looked at him to see if he was judging her, then continued, "You told me there was no chance for us. You even told me to go back to the matador. Well, I did, and he is amazing. But I'm confused. I don't think I can live with the danger of what he does for a living."

Once he could move about the cabin, he came over and said quietly, "It should have been me. I have been in agony since we parted, knowing you were going to him."

Annie's head was spinning. "I can't listen to this. I am going home and not even stopping at Marbella. He expects me, but I have to figure out what is happening."

El Amir went over to his briefcase, pulled out a newspaper, folded it to the second page, then handed it to Annie without a word.

Before her eyes, the headline read, "STAR MATADOR IN SERIOUS CONDITION AFTER GORING."

With that, Annie swooned into a faint. El Amir immediately regretted handling that so poorly. He called for his attendant to help revive her.

When she finally regained consciousness, she tentatively asked, "Is he dead?"

El Amir put the article in front of her. "It was Antonio. He was the one gored. Read the article." The article read:

ANTONIO SANCHEZ was seriously injured in the abdomen according to medical staff who

confirmed the matador, who hails from one
of Spain's most famous bullfighting dynas-
ties, might never fight again. The incident
took place during the bullfighting festival that
welcomes some of the biggest names on the
bullfighting circuit. As Antonio was passing
his cape, there was a loud noise in the stands.
For just an instant he was distracted, and the
bull charged, defeating him during one of his
passes. The bull took hold during several seconds, which seemed to go on forever. Antonio's
brother, RAMONE SANCHEZ, is scheduled in
the ring this week in Sevilla.

"Ramone's brother!" Annie sobbed.

She remembered that frisky younger brother. "He must
be so worried...he said worry and distraction are the kiss of
death to a matador. Oh no, what have I done? He may or
may not know yet that I am not coming back. What will he
do?" Looking at El Amir with despair, Annie felt helpless to
give Ramone any comfort. "What am I to do?"

El Amir strived to hide his raging jealousy and asked,
"What can I do to help?"

Nausea running rampant, not having a clue what to
do, Annie reasoned she had two choices—one, to get on the
plane and go home, or two, to get to Marbella. *What to do,
what to do? What is the right choice?*

"Give me a few moments..." Annie implored. El Amir
wanted nothing more than to hold her, but she was very
possibly with child and thus very much off-limits. "Can you
change our course and land the plane in Marbella?" Annie
asked.

With an acquiescent sigh, El Amir said, "Yes, if that is
what you want to do."

She then asked, "Is there any way to change my Madrid
to Portland ticket?"

"I can make that happen." El Amir answered and added, "But, Annie, are you sure this is what you want to do? Where will you go? Ramone is already in Sevilla. He cannot cancel his fight. Your grandparents are there by now too."

Annie, feeling anything but rational, tried to think. Aloud she said, "Oh my god, Ramone told me the two biggest dangers for a matador are worry and distraction. He must be worried out of his mind about Antonio, and if he saw me, I would be the distraction. I can't go, can I?"

El Amir sought to calm her. "Your matador will be fine. Spain will not take kindly to losing two of its heroes and will be there in force to support him and urge him on through the fight. Yes, you would be a distraction. Let him do what he was trained to do."

Eyes wide with confusion, Annie cried, "What if I am carrying his child and something happens to him? I couldn't bear it!"

As she said the words, she remembered Ramone saying the same thing about her rock climb. Right now, she needed to pull herself together and get the worry off El Amir's face. It was at that moment Annie realized the irresistible attraction to El Amir was gone. It most likely was erased in Karpathos. *Could I be in love with Ramone?* Shaking her head, she wondered how this was ever going to work out.

Trying to distract herself for a few moments, Annie asked El Amir bluntly, "How are you able to do all these things? You are young, and I have never heard you speak of any family other than your father. Your lavish generosity speaks of great wealth."

Not used to being questioned but unable to deny her request, El Amir began, "I was born and lived my early years with my parents and two sisters in Dubai. My father was caught up in the border dispute between Dubai and Abu Dhabi. When the British came in to arbitrate, my father was helpful in securing a cessation of hostilities. The British were very impressed with my father and offered him a distinguished position in North Africa to keep the insurgents at bay.

"Oil had just been discovered off the coast of Dubai, and the city was on the brink of an infrastructure boom. My mother, with relatives in Saudi, was wealthy in her own right. She insisted on staying in Dubai and keeping my two sisters with her. It was a hard decision for my father, but this was a great opportunity for him. The Saudi relatives and my father's death resulted in a significant inheritance left to me. My sisters have both married well, and I have five nieces and nephews. I do miss them, but I have been away so long. Morocco is home for me. I do try to visit them at least once a year."

Sensing this was a subject El Amir rarely spoke of, Annie thanked him for being so open. "You have done so much for the people around you. When will it be your time to seek happiness?"

"My time will come when it is right. For now, what is your plan?"

Taking a deep breath, she said, "I will write Ramone another letter. Is there any way for you to arrange for him to get it after the fight?"

He nodded, and Annie went to her journal to tear out a sheet of paper. A jolt of turbulence knocked the journal and paper out of her hands. As he reached to pick it up, El Amir noticed his own name. He quickly glanced at her writing of her attraction to him, then comparing him to the matador. He looked at her with questions in those golden eyes of his.

She took the journal from him. "My journal holds my private thoughts. What you read was written shortly after Paris. A lot has happened since then."

El Amir, gazing at her abdomen, would have to agree with that. "It could have been me, Annie."

Fighting the nausea that was steadily rising in her, Annie answered, "You were right. Our cultures are too different. It would never have worked for us." *How is it when you* *least expect it, things seem to spin out of control? Breathe in, breathe out...*Annie tried to concentrate on her letter to Ramone:

> *'Dearest Ramone, as I reached Madrid to board the plane back to the States, I heard about Antonio. I am so sorry and am praying for his speedy recovery. You must be so worried about him! I know you must fight. As I am sure you realize, this is my biggest fear for us being together. I pray for your safety as well. Please try to understand my need to go home and see my parents for a while, just as you will need to be with your family after your fight. At the very least, I will be in Maine through the wedding. I am unsure after that. You have found a place in my heart. I need time to think. Be safe, my love. Annie'*

She sealed the envelope and gave it to El Amir. "Do NOT let him open it until after the fight."

"You have my word," El Amir responded. Staring intensely at her, he continued, "If you ever need anything, Annie, you have but to call. I will be there."

Wondering how she was blessed to be loved by two such men, Annie could only think to say, "Thank you." She waved as his plane took off, headed for Sevilla.

Chapter 35

Home to Boothbay

Annie boarded her plane for the international flight. It seemed as if long flights inspired her to reminisce, even more so than being at sea—perhaps because the sky was not her domain. Here she was not required to be at the helm and at-the-ready. She could relax and remember. Her mind gently massaged the travel memories from Africa to Thailand, Bali, and Australia, then Scotland, England, Ireland, France, and, of course, her beloved Spain and Andalusia. And now, a most unforgettable time in Greece. WOW! Annie took out the amethyst stone Sarah had given back to her and absently rubbed it. Never part of the plan, Annie rested her other hand on her stomach. *This might be the most surprising journey yet.*

After a change of planes in New York, Annie finally made it to Portland, exhausted. Both her parents were waiting for her. Seeing her father finally reunited with her mother and the two of them meeting her plane together, her exhaustion gave way to overwhelming joy. Everything mental and emotional fell into alignment the moment they wrapped her in their arms. Whether her tears were of joy, worry, or exhaustion ceased to matter. She was home. Her parents were wise enough to shower her with love rather than questions. They would find out about her need to come home in due time.

On the ride home, Annie hesitantly asked her father, "How long are you staying here this time?"

Celeste looked at Alex too, waiting for his response. "Being back here with your mother after such a long absence has me quite comfortable staying put. I have asked for a permanent relocation to this area. If that cannot happen, then it might be time to retire. I will not leave your mother again, and if I have the urge to go somewhere, then I will have to entice her to go with me!" He finished with a laugh.

Celeste added with a twinkle in her eye, "He'll be going nowhere in the future without me."

Although happy to see her daughter smiling, Celeste saw her covering a yawn.

"Let's get you home and in bed...you have to get this jet lag out of your system. We have a week before Tomás and Meghan arrive. Then another few days before Dom and Gennie and the other guests get here."

Annie added, "I spoke with Sabine. She's trying to fly over with Tomás. Have you heard why she needs to fly with someone?"

Her mother answered, "No, we haven't. We're just happy she is well enough to travel to get here and be with us!"

Alone in her room, among her familiar things, Annie allowed herself to think of Ramone. He should have finished his fight by now. Surely if anything happened to him, her grandparents would have called. She wondered pensively how El Amir planned to get her letter to him. Then her thoughts shifted to El Amir. She realized how unusual and out of character it had been for him to open up about his family. *How different things might have been if he hadn't stayed strong that night in Paris.*

But Ramone had stepped up the romance, as well as intensity, and there was no question he was her man. It might be too early for her to take the test and get an answer that would most likely affect her entire future. Fortunately, her nausea had calmed down since Madrid. Tomorrow, she would get up for her walk and insert a stop at the drugstore into her itinerary. It would soon be time she knew for sure.

Annie slipped out of the house early, felt the brisk air, and ran back for a sweatshirt. Walking out to the rocky shoreline, she felt that familiar and unique appeal this area held for her that even the most exotic ports could not surpass. This place was home. Annie let her internal clock unwind to the pleasing New England pace. Quaint harborside towns and the hypnotizing loneliness of their lighthouses...these were reminders of her childhood and the core of what made her the seafarer she was today.

As she watched the fog roll over the old Boothbay lighthouse, Annie felt her decision to return home early was the right one. Then just when Annie thought the nausea was behind her and there was no need to stop at the store, a huge wave came over her. Guess she was stopping after all. With the decision made to find out, hoping it wasn't too soon, she was ready to end the anticipation!

Trying to slip back to her room, Annie changed plans when Celeste saw her and called out. Walking toward the kitchen, Annie saw her mother working on a large breakfast. Very much like her own mother, Celeste enjoyed the kitchen and creating different delicacies.

"Mom, I'm not feeling well and thought I might go lie down for a while. The meal looks wonderful! Would you save me a plate for later?"

"Of course, sweetheart. You do look a little run-down. How about a cup of tea to take with you?" her mother asked.

"That would be great, thanks." Annie answered.

Pouring the tea, Celeste suggested, "When you get up and feel better, why don't we have some mother-daughter time. I have missed you and our talks so very much."

"Yes, I look forward to that too," Annie said as she left with the tea. Her mother didn't miss that she picked up a bag she had dropped off by her door. Celeste, wise to the moods of her daughter, thought back to the days after Sabine's accident. This, thankfully, did not seem the same.

Pacing will not help! Annie scolded herself as she paced back and forth in her room, looking at the pregnancy kit. Did she want to know? Was it too early to find out? After all, her monthly cycle was only a few days late. How could so much be riding on a simple positive or negative mark? In a leap of faith, she grabbed the kit and waited for the result. False positive, false negative? Would the test give her the right answer? The answer...*negative.*

After the initial sigh of relief came an unexpected sadness. This child would have originated in the most romantic place in a union between two people in the early stages of falling in love. Annie gave herself a chance to shed a few tears for this negative test result and the unborn child who might have been. It was time to find her mother. Celeste was out in the garden. Alex had to run some errands in Portland and wouldn't be back for a while.

Finding her mother, Annie asked, "Is that plate ready to heat up? I can get it."

Celeste came in as Annie was heating her meal and asked, "Are you ready for our talk?"

After her third bite of sausage and eggs, Annie's nausea returned with a vengeance, and she rushed back to her room. Her mother anxiously waited at her door until Annie came back out.

Annie, tears rolling down her face, looked at her mother and said, "Oh, Mom, I don't know if I have picked up a bug of some kind." Brooding, she added, "I am just trying to make sense of what's happening in my life."

Celeste, putting her arms around her daughter, gently said, "Perhaps we should start at the beginning."

Breakfast forgotten, they moved over to the comfortable sofa and chair in the salon.

Annie wiped her tears. "I don't even know where to begin...so much has happened!"

"Sweetheart, you've been gone a long time. Do you think the places you discovered or the people you met along the way have influenced you the most?" her mother asked, bringing Annie another cup of tea.

"Both really. I have made close friends, but I have also been fascinated by the countries and cultures I have experienced, while the history and architecture obviously struck a true chord in me."

"Your father told me what your young men did to get him released. Why don't you start there and tell me about them?"

Warming to the subject, Annie began, "I met Ramone in Marbella. He's a famous matador, a Spanish hero. Part of Salvador's plot was to have his brother court me to allow their father to kidnap me. But Ramone stepped in instead and, in the end, betrayed his own father to protect Dad and me. I then met El Amir in Morocco and met my new close friend Sarah, a painter in Africa, through him. It was El Amir who had the influence and contacts to make the escape happen. His father owed Dad a personal debt for saving his life in North Africa, and El Amir wanted to repay it. In that one dramatic room in Paris, all three of us were dealing with our fathers in some way.

"Both men are exceedingly handsome," Annie continued, smiling. "They have some of the same features. Both have darker complexions and dark wavy hair. Their eyes, although different in color, are mesmerizing and expressive."

Celeste, curious, asked, "Did one of these men become more important to you?"

Annie loved the easy rapport she always found with her mother. She never felt judged, and it was easy to be truthful.

"In the beginning, I was honestly attracted to both. Ramone was so romantic from the first meeting. El Amir was mysterious with a hypnotizing allure and filled with generosity. The entire setting in Paris when Dad escaped was so confusing. I lost track of who was good and who was not. But it turns out both men are good. Ramone returned to Spain. I remained with El Amir and Sarah in Paris to do a little sightseeing. During that time, I got to know El Amir better and thought there might be something between us. In the end, though, he told me his culture and traditions would not allow him to be with me. I had no choice but to respect that."

"That was wise of you, sweetheart. I know your father asked him to send his plane for you. Did you know the plane was his?" Celeste asked.

"El Amir came with the plane."

Sensing Annie did not want to speak of the ride with El Amir, she moved on cautiously, "And what became of the matador?"

"After I returned to Marbella, Ramone and I became close. He has such a way about him that combines sheer strength with unbelievable gentleness. I joined him on the island of Karpathos at the end of the Greece trip while we waited for the *Porto Banus* to arrive. Oh, Mom, I can't even describe the closeness we felt on that island. Both Ramone and the island are etched in my heart forever."

"Have you found love with this man, sweetheart?" Celeste was putting the pieces together.

"Yes, I think so, but I can't live in fear every time he goes into the ring. It's impossible not to think of Jeffrey. Even though there was fear in his heart, he sacrificed himself for a comrade while trying to get him to safety. The difference is, Ramone shows no fear when he faces these bulls, yet his scars tell the true story. His brother, Antonio, who is also a well-known matador, was just critically injured last week. Ramone couldn't even be by his brother's side because of the honor he felt not to cancel his fight in Sevilla. Dom and Gennie were at that fight. What if it had been Ramone?"

Celeste thoughtfully asked, "When did the nausea start? Had you eaten something unusual?"

Thinking back, Annie replied, "The food in Karpathos was excellent. I don't think that could be it. The first round of nausea started when we were out at sea during a storm."

"You are certainly not prone to seasickness," her mother said.

Annie quickly answered, "Of course not. And I was equally sick on land in Crete and even now. Do you think I might have some dreadful disease?" Annie looked at her mother with alarm.

"Perhaps we should get you an appointment with the doctor." Then as an afterthought, she asked, "Were you and Ramone intimate on the island?"

"Yes...we were, and there was one time we missed using protection. I thought I might be pregnant. But I took a test this morning, and it showed negative."

Trying to absorb all this, Celeste calmly asked, "How late are you, sweetheart?"

Mentally calculating, Annie replied, "Only about three or four days. I feel like it should start any time now. What can it be?"

Annie told her mother about the oils and ginger bought in Crete. They seemed to help somewhat. She had no fever.

Finally, Celeste said, "Maybe it was too early for the test. Why don't we give it a few more days to see what happens? But, Annie, are you prepared to face the chance you might be pregnant with Ramone's child?"

"Mom, that's why I needed to be here with you and Dad. I wasn't ready to face Ramone with the possibility. But this morning, when the test showed negative, such a feeling of sadness came over me."

Giving her daughter another hug, Celeste said, "I understand what a gift a child can be. Let's take things as they come. No reason to worry your father at this point. In the meantime, get lots of fresh air, rest, and rejuvenate."

Chapter 36

A Fateful Letter Arrives

This was precisely what Annie needed, and she marveled at the clearheaded insight her mother always shared in their conversations. Although she was determined not to focus on it, a small bubble of excitement grew with the thought she might get a "positive" result soon. The nausea didn't totally go away but became more manageable. The next few days were spent catching up with family and reuniting with her sailing friends.

Her father accompanied her often on her early morning walks. Each time, the gratitude she felt was endless for those men who helped him (and her). She was so relieved he had recovered from Salvador's nearly mortal gunshot wound.

Robert came around daily, and he and Annie fell into their earlier easy banter. Knowing Sabine was better was a huge weight lifted from their friendship. Robert told her he had been by the museum and that she was missed. It sounded like her job was waiting for her if she wanted it. However, Annie simply couldn't commit to such a permanent responsibility right now. Deep within her, she also now understood this position was not the best use of her talents.

Celeste mentioned Todd Middleton had returned. Her mentor had shared such inspiration with her in Thailand, and she was excited to see the professor again. Annie called him to meet for lunch at one of the dockside restaurants along the pier. They were both fans of the fresh catch of the day. It would be a seafood feast.

Annie told him about the places she went after Thailand. From her descriptions, Todd vowed to go to some of them. He had never been to the Greek islands. She gave such life to the history and beauty there the professor knew that it would be one of his next destinations.

He then asked an intriguing question: "It sounds like it has been quite a journey! Do you think the architect or historian were awakened more during these months?"

Annie pondered for a moment. "Both actually. I find myself fascinated with lands and cultures formulated through so many generations. Often, I would pull out my journal to rough out a drawing of something unique. The D'Orsay Museum was interesting. But honestly, when I heard the story of Colossus in Rhodes at 157 feet tall, built in 280 BC, I was astounded. And the sophisticated engineering of the Minoan cities in Crete creates so much speculation in my mind about the people and what they thought and experienced! But I think beyond the architecture and history, I began to find myself...through diverse new friendships, adventure, intrigue, traditions, and possibly love."

Todd was always enjoyable to be around, with his insight, and they thoroughly enjoyed the afternoon.

On the walk home, appreciative of both the professor and the delicious Maine seafood, Annie was thankful to be at home with family and friends. The walks along the coast had been a balm for her emotion-weary soul. But now, as she looked over Boothbay Harbor, she felt a spirit of renewal flow through her. Her monthly time had not come as yet, and she wondered whether a small peanut of a person might be growing inside her.

For some reason, Annie no longer felt the urgency to know. Nausea had subsided for now, but Annie felt she already knew what another test would tell her. Her mother never pushed her. Everyone's focus was now concentrated on the wedding. Sabine would arrive the next afternoon with Tomás and Meghan, then everything would move forward in preparation for the special day.

The following morning, Celeste gently knocked on Annie's door to wake her. There was a letter from Ramone. He had not contacted her since his fight, and she prayed he was not angry at her. She opened the letter and glanced down...strange. He never used her real name.

> 'Annie, your letters arrived. I was told you heard about my brother, yet you left without seeing me or showing any support for me or my family at such a difficult time. After all we experienced together, I am deeply hurt by your actions. If you are even interested, my brother is strong and is healing. It is still a question whether he will walk again, much less fight. Can I say it was bittersweet seeing your grandparents at a fight when I needed you at my side? I hope your cousin's wedding goes well and that you find what you need there in Maine. Ramone'

Stunned with grief, Annie handed the letter to her mother. Celeste quickly read it and, for once, had no words. All she could do was hold her daughter, who was now sobbing relentlessly.

Hearing the crying, Alex came into the room and, looking at Celeste, said, "I refuse to be kept in the dark any longer! I know I have not been here for you in the past, but I'm here now. Let me help."

Annie was in no condition to talk. Celeste summed up the situation for him, "Our girl has fallen in love with the matador. She is very possibly carrying his child. Between that and her fear behind the danger he faces each time he goes in the ring, she needed to be around us. I think that about sums it up."

Annie nodded and looked so desolate, watching her

father try to absorb all that her mother said in just three sentences. She passed him the letter.

Still sniffling, she added, "He always calls me *querida*... he hates me now."

Alex read the letter and said with reason, "It sounds more like he's hurting and confused. He is dealing with his brother's injury, probably still reeling from betraying his own father, and feeling as though he's lost the woman he loves."

Sitting next to Celeste and holding Annie's hand, he continued, "Nothing's really over until the moment you stop trying, sweetheart. It's okay to admit you are less than perfect. Taking chances is how you learn to be brave. You don't want to shut love out of your heart by saying it's impossible. It is okay to dream, Annie. To be without dreams is to live without hope, and to be without hope is to live without purpose. I wouldn't give up on this man, sweetheart. He will find his way back to you if he is your destiny. But at some point, you will need to meet him halfway."

Celeste held his other hand. "Well said, dear."

Looking at Annie, she said, "Your matador does not know all the background of your decision. Perhaps after the wedding you should go back to Spain with Dom and Gennie to see if there is a future with Ramone."

Drying her eyes, she looked at them lovingly. "I am so lucky to have you both in my life. And, Dad, I want to believe you can transform possibility into reality...to bring your dreams to life."

"That's my girl," Alex said. "With everyone arriving, you won't have the quiet time you need to process. For now, your challenge is to make the moments count with Sabine, Tomás, and Meghan. This is their time to shine in the spotlight. Your time is right around the corner. I'm sure of it."

Hugging both her parents tight, Annie left for a walk to digest Ramone's letter and all her parents had told her. They were right. The next few days were not about her. She desperately wanted to call him to try to make it right but knew in her heart that it would be better in person. Ramone's letter didn't sound at all like himself. She could feel the hurt and disappointment she had caused him. Yes, after the wedding, she would return to Marbella, and they would figure it out.

Chapter 37

Wedding Preparations—Boothbay

Annie jumped out of bed when she heard preparations already underway to greet Tomás, Sabine, and Meghan. She had her list and was ready to get started. Her father was right. Annie's time could wait. She would see Sabine today! Her mother was busy in the kitchen and smiled a good morning when Annie came in to get a blueberry bagel.

Annie shared, "I plan to gather flowers from the garden to place arrangements around the house, then go to the market for the fresh lobster rolls and corn. Do you want the lobster meat on brioche rolls? That's the way Sabine always loved them!"

"That sounds great. Would you also pick up some fresh spinach and blueberry muffins while you're there?" Celeste asked.

Annie replied with another question. "Sure. Are you making that cabbage slaw we all like?"

Pulling out the two heads of cabbage, Celeste said, "Starting it now."

Grabbing a large straw basket and clippers, Annie headed out to the garden to look for unusual combinations of colors and textures. Careful not to over-prune any one area, she filled the basket to overflowing, then came in to start the arrangements. Music was softly playing in the background. Annie let her creative side take over and was fascinated with weaving together the unlikely blend of colorful flowers and greenery.

While she was working on her fourth arrangement, Celeste came in and raved, "Annie, sweetheart, those are lovely!"

She took the ones that were finished and began placing them strategically around the house to best showcase each arrangement's color combination.

Next was the market. Annie decided to take the bike with the big basket attached to the handlebars. As she rode along, she thought about the history of Boothbay. After being in countries that have gone through century after century of history and cultural blends, this area was very young, basically founded by English fishermen and farmers in the early 1600s. When the Pilgrims were low on food, this was where they came to resupply. The Indian Wars forced these mainland and island settlements out in the later 1600s. Annie remembered as a girl hunting for arrowheads with Tomás and Sabine.

It was the Scotch-Irish families who resettled the area. They were industrious people who principally exported lumber, firewood, and fish for cash to buy what they couldn't create themselves. It was that background that appealed to Meghan's Irish heritage. Annie wanted to be sure to take her to the shipbuilding museum to see what knowledge these early settlers had brought from her homeland.

The outdoor farmers market seemed low-key compared to the market she experienced in Crete most recently but also the individual markets of some of the more exotic countries she visited. Somehow, however, the similarities shone through...a common place filled with workers selling produce or homemade delicacies from their own harvests. She saw a huge barrel overflowing with husk-on ears of corn. Several people were standing over the barrel to pull back a husk to check for freshness. They looked perfect, and Annie couldn't wait to try them.

Loading up her bag, she moved over to the booth with the fresh lobster meat. The plate of samples on the counter were impossible to resist. She knew there was nowhere else that had better lobster than Maine. Getting the brioche rolls, she also found the spinach and muffins.

Returning to her bike with arms full, she laughed out loud at how she thought she could carry all this in the bike basket. She looked around and saw Robert in the distance.

Calling out, "Hey, Robert, can I get some help?"

He walked over and looked at the load in Annie's arms, then at the basket that wasn't looking so big right now. They lined the bottom of the basket with the ears of corn, but once the lobster rolls were in, that was it. They laughed and shook their heads.

Robert said, "Wait here. Let me grab my bike. I'll help you get this home."

Riding home, they talked of Sabine's visit and the upcoming wedding. Annie was pleased they had rekindled their friendship. They both had felt an enormous weight of guilt after the accident.

Realizing that, she said, "I'm sorry how I acted after Sabine's accident. Somehow seeing you reminded me of her injury and the guilt I felt about it. You were hurting too. Will you forgive me?"

Robert took a moment before he responded, "Annie, seeing you so distressed was as bad as being there helpless at the accident. Hopefully, your travels have given you some peace." When she didn't answer, Robert went on, "I can't wait to see her. Is it okay if I help out at the house until they get here? I meant to ask you if I could be there when they arrive."

Annie smiled at him. "Of course. Robert, she's still recovering. All I know was that she had to fly with someone else over to Portland, and I'm not sure why. She is flying with Tomás. They meet Meghan in New York to make the last leg to Portland. Dad had some business in Portland today and plans to pick them up." Looking at her watch, she continued with growing excitement, "It shouldn't be too long now."

At home, they unloaded. Celeste waved hi to Robert, and he said, laughing, "How she thought she was getting all this in her bike basket, I do not know."

Celeste looked at the corn, pleased. "Sweetheart, would you like to grill it in the husk or boil it?"

Annie answered, "Oh, either is so good." To Robert, she asked, "Do you feel like firing up the grill?"

"Sure!" Robert headed out to the patio to get started.

Celeste observed to Annie, "I'm glad Robert is here. Sabine always had a bit of a thing for him, but I think she never acted on it since he was your friend." Reflecting further, she said, "You know, I saw the friendship between you and Robert, but I could never see you two together romantically. He is a very nice young man with a big heart, but you need a strong man beside you."

Refusing to tear up, Annie said softly, "You will like Ramone, Mom. Even when he displays his strength, he has amazing tenderness. I hope you get a chance to meet him."

To change the subject, Annie went to sneak a bite of the cabbage slaw and said, rolling her eyes in pleasure, "Ah... just like I remember."

Annie walked out to join Robert while her mother set the table. Everything looked perfect. Annie was particularly pleased with the floral centerpiece. She had mixed white lilies with purple roses and orange sunflowers, then added some green button poms and other greenery to pull it all together. With a satisfied sigh, she sat down on the patio and waited for Robert to finish.

Grill heating up, they heard her father call out, "We're home!"

Chapter 38

Wedding Party Arrives

In typical fashion, Tomás excitedly bounded into the house, carrying the bags. Dropping them, he headed straight for Celeste. "Aunt Celeste, how do you get more beautiful every time I see you?"

Giving him a big hug and a wink, with a glance toward Alex, she answered, "Maybe it's having my husband back."

"So that's it. Meghan, come meet the other woman in my life. Aunt Celeste, I'm afraid you have finally been replaced. Meet the love of my life and soon-to-be bride, Meghan."

Annie caught the jovial spirit, delighted to see them both. Looking around, she saw Sabine coming in with her father. Annie smiled and reached out to hug this girl who was like a sister to her. What she noticed was that her actions and speech were just one beat behind normal. Celeste came over to welcome Sabine, who seemed overly quiet.

It was when Sabine shyly looked over at Robert, and Annie turned to look at him, that she saw the compassion and love on his face. He came over and took Sabine's hands in his. Annie looked at her mother, who was smiling, in utter disbelief. Tomás winked at her. *What just happened...when did this happen?*

Meghan walked over to Annie and shook her shoulders. "Hey, remember me?"

Snapping out of her shock at seeing Robert and Sabine, she refocused on Meghan.

Looking at her, Annie said, "Oh my gosh! You are glowing. Look at you." Then to Tomás, she said, "What a lucky man you are. She is beautiful."

Back to Meghan, she added, "I have so much to tell you! There's a village on an island in Greece that is so like Dingle. Maybe we can slip away with Sabine tomorrow so I can tell you about it? Also, there's a shipbuilding museum here in Boothbay where I used to work that has Irish origins. I'd like to show it to you if Tomás will let you out of his sight."

Looking over at Sabine, Annie added, "Would you like to go?"

Sabine answered enthusiastically but slowly, "Yes, I would love that! When I stopped in Marbella, Gennie gave me your dress to bring with me. What a surprise when Tomás and Meghan found out I could come; they asked if I would be a bridesmaid too. So I have mine as well."

Annie smiled lovingly at Tomás and Meghan, so incredibly thankful this beautiful miracle was here with them. Sabine (cousin, sister, best friend forever) was here talking with them and about to be part of the wedding.

To Sabine, she said playfully, "Hey cuz, we're roommates as usual."

Robert jumped in with, "I'll take your bag in." Sabine thanked him and looked at Celeste with the obvious question.

Knowing her niece well, Celeste asked Robert, "Can you stay for dinner?"

Delighted, Robert looked at Sabine and answered, "Of course, I'll grill the corn."

Sabine wandered out to the patio with Robert to check the grill. Annie looked at each of them. "What is going on between those two?"

Everyone shrugged but Tomás. He started, "Sabine and I had a long time to talk on the plane. She is still self-conscious about her voice. It seems our boy, Robert, began to write Sabine after the accident...every day."

Celeste added, "Yes, I remember he came by to get her

address right after the accident. Annie, you were still here at that point."

Tomás continued, "Right, Sabine said the letters talked to her like he was in the room. Her mother would read them to her each day while she was in the coma. Sabine told me she felt she might have heard them. Robert continued writing encouragement even after she regained consciousness and was in rehab. When Sabine couldn't write back, her mother did. She now has a box full of those letters she holds so precious and rereads them whenever she has a bad day. It sounded like she was really looking forward to seeing him."

Every word Tomás was saying made Annie feel more wretched than the last. Had she been so caught up in her own self-pity that she wasn't there for Sabine? Instead, she was off traveling the world. *Now I have done the same exact thing to the man I was falling in love with...a man with whom I might be having a child. I am pathetic.*

Interestingly, it was Meghan who saw through what Annie was feeling. "Let's go for a walk."

They didn't want to go to the patio, so they went out the front door. Headed to the coastline, Meghan was the first to speak. "Annie, we all handle grief differently. Tomás did not share her story to make you feel bad."

"I know, but the fact remains that I am letting down the people closest to me in their time of need. I thought I was learning in my journey. How can I be so self-absorbed?" she asked. Shaking her head, she shared with Meghan, "Remember the matador, Ramone? He betrayed his own father to protect my father and me, then worked his way into my heart...mentally, emotionally, and sexually." Looking at Meghan, she added, "There is a good chance I might be carrying his child, yet I have screwed it all up."

Meghan felt her Irish temper flaring. "We're not perfect, Annie. We make mistakes. Yes, maybe Sabine is here with gratitude for what Robert did, but she is still here for you. She loves you as much as you love her. Show her, Annie.

And as for the matador, from what I hear, you had your reasons for your choice and he might be alive today because you made that choice. You have affected so many people in a positive way, including me...don't lose sight of that."

Annie had to smile and raise her eyebrows at her soon-to-be cousin in law. "You are a feisty woman. And exactly what I need right now. Enough about me...let's go back for dinner and prepare to get you married."

Dinner was perfect! The lobster rolls were devoured, as well as the corn and cabbage slaw. The new arrivals were naturally all a little jet-lagged. Robert left, and Annie joined Sabine in their room to help her unpack.

"Sabine," Annie started, "I know you probably think I haven't been there for you, but the accident crushed me to think I might have hurt you permanently."

Sabine stopped her unpacking and came over to hug Annie. "Dearest cousin, do you not think I know all the times you checked on me? The accident was not your fault. Those earphones were a mistake." Then as a second thought, she added, "I think I always wondered if you and Robert were just friends. There were a couple of times when he looked at me, I played our game of 'what if.' Annie, he seems to accept me for how I am. The last thing I want to do is hurt you."

"Sabine, sweetie, I could not be happier for you and Robert. I actually met a man that I might be in love with, but I think I've screwed it up." With a pause and a sigh, Annie knew she wanted to tell Sabine. "I might be carrying his child."

Sabine seemed genuinely excited when she asked, "Have you done the test to be sure?"

Annie rolled her eyes. "Yes, about a week ago. It was negative. But honestly, I feel like I am."

Sabine had already come over to sit next to Annie like old times. With a little giggle, she said, "We'll get another kit tomorrow. Life is messy, Annie. We can't change that, but every now and then, a miracle happens. I am here with you today, and I will be in this wedding. That is our miracle."

Then crossing back to her bed, she closed with "I am exhausted! Jet lag...good night, Annie."

While Sabine slept, Annie thought about sending a letter to Ramone. The reality was she didn't know what to say. If she was to do the test again tomorrow, no matter the result, she needed to learn from this turn of events.

Chapter 39

The Discovery

Sabine woke up first and poked Annie like they used to do. "Let's go get the kit!"

"OMG, it is so good to have you back here. So what are we going to do if we find out?" Annie asked.

"Nothing, really...except there would be no champagne for you at the wedding," Sabine said with a little of her old devilish ways.

Happy to see that, Annie answered back, pulling the cover back over her head, "Ah, then it's no hurry. I may sleep in a bit."

Sabine poked her again, "NO WAY!" Shoving her now, Sabine loved torturing her cousin. There was not one moment she wasn't grateful to be able to do this. "Am I dealing with a pregnant woman or just a prima donna who wants to sleep all day?" Sabine, feeling better than ever since the accident, got dressed and told Annie, "Five minutes! Front door."

Annie, not sure she really wanted to know the result, reluctantly dressed and met her cousin at the door. It was a brisk morning. Annie grabbed a jacket for her and one for Sabine. Although Sabine walked a little slow, Annie was perfectly happy matching her pace. They walked into the quaint town of Boothbay via their favorite trail through the meadowlands with beautiful views of the various lighthouses. Their talk was mostly about the wedding. They both were crazy about Meghan and so happy for Tomás.

Annie suggested, "I think Meghan wants to go out to

Ocean Point to see Stone Chapel where the wedding will be. She has an appointment with the planner who is coordinating the flowers and reception this afternoon. I think I will go...do you want to?"

"If it's okay, Robert asked me to a clambake this afternoon. He says I got cheated out of the one the day of the accident," Sabine answered.

"Very true. So you two are going to give it a try? I should have seen it before. I honestly think Robert is such a great man, and he obviously cares about you."

They got the kit and stopped on the way back to get a bite to eat. Sabine excitedly said, "Can we get that avocado toast that has the goat cheese and smoked salmon on it? It is one of my favorites!"

Annie pointed to one of the cafés. "This one has it." She wasn't overly nauseous but still felt the need for something plain. Annie decided on an egg white frittata with sundried tomatoes.

Sabine looked around at the people who all spoke to one another and were so friendly. "This is such a special place. I'm so happy to be back."

Annie smiled. "Awww, it's so great to have you here... more than you know. But I guess you won't be going out on the sailboat this trip."

"Well, if I do, I won't be wearing earphones and will stay alert!" Taking a bite of her toast, Sabine simply smiled in delight.

The sun had warmed the temperature for the walk back, and they no longer needed jackets. Their talk naturally veered to the expected results of the test.

Sabine thoughtfully said, "You know how we talk about crossroads in our lives. This is one for you. The direction of the paths may change, but you always have a choice. The challenge is to step back to get a clear view of the situation before making any rash decision. I tried to do that when I was in rehab. I was embarrassed by my infirmity. Because of that, I almost didn't come on this trip. Think what a difference the direction my path took by making that one choice."

Meghan and Tomás were chatting with Celeste and Alex when the girls came into the house.

Annie asked Meghan, "What time do you want to go out to Stone Chapel? I'm planning to go, but Sabine has other plans," giving Sabine a little jab with her elbow.

Celeste laughed, glad the girls were past any drama. She also noticed the drugstore sack. So did Meghan.

Meghan said, "Tomás wants to go too. If we are going to walk, we should start in about an hour. In the meantime, I would love to take another look at your bridesmaid's dresses so I can be sure about the flower colors of your bouquet."

The three of them went to Annie's room.

Annie looked at Meghan, "Very sneaky...you didn't really need to see the dresses, did you?"

"Well, no, but you are not leaving me out of this big moment. Get in there."

Coming back out with her face dazed, Annie handed the stick over. Both girls squealed, "YES!" Annie rubbed her temples. Although she'd felt like she was, the reality was still a shock.

Celeste knocked on the door. "How are those dresses? May I see?"

After Annie nodded, Sabine came to the door. "Of course, Aunt Celeste."

When the door closed behind her, Annie showed her the results. Celeste wrapped her arms around her daughter and said, "It appears I am going to be a grandmother!" All four of them were giddy and indulged in a group hug.

Annie finally spoke, "Just having the three of you here with me and not having to find this out alone means the world to me."

More hugs. Mentally, she felt a pang of loss that a certain matador was not there with her to hear the news. Annie knew her mother would tell her father, but she didn't want Tomás or Robert to find out before Ramone. Meghan and Sabine understood.

When the ladies came out, they were all talking about the dresses. Alex raised his eyebrow at Celeste, who gave him a very subtle nod. Spirits were high in the group as they discussed the venues for the rehearsal dinner and wedding. Dom and Gennie would arrive the next day, then the festivities would begin. There was no time for Annie to absorb her results. That would have to wait for later. Sabine left with Robert and Annie, Meghan and Tomás prepared to walk over to Ocean Point and the chapel.

Tomás couldn't wait to show Meghan one of his favorite places—the Stone Chapel built in the early 1900s. The chapel's original dedication was extremely meaningful to him. Dr. Elliott had said, "We are associating this place with a certain clearness of spirit to perceive the very best in things and in people." Annie had always liked that about the chapel too. Though she knew she would forever have the soul of a mariner, she thrived on being enveloped by family and loved ones. The thought of staying flitted across her mind.

Annie's parents had offered to check out the location of the rehearsal dinner to be held in an authentic nineteenth-century farmhouse in Wiscasset. The owner was a dear family friend and particularly special to Tomás and his deceased parents.

Celeste's older brother, Jorge, and his wife Maria, used to bring Tomás to Maine to visit during the summers. After their tragic auto accident when Tomás was just a boy, Dom and Gennie brought him to live with them in Marbella. But Celeste insisted he come back and stay with them each summer.

Emily Weston was Maria's best friend, and she made a vow after losing her friend to always be there for Tomás. Tomás and Meghan shared that unfortunate loss of parents. Her father had died when she was a young girl. Then she lost her mother to breast cancer two years ago. That was the main reason they decided to marry in this part of Maine and introduce Meghan to the people who were his family, knowing they would accept her as their own.

Chapter 40

Everything in Place

Alex and Celeste both went to Portland to pick up her parents. After all, Dom and Gennie hadn't seen their daughter in over eight months and Alex since before he left Maine on assignment. They already loved Meghan from her visits to Marbella, and they were especially excited to see Sabine. Everyone was waiting when they got home from the airport. Loving hugs and tears of joy all around, Dom and Gennie quickly saw Sabine's affection for Robert, and they readily accepted him like family. Annie's hasty retreat from Crete had caused them some concern. However, they were pleased to see her happy with her family around her.

Annie left the group to get some appetizers from the kitchen. When she reentered the room with the tray of pimento cheese fritters she and Sabine had made, it hit her hard. Meghan was arm in arm with Tomás. Sabine was holding Robert's hand. Her mother looked ecstatic, standing next to her father and, of course, Dom and Gennie with their long-term love and friendship, surrounded by loved ones. Herself? She wasn't alone either—she had this little person growing inside her.

Without realizing it, she took one hand and placed it on her stomach and thought, *You and me, my precious child.* But in truth, there was an ache, a void in her heart. Passing the appetizers, she noticed Tomás going to the door to greet Emily Weston.

She greeted him with "Son, I could not wait another second to see you. Introduce me to your girl."

Emily easily fit right into the group. At one point, Annie looked over at Meghan and could tell she was genuinely happy with her new family. She had a gracious spirit (when her Irish temper wasn't flared) that Annie loved.

Sabine came over to put an arm around Annie. "Don't feel left out. The answers will come soon enough. Everyone in this room loves you so much." Annie could feel the tears start but forced them down.

Finally, deciding she needed to know, Annie approached Dom and quietly asked, "How was the fight in Sevilla?"

"Ramone fought well, Annie. He started out with a heartfelt dedication to his brother. All of Spain was behind him, and the cheers were deafening. His slight nod acknowledged we were there, but he never came up to us after the victory. When I think back, he didn't stay to receive his roses either."

The rehearsal went well. Annie and Sabine were the two bridesmaids. Alex was to be Tomás's groomsman, but last minute, Tomás asked Robert to stand up with him as well. They met through Annie and had been acquainted over the years. Knowing what Robert did for Sabine was the motivation to make the friendship stronger. Now they had a balanced wedding party.

The rehearsal dinner at the farmhouse was the perfect blend of rustic chic and manor elegance. Annie was seated next to a friend of Emily's that Tomás knew but she had never met. Her name was Deidra. Such an interesting lady. It turned out Deidra lived in Martha's Vineyard half the year. She had met Emily while student teaching in Rio de Janeiro. Deidra had then gone on to explore and teach in other South American countries, including Ecuador, Uruguay, and Columbia. This was exciting enough, but when Annie heard what Deidra was doing in Peru, she was spellbound.

As Annie listened, she recognized the profound respect

for and curiosity about distant cultures, along with a fierce personal independence that seemed just a few of the commonalities between them. Deidra's project in Peru, combined with a family here in Martha's Vineyard, was incredibly intriguing to Annie. It was clear there was much she could learn from Deidra.

She met her husband here in the States while visiting Emily eighteen years ago. Seemingly an impossible relationship on the surface, she showed her husband-to-be how she had built a thriving business in Peru. He was impressed with her accomplishments and worked with her to find a life together that worked for them both. Similarly, Tomás and Meghan agreed to share time between Ireland and Spain. It seemed both couples had achieved that elusive balance that Annie sought. She agreed to meet and hear more about Deidra's story after the wedding. Before they parted, Deidra said to her, "Maybe someday you will visit me in Lima."

Annie sincerely answered, "I would love that. When do you go again?"

Deidra said, "In about two weeks. This should be an interesting trip. Let's do talk more after the wedding."

The day of the wedding arrived. Annie ventured out to the patio and found Meghan calm and enjoying each moment. "How can you not be nervous?"

"Annie, I love Tomás, and I am lucky to have him love me in return. I now have a new family. All of you are beyond what I could hope for. Why on earth would I be nervous?"

"Have you decided where you will honeymoon?" Annie asked.

"Tomás found a bed-and-breakfast on an island close by, so we plan to go there for a few days. Do you plan to stay after the wedding?"

Annie thought for a moment before responding, "I'm not sure. I might go back to Marbella in hopes I can mend the situation with Ramone. With him so hurt and angry and my carrying his child, that seems a bit overwhelming. Deidra from last night offered a visit to Peru to see the work she is doing with the knitters there. That seems very intriguing to me."

Cryptically Meghan said, "Destiny is knocking on your door, Annie. Don't get in the way."

Sabine found them and said it was time for Meghan to start getting ready. Alex took Tomás and Robert to play a round of golf, then they were going to the church after to change.

Looking at Meghan, Annie said, "You are such a natural beauty. It seems a waste to go all out with hair and makeup. Oh well, let's have fun with it and all spruce up a little."

The makeup artist and hairdresser arrived. Celeste poured a mimosa for Meghan and Sabine and smiled when she handed the champagne glass with pure orange juice to Annie. Sabine wanted her long brown hair in an updo, so Annie decided on something similar. That way Meghan's fire-red hair could stream long in soft curls as a contrast.

The bridesmaid's dresses were a stunning emerald green, bringing some Irish influence to the wedding. Floor-length, the solid chiffon flowed from the waist. Attached to the fitted bustier top was a cap sleeve with beautiful open-lace trim that gave the dresses a demur but elegant look. Meghan's bridal dress took everyone's breath away. Ivory satin covered in a slightly darker lace fit sleekly down to her knees, then ruffled from there to the floor. Sleeveless with a deep V-front, the dress needed no train. Meghan had a most simple claddagh clip with a crystal-edged bridal veil attached. Stunning!

Celeste arrived dressed in a soft shade of aubergine. "Oh my, you girls look beautiful. Meghan, you are going to make a spectacular bride, and Tomás will feel like the luckiest man alive!"

Radiant and Irish eyes smiling, Meghan answered, "Tis I'm the lucky one, Aunt Celeste. Thank you for welcoming me to the family."

The driver gave a loud whistle when he saw the women he would be driving to the church. Ocean Point wasn't far, and Stone Chapel looked particularly welcoming today. The florist had created a wedding wreath for the chapel door, weaving emerald green lace and ribbon through white roses and baby's breath. Inside, the pews had simple emerald bows on the ends with two beautiful arrangements at the altar. Annie knew Meghan was pleased. Everything looked perfect!

Chapter 41

The Wedding

The ladies retired to the bridal room as guests began to arrive. Emily and Deidra came by to see the girls and give their best wishes to Meghan. They had just seen Tomás and said he was counting the seconds! Everything had been leading up to this special day that would join the two lovers in matrimony. Celeste left them to go take her seat. The florist had given her an orchid corsage with a touch of green that was perfect with her dress and coordinated with the wedding party. Annie and Sabine had simple bouquets of the same orchids. Meghan's bouquet was gorgeous. A mini version of the wreath on the door, the bouquet was interwoven with the large white lilies and sprays of orchids down the sides. They were ready.

Sabine walked down the aisle first, giving a reassuring smile to Tomás. The men looked so handsome! Dark-gray cutaway suits with their white-on-white bow tie and emerald green cummerbund tied the entire wedding party together. Sabine hadn't seen Robert all dressed up. He looked dashing to her. Next, it was time for Annie. She agreed wholeheartedly about the men, and she was reminded again how lucky she was to have her father with them today. When the organ began to play the bridal song, everyone stood up and looked to the entrance. Meghan looked around the room and smiled her radiant smile at her guests. An orphan, she had found family and friends here in this quaint town. The joy and happiness she felt could hardly be contained, and the love in her eyes when she looked at Tomás said it all.

The thoughtful and inspiring vows they exchanged touched the hearts of all present, but not as much as when Tomás held up the custom-made claddagh ring to give to Meghan and said, "This traditional Irish symbol of love, loyalty, and friendship elegantly captures the sentiments at the core of marriage. My beautiful Irish treasure, please be mine forever."

Meghan's tears could not be contained. She hadn't known about the ring, and she was overwhelmed. There wasn't a dry eye in the chapel when the newlyweds came down the aisle arm in arm. Annie and Sabine followed... Annie with her father and Sabine with Robert. Alex went back to escort a teary Celeste down the aisle...a most memorable ceremony.

The large tent set up behind the chapel was ready for the reception. The florist had exceeded expectations there as well! Guests began to wander out, and the photographer took over with the wedding party. Annie could see Meghan looking about and wondered if she was missing something she needed for the pictures. However, she forgot it as they were all caught up following the photographer's instructions. What a beautiful day they were having together. The photographer, finally finished with the posed photos, allowed the wedding party to join the reception. Tomás and Meghan led the way to a round of applause as they entered. Meghan nodded to the photographer.

Logic told Annie that the wedding brought with it a natural point of departure, and she knew she would have to decide her next steps. Yet she wasn't so anxious to leave this time. So much of her life belonged to Marbella and the sea itself. Lost in these musings, Annie absentmindedly caught the wedding bouquet. Surprised and laughing, she whirled around, and there stood Ramone! Her mind was bombarded with questions, yet all she saw was her matador, dapper and handsome as ever in his perfectly fitted dark suit.

"W-what? H-how?"

The bride came over between them. Meghan said, "May I assume this handsome man is Ramone?" To Ramone, she said, smiling, "What took you so long?"

Everyone's attention at the reception turned to Annie and Ramone. He had not spoken a word. Alex came over to shake his hand and introduce him to Celeste. Annie's mother scrutinized this man who had stolen her daughter's heart and saved her husband. She definitely looked forward to the opportunity to spend time with him.

Dom and Gennie came over next. "Excellent fight, Ramone. How is Antonio?"

Ramone glanced at Annie and answered, "Much better, thank you."

Meghan saw the dazed look in Annie's eyes and took charge. "Okay, everyone...enough. This is Ramone Sanchez, the famous Spanish matador. He got here a little late. That's all. Let's get the dancing started!"

Taking Tomás's hand, they went out to the dance floor for the first dance.

The guests turned their attention back toward the bride and groom. Annie looked at Meghan in question, then Ramone—totally confused. He walked toward her and pulled her outside. She sensed the intensity in his stare.

All she could say was "Your letter?"

"When I heard the Arab brought his plane to get you in Crete, I could not believe it. HE was the one to deliver your letter to me?" Ramone answered. "It was Meghan who finally reached out to me. She called to ask why I was not coming to the wedding. The answer was simple. 'I wasn't invited.'"

"Ramone, I never intended any of this. My father arranged the flight quickly. El Amir was not supposed to be on it. I got sick at sea. I am so sorry I let you and your brother down when you needed me. Somehow, I was con-vinced I would be a distraction to you in the ring. With your worry about Antonio, I didn't want to make the fight more difficult and dangerous." Annie knew she was rambling.

"We obviously need to talk. Meghan told me there were circumstances I didn't understand. She asked me to come. I got on the earliest flight I could," Ramone continued.

Annie honestly didn't know whether to be furious at Meghan's audacious nerve or kiss both her cheeks in thanks. Looking at Ramone, Annie could do nothing but wrap her arms around him and say, "Whatever got you here...I've missed you terribly."

Ramone was not prepared for what he would feel holding her again. Although there were still many unanswered questions between them, he had his woman back in his arms. Pulling her close, he kissed her deeply with the most hypnotic combination of need, desperation, and urgency.

Where this was leading got interrupted by a polite cough. Both Annie and Ramone turned around to see her father. "Perhaps you two would care to rejoin the wedding party. The toasts are beginning." Then he left.

Awkwardly, Annie shook her head and said, "Geez, my father? How does everything keep spinning out of control?"

Ramone turned her toward him. "One step at a time. Let's go in."

Obviously, their absence was noticed. The looks they got from all over the party were palpable. Annie was sure she was blushing to be the cause of such a display. While they were outside, an extra seat had been placed at the wedding party table so Ramone could join them. Annie tried not to notice the look from Robert and smirk from Sabine. With this recent turn of events, her rather vanilla toast no longer seemed appropriate.

One by one, toasts were made, glasses refilled. Ramone noticed Annie was drinking sparkling cider rather than champagne but did not feel a need to question it. Sabine's toast was particularly touching, especially knowing how self-conscious she was about her speech. It was finally time for Annie. Looking around, she tossed her well-rehearsed toast away and went ad lib.

"Meghan and Tomás, I want to start by returning the comment made to me earlier today, 'Destiny is knocking at the door.' You are two of the lucky ones who have found your destiny together. Tomás, you have discovered the infamous 'pot of gold' with this Irish beauty full of spunk and sizzle. Don't expect a smooth sail every time with her." Polite laughter. "Instead, embrace those times when a touch of devilish trouble enters the mix. Meghan has many layers that will take a lifetime for you to explore in depth, but I can tell you from the little time that I have known her it will be well worth your while. And Meghan, to see how deeply you love Tomás is a balm to all of us. Tomás can be light-hearted and charismatic, but his sensitive heart and love for you is your own 'pot of gold.' Together, you will face life's challenges. Embrace those challenges jointly, and you will find the possibilities to conquer them and so many more. To some, it might seem now is your moment. It is not just now. But tomorrow and every day after that, you have a chance to love each other, appreciate each other, sacrifice for each other. I love you both and wish nothing but joy for you in your marriage."

The applause was deafening. Meghan had tears streaming down her cheeks. Annie, herself, had tears welling up. Even Tomás was misty-eyed. The shock was from Ramone, hearing this toast from his woman (his own eyes glistening). He turned her to him and kissed her soundly. More applause from the guests.

Meghan came up to Annie, tears still in her eyes, and said, "Please don't be cross with me for my interference. Tomás had no idea I called. Ramone needs to be here with you. Are you okay?"

Am I okay? Time would tell. Every thought, every action brings an opportunity, and I need to be prepared to increase my efforts in that regard.

Chapter 42

Annie and Ramone—Maine

B ack at home, the atmosphere was totally different from the prior evening. Celeste offered Ramone the room Tomás and Meghan had just vacated. Dom and Gennie excused themselves and retired early. Celeste looked at her daughter with concern. Annie looked emotionally drained; and Celeste, who knew her daughter well, realized a deep intensive conversation between Annie and Ramone would not go the way they hoped at this late hour. While she was remaking the bed for Ramone, he brought in his bag. Annie stood in the doorway with no idea how to proceed.

Celeste gently said to them both, "Everyone is tired. Ramone has traveled many hours. Perhaps it would be a good idea for you both to get some rest before tackling your emotions."

Walking over to Ramone, Celeste hugged him and said, "Ramone, we're so glad you are here, and I look forward to getting to know you."

He hugged her back and with a glance over at Annie. He too could see how tired she was.

To her daughter, Celeste said, "Get some rest, sweetheart. You will have a much better talk if you wait until the morning."

Annie seemed relieved. Ramone wasn't so sure he liked Celeste's interference, but honestly, he was coming off some jet lag himself. Celeste left them. Alex had already gone to bed; Sabine and Robert were talking out on the patio.

Ramone went up to Annie. "I am here and not going anywhere until we are settled. Get some sleep, *querida*."

Annie felt such relief at the sound of that one simple word and smiled. "Good night, I'll see you in the morning."

Ramone watched her quietly close her bedroom door. He felt too restless to sleep and wandered out to the patio where Sabine and Robert were talking.

"I don't want to interrupt," he said as he approached them.

Sabine answered, "Of course you aren't interrupting. Please join us." Sabine's speech was getting better every day, perhaps because of being surrounded by people who made her so comfortable.

Ramone studied Sabine for a moment and said, "Annie has been so worried about you. She spoke of you often. It must make her heart full of joy to have you here."

"As it does mine," Sabine answered, smiling.

"Robert, you were there when the accident happened. Was it an accident? Annie felt such guilt that she in some way caused it." Ramone was curious to know what really happened.

Both Robert and Sabine protested. Robert explained, "Annie was at the helm. She called out that we were doing a gybe, which would force the boom over in a hard manner. What she didn't notice was that Sabine had earphones in and hadn't heard the warning."

Sabine added, "I knew better. I have sailed since I was a little girl. It was totally my fault. I do think Annie and I have been able to come to peace with it."

Not wanting to get too serious or somehow interfere with Annie's conversation with Ramone, Sabine and Robert told him a little about Boothbay and how special it was to all of them. Ramone came straight from the airport to the wedding, with a quick stop to change clothes, so he hadn't seen much of the landscape or the town. Robert told him about all the hiking trails and that he and Sabine were doing an early morning hike the next day.

"Get Annie to take you on one of her early morning walks. They mean a lot to her. But what you will really want to experience is why this is the boating capital of New England," Robert suggested.

Then Sabine added, "And don't forget to eat lobster— lots of it! There's nothing like it. Have it on a roll, in a salad, in a soup...it doesn't matter which way. It's delicious."

To Sabine, Ramone asked, "How long are you staying?"

With a glance at Robert, she casually answered with a smile, "Still up in the air, I suppose. What about you?"

"I fight again at the end of next week, so I have to be back before that time. My ticket is open. I still do not know how I will be received."

Robert got up and said to Sabine, "Let's get some sleep. We have an early morning."

Annie was still sleeping soundly when Sabine woke up the following morning. Sabine lightly shook her, "Hey, sleepyhead! You might want to get up. There is most likely a handsome matador waiting for you."

Annie bolted up, "Oh no. What do I say?"

Sabine said calmly, "He seems like a good man. If he weren't, you wouldn't feel as strongly as you do about him. Trust your instincts, Annie. Remember what Captain Luis taught us...that we cannot control the wind or the sea, but we can adjust the sail to find our direction. You can do this."

A quick hug for Sabine, and Annie grabbed her jeans and a white shirt. *Hmmm*, Annie pondered. The tightness at the waist of her jeans might not be just from the wedding dinner. Sabine smiled knowingly then waved as she left to meet Robert.

Ramone was in a conversation with her parents and grandparents when Annie walked out to the patio. He stood when he saw her.

Everyone greeted her, and Celeste added, "We were having a lovely chat."

Looking over at Gennie, she said, "Why don't we go into town for breakfast?"

"*Mais oui*, lovely idea!" Gennie responded, catching Celeste's implication to let Annie and Ramone have some time alone.

Once they left, Annie picked up Ramone's cup. "More coffee?"

"*Si, querida*, another cup would be good." Ramone followed her to the kitchen and took the cup from her. Picking her up, he sat her on the counter. With her legs apart, he leaned into her and whispered, "The awkwardness must stop, *querida*. Talk to me."

Annie sighed and began, "It seems each time things get settled and I might be heading in the right direction, life randomly puts chaos in the mix, and I have a difficult time knowing where to turn."

Ramone tried to understand and asked, "Start when we left Karpathos. What happened on the *Porto Banus*?"

"It felt good to be at sea again. I missed you terribly..."

Holding her closer, Ramone encouraged her, "Go on. What changed?"

"I began to think about the possibility of us together, which led to the reminder of the danger you face each time you enter the ring. The fear I felt about your fight coming up in Sevilla was paralyzing. I reasoned that if I fell too hard for you, I would have to face this fear regularly, always wondering when or if there might be an injury. On board, we went through a big storm. I got sick. I wasn't sure whether I had made myself sick with worry since I rarely get seasick, but it didn't seem to calm down after the storm."

Annie continued, "Feeling sick and confused, all I could think of was seeing my mother and father and being home to sort things out. The captain stopped in Crete so I could have a couple of nights on land to see if that would settle the nausea. When I called my parents and heard their voices, I knew I had to go home. That's when I wrote you the first letter. I swear I did not have any idea my father would contact El Amir to use his plane."

Ramone lifted her down from the counter, and they moved to the sofa. He could see the tired look on her face. Thinking back, he said, "I had already left for Sevilla before that letter came. What happened next?"

Annie took a deep breath and went on, "I certainly did not expect to see El Amir. I was still sick and not thinking clearly. He showed me the newspaper with the article about Antonio's injury, but all I saw was the headline. I thought it was you, and I fainted."

Putting his arm around Annie, Ramone closed his eyes with understanding. "*Querida*, we have spoken of this before. It is what I do and what my family has done for generations."

Annie looked at him pitifully. "I know, but the deeper my feelings for you, the harder it becomes. You said worry and distraction are the greatest dangers. I knew you would be worried about Antonio. I was afraid I would be a distraction. I just don't know how to deal with this properly. I'm sure you are angry with me...it must have seemed like I was running away. I suppose I really did run away."

Annie's eyes began to glisten. "And Ramone, there is one more thing..." With a big breath, she added, "I am carrying your child."

Chapter 43

Traditions Explored

Annie watched Ramone's reaction as her last statement sunk in. Shock turned to excitement, then the questions. "What! How? We were careful."

Annie simply said, "Gypsy Beach."

He nodded and placed his hand on her stomach. "How long have you known?"

"My nausea was the first sign, but the initial test I did was negative. I just found out...that must have been when Meghan called you. Ramone, I am so sorry for everything."

Huskily, he said, "*Querida, mi amor,* my blood flows through you now. My child rests within your womb." Ramone turned her toward him for a kiss. "Never regret this child that has been created through our love. Let me spend the time I have here to get to know your family and understand your love of this place. Will you show it to me? All I ask in return is that you meet my family and try to understand what I do and why I do it."

Annie could merely hug him and say, "That seems only fair."

From there, they fell back into the easy rapport they had in Greece, planning their time in Maine. They spent the next few days exploring...Annie eager to show her Maine to fresh eyes. Sailing, fishing, hiking, and enjoying the quaint harbor town were interspersed with warm meals with family and picnics with Sabine and Robert. Annie was pleased to see Ramone revert to the easy-going man he was in Greece, and he seemed to genuinely enjoy both her family and her home.

Knowing Ramone's role in freeing Alex, plus seeing the interaction between he and Annie, it was easy for the family to accept him. Annie and Ramone agreed to postpone further discussion about the baby for the moment. They needed to breathe each other in right now, and they both understood Annie's fear had to be dealt with. Dom and Gennie flew home after tearful goodbyes. They asked Sabine to fly with them, but she wasn't ready to leave yet. Meghan and Tomás would be back from their honeymoon in a couple of days before returning to Marbella. Sabine could fly home then or wait until Annie flew back. She knew Annie had committed to meet Ramone's family.

Ramone was leaving the following day to get back to Marbella in time for the bullfight in Malaga. Right before Dom and Gennie flew home, Annie told them she could not go back for the fight.

Without hesitation, Dom patted Ramone on the back and said, "We will be there, son. Look for us."

Dom and Ramone had formed a bond created from an understanding of Spanish tradition combined with a love of Annie. Dom committed to help Ramone bridge that gap if he could.

Annie and Ramone spent their last day in Boothbay watching a fleet of windjammers under sail in the harbor, listening to a concert in the park, and stopping for ice cream... with a show-stopping display of fireworks as the finale.

Once the fireworks ended, Ramone pulled Annie into his arms. "I cannot bear to leave you tomorrow, *querida*, but I must go back. The last few days have given me an understanding of the closeness you feel with your family and the love you have for this seafaring town. The child you carry is growing, *querida*. Do not wait too long to come back to me."

Ramone's arrival in Maine had been a shock when he appeared at the wedding after she caught the bouquet. She was deeply touched by his desire to know her family.

Sharing her old haunts and favorite parts of New England with Ramone had been utterly fulfilling. His anguished sincerity should have been enough to assure her of his feelings. But now, Annie knew something was still undone for her before any commitments could be made. She needed time to reflect and absorb the enormity of her pregnancy and her fear of losing her baby's father.

To Ramone, she said, "There is something I must do before I come back. My hope is that it gives me some clarity. I will take care of our child...please do not worry. Just promise me you will take care of yourself."

Ramone nodded in agreement as he pulled her into his room and into his bed for the most achingly tender lovemaking they had ever experienced. When he parted the following morning, his final words were "Come back to me, *querida*..."

Celeste watched her daughter come in after Ramone left. "Are you okay?"

"Mom, I love that man. I just don't know if I can live a life with him in constant worry. He gave me a note once...I keep it with me always."

Annie took the note Ramone had written back in Scotland and showed it to her mother.

> *'Sailing maiden, thornless rose. Adventurous heart the sea best knows. The same love that draws me to you lets me set you free. Your journey's end waits next to me.'*

"That is beautiful. Ramone has a poet's heart, filled with romance. Perhaps that gives him the complement to his bravado side he needs to fight?" Celeste questioned.

Annie wondered if that might be so. To Celeste, she said, "I think I will go visit Deidra today. I met her at the rehearsal dinner, and she might still be at Emily's. She was fascinating, and I'd like to hear more about the balance she has maneuvered into her life."

Pulling out her journal, Annie tried to write from her artist friends' perspective:

> *Is there a healing canvas on which I could paint a perfect picture of my future—one that could contain the man, the children, the world, and the oceans that I love? What is in store at my journey's end?*

Annie walked to Emily's house and found the two ladies coming in from shopping.

Emily saw her first and called out, "Annie, come in for a cup of tea. We hoped to see you and find out a little more about your handsome Spanish matador."

Annie smiled and shook her head at how quickly news got around this small town. "He left this morning." Looking at Deidra, she asked, "How long are you staying?"

Deidra answered, "I drive back to Martha's Vineyard tomorrow. Emily and I rarely get time for just the two of us. This has been such a great visit. I leave for Peru by the end of the week. My husband and son will also go with me on this trip."

Emily brought the tea out to the garden where the ladies sat.

Annie asked Deidra, "I'm curious. Can you tell me more about what you do and how you manage two such different lives?"

Deidra, warming up to the subject, began to share her story. As a young teacher in Brazil, Deidra had adopted the love of knitting that was inherent to South Americans. On buses and trains, to and from teaching school, she would knit...for herself, family and friends. Several years later when she later ventured to Peru, she got to know some of the native roadside knitters with such incredible hidden talents. The way they dyed their wool to get hundreds of colors was part art and part science.

Deidra learned the Andes were filled with a great diversity of plant life, and the Andean people carried a rich knowledge of the use of these plants for natural dyes for their cloth. Their spun yarn, usually alpaca, was boiled for varying periods of time, depending on which dyestuff used, the quantity of yarn to be dyed, and the desired color. Fixatives such as mineral salts or even urine were necessary to create colorfastness, alter hues, or intensify color. Then after the yarns have dried, they were respun, plied, and wound into balls of yarn ready for weaving. An idea was born...Deidra could bring these craftsmen together and produce top-quality sweaters while creating a local community for those who needed it desperately.

Annie was enthralled with her story. "What are the people like? How do they accept you?"

Deidra answered, "When I'm there, I usually live with a family of knitters. Their home is primitive...adobe-like walls and shower-curtain doors, but their warm hospitality never allows me to feel like an outsider. My love of knitting and reasonable ability has led to an easy camaraderie with these Peruvian knitters. But it is the trust that these proud, quiet people give me that humbles me."

Deidra continued, "In return, I try to teach them about better health and living conditions and to give them a business knowledge they didn't know existed. But I never cease to be amazed at what they can teach me and how extraordinary their hearts are. And that is what I bring back to my family and to my home here in the States."

As Annie listened, her mind found a quiet sense of peace, pondering the Peruvian people. As the consummate explorer, Annie was always open to new cultures and experiences. But her brain was already processing what she had learned over the last months, assimilating it and making plans.

To Deidra, she said, "I think I would love to go to Peru one day."

They all agreed to keep in touch, and Deidra gave Annie an open invitation to visit.

On the walk home, Annie reflected. *How is it possible for me to accept so many cultures and traditions, yet I can't accept one of the oldest traditions in Spain?*

It would clearly be an emotional investment to officially meet Ramone's mother, but perhaps she could help give some clarity and understanding to living as a woman in this dynasty of matadors. Although it had not seemed important before, she also wanted to comprehend the impact of Salvador's decisions...first, to not join the generational family tradition of becoming a matador, and second, the close friendship he had with her father followed by his betrayal and murder attempt. There was something unsettled there that Ramone's mother, Marguerite, might possibly enlighten. Her father had not discussed it other than to ask Ramone how his father was. According to Ramone, Salvador was still detained by the British military.

At home, Annie affectionately told her mother about Deidra's lifestyle and how she would like to visit Peru someday and see these indigenous knitters.

Celeste wisely added, "Sweetheart, it appears you have found a kindred spirit in this woman who has a passion for travel and everything Spanish. Did talking with her help you make a decision about the choice you have at this crossroad?"

Annie shared, "I think her story opened my eyes to how important Spanish tradition is to Ramone's family. I want to understand how the women in the family cope with their men in danger. I believe it is time I went back to meet his mother."

Celeste agreed. "Throughout time, men have fought in battles, gone on dangerous expeditions. Think about the Greek sponge divers who free dove hundreds of feet and, as they left the harbor, didn't know if they would return. How about our own astronauts who fly up into outer space? Any number of dangerous activities where a spouse or a child might be left behind are done for such a variety of reasons—bravery, power, and adventure are just a few. You are not alone. The choice will be yours whether to accept this man for who he is or choose a different path. But, sweetheart, do not let fear rule your destiny."

Annie nodded and hugged her mother, who always seemed to have the right thing to say. "Yes, I'll go arrange a flight."

Chapter 44

Alex's Revelation

Before she booked her flight, Annie wanted to have a quick talk with her father. She found him out on the patio. "Dad, can you talk for a few minutes?"

Alex answered, putting his book down, "Of course, what's on your mind?"

Annie gave some thought about how to start. She quietly began, "You haven't spoken much about Salvador. He was supposedly your best friend. Of course, you know I'm having Ramone's child. I am seriously considering going back to Marbella, and I would like to better understand some things about his father. When did you become friends? Why did Salvador not want to be a matador but his sons did? Salvador is Spanish. Why is it the British military has him detained?"

Alex got up and paced a little. "This is not an easy subject for me. There were times while Ramone was here that he looked so much like Salvador, with even some of the same mannerisms, it made me very sad how things unfolded for us.

"I met Salvador when we were both boarding students at King's College in Madrid. We were around eleven years old. It's an excellent English-speaking school. My parents wanted me to grow up in an international setting. Salvador's father and grandfather were matadors. Everyone expected him to be one also. It was his father who urged his son to expand his horizons and go to this school in Madrid. Salvador loved his father. Their connection was very close. I met him the first day of school. He didn't speak much English, and I didn't speak much Spanish. So we made a pact to teach each other. Years went by. We visited each other's homes frequently. Salvador's father, when he wasn't scheduled for a fight, would take us hunting. He is the one who taught us to be such good marksmen. When we were sixteen, Salvador was to spend the summer at bullfighting school. I remember he was so excited.

"Fate stepped in at the beginning of that summer. Salvador went to see his father defeat the bull and be awarded the bull's ear for a great fight. Instead, he saw the father he loved so much gored and mortally wounded in front of him."

At Annie's gasp, her father stopped. "That's what you are afraid of, right?"

Annie closed her eyes and answered, "Yes, exactly. How horrible it must have been for him."

Alex continued, "Everything changed for Salvador that day. He did not show up at the bullfighting school. His older brother had already been to the school and wasn't there the day of their father's fight. He tried to counsel Salvador to get him to reconsider his place in their family tradition, but there was no way my friend was going to enter the ring. It wasn't fear in him...it was anger."

"What happened?" Annie asked.

"I think that anger somehow took root in him. When I graduated and went into the military, Salvador enlisted in the British military as well so we remained close. I was more of a brother to him than his own. We were young. I heard he took you to Aero Bleu in Paris. We spent many a night there when we were single and drank far too much. It was at that club where people of questionable character propositioned us to spy. The military found out about their interest and asked us to accept and be part of the counterin-telligence community. It was dangerous work, and we often found ourselves in trouble. But we covered for each other when we could. That is when we met Ernest and Peter, the colonel you met in Scotland. The four of us vowed to have one another's back."

Astounded with her father's history, Annie asked, "What about us?"

Alex went on, "Salvador and I were due for a leave and decided to spend our time off in Barcelona. I met your mother at a club she had come to with Dom and Gennie. She captivated my heart at first glance, and I had to meet her! Everything was quite civil, of course. I was British, after all. With Don Marco's permission, I soon began to court her. That same trip, Salvador met Marguerite. She was a most stunning flamenco dancer, and he was crazy about her. The four of us went out a couple of times."

Annie interrupted, "Wait, Mom knew her?"

Alex explained, "We were young. Your mother was society. They moved in different circles."

Annie said, "Ah, that might explain Antonio's choice of a beautiful flamenco dancer at the party we attended."

Her father continued, "After that vacation, we lost touch. I was sent to North Africa, and Salvador to Hong Kong. We both managed to marry. I knew he married Marguerite but never knew about his two sons. I married your mother in Marbella at Dom's villa shortly after. You were conceived there. Maybe that is why you feel so at home in Marbella. There was nothing more important to me than keeping you both safe. As our situation in North Africa began to heat up, I was worried. When I approached my commanding officer, he suggested I move you both to a remote area in the States. I told you in Paris how Peter helped us. That's when I moved you and your mother here to Maine.

"I knew she would want to be by the sea. After we visited several areas, she chose Boothbay. I wanted her as happy as possible raising you with me often gone. Once I got the two of you settled in, I had to leave for a variety of counterintelligence assignments and, finally, the most recent one in Hong

Kong. I looked for Salvador, but no one seemed to know of his whereabouts. Britain was struggling with Chinese counterintelligence in Hong Kong. It is still a British colony and will not be released and handed over to Beijing until 1997. However, there is a force inside Hong Kong trying to speed up the turnover against great resistance. Salvador got involved with that group and met Kung Li. I think you know the rest." *Oh my gosh, my father, Ramone's father, Salvador's father, El Amir's father. How very Shakespearean!*

Chapter 45

Back to Marbella, Spain

Sabine walked in while Annie was packing. "So you are going back to Marbella? You and Uncle Alex talked for a long time."

Annie looked up at the cousin she loved so much. "Yes, Dad cleared up a lot of things for me. The story of what happened with Salvador was important for me to know. I think I owe Ramone and the baby an attempt to understand his traditions. Maybe his mother will help me, although now I am curious about her life with Ramone's father, who chose not to become a matador. I wonder if he regretted that decision." As an afterthought, she said, "Why don't you come with me to Marbella?"

It was a few moments before Sabine answered, "I think I would like that. Robert and I have formed a close friendship, but he doesn't seem to be pursuing a romance. With you gone, it might be time for me to leave as well."

Annie nodded. "Robert is such a considerate man, and he seems to genuinely care about you."

Sabine answered thoughtfully, "I know he does, and I'm grateful for his kindness. I care for him as well."

Annie responded, "As long as I have known Robert, I have never seen him even close to having a girlfriend. That has changed with you. Perhaps he could visit you in France and you could spend some time there?"

"Yes, we talked about that. Possibly over the holidays. We'll see." Sabine smiled.

The girls scheduled their flight for the next day. They would arrive in Madrid the day after. Sabine decided to return to Marbella with Annie rather than go back to France, at least for a while. Her parents were traveling in Switzerland and wouldn't be home for several weeks, so there was no real rush to get home. Decision made, she arranged to have dinner with Robert that night to say goodbye. Annie put a call into Ramone but had to leave a message asking him if he could pick them up from the train in Malaga. Everything was set.

Annie was writing in her journal when Celeste came in to see if she wanted a cup of tea.

Putting the journal aside, she accepted the tea and told her mother, "I will miss you, Mom...so much. Seeing you and Dad here together has been the best gift ever. This trip home has been like its own island in time for me. Even with all the festivities, there was time to think and be with family but also to gossip, laugh, cry, share our talks...even gaze at the stars. I won't be gone so long again."

Celeste smiled lovingly at her daughter. "I would hope not. You are carrying my grandchild. Seriously, sweetheart, if you need anything, call us." Tearful hugs were followed by Celeste's question, "Do you know what you plan to do?"

Annie shook her head. "Not really...one step at a time and try not to get in my own way, I suppose."

Final goodbyes at the airport, and the girls were on their way to Spain. On board, they giggled with excitement. Sabine was telling Annie about her dinner with Robert when a flight attendant handed Annie a small package. Surprised, she opened it to find a little baby red rose with a note:

'Querida, *I got your message...you can count on me always. I will be there. Ramone*'

Sabine looked too. "Awww, a baby rose. That is so sweet. Your matador is amazing. What man would take the time and effort to do that?"

Annie was so touched and, for a moment, could visualize Ramone holding their child. *Wow!*

Delighted to have Sabine as a travel partner, Annie was overjoyed that her speech continued to improve daily and was almost back to normal. She was tanned from her outdoor activities and had a much healthier look than when she arrived in Boothbay. They enjoyed the flight together, and before they knew it, they were on the train to Malaga. Annie knew Ramone's fight there was over. She was grateful for that since she wasn't ready to face watching him fight again.

Dozing with the gentle rocking of the train, Annie allowed herself to daydream, thinking back to the last time he greeted her at the ferry dock in Karpathos and that first scooter ride. She couldn't help a devilish smile, and Sabine elbowed her.

"I don't even want to know what that grin is all about." Annie just smiled even wider, rolling her eyes.

They changed clothes while on the train to freshen up. Annie chose a formfitting cobalt-blue dress with a multicolor belt. Sabine wore dark-purple slacks with a pale-pink tank top. As they approached the station, Annie looked out the window. Ramone was there waiting for her. He saw her and caught her eye. With the look they exchanged, Annie somehow felt as though she had found her soul mate. What Annie hadn't noticed was that Ramone was not alone.

Annie and Sabine stepped off the train platform to a loud appreciative whistle. Finding the source, Annie saw Antonio there beside Ramone...in a wheelchair. However, that didn't seem to stop his playful grin that showed off his dimples. Annie hugged Ramone with a lingering kiss.

Then while Ramone hugged Sabine, Annie reached down to hug Antonio. "I heard about your accident. I am so sorry."

Shrugging off her sympathy, Antonio was looking over at Sabine. Loud enough so she could hear, Antonio said to

Annie, "My brother told me about your beautiful cousin with the chestnut hair and dark-blue eyes" Looking at Ramone, he winked, "She's even more stunning than you let on!"

Sabine blushed profusely.

Ramone, shaking his head with a laugh, looked at Sabine and said, "Sabine, may I present my wayward brother, Antonio?"

She reached over to shake his hand, and he shocked her by pulling her into an embrace. "After all," he sheepishly said, "we are like family."

Caught entirely off guard by this rogue of a gentleman, Sabine straightened and looked over at Annie for help.

Annie laughed and quickly said, "Don't mind him. Antonio is a notorious flirt!"

Ramone chimed in looking at his brother, "Leave the poor girl alone! Let's get the bags and be on our way."

Not so gently, Ramone tossed a couple of bags onto Antonio's lap and was satisfied to get a loud "Ouch!" from him.

Although affectionately rough with Antonio, when it was time to move him from the chair into the car, he was exceedingly gentle.

There are so many layers to this man. It made Annie appreciate him even more.

Sabine had noticed the brief look of pain on Antonio's face while getting into the back seat. She went around to the other side and got in beside him. Annie and Ramone were talking and catching up in the front.

However, Sabine and Antonio were quiet for a while. Sabine finally said quietly, "I'm sorry about your accident. Is it bad?"

Antonio was about to wave it off but changed his mind and said, "I heard you were in a bad accident a while back."

She answered, "Yes, I am still recovering."

Antonio patted her hand. "You seem good to me." He continued, "The doctors tell me I have at least a few more months in the chair before I can move to crutches. Time will tell if I will be able to walk without help, much less if I will be able to fight again."

Sabine thought about her coma and the excruciating rehab after, then said, "It must have been horrible. I can't even imagine. My body went into a coma, so I never really felt intense pain until rehab."

Neither Sabine nor Antonio noticed the glance Ramone and Annie gave each other.

Chapter 46

Meeting Ramone's Mother

Antonio was staying at his mother's house during his recuperation. They all decided to drop Annie and Sabine at the villa to let them rest after their long trip. Ramone would then take Antonio to their mother's house. All Ramone wanted was to get Annie alone, but he graciously offered to take both Annie and Sabine to dinner. Right away Sabine declined, saying she wanted to rest and catch up with Dom and Gennie. It was understood that Annie wanted to meet Marguerite. They each wanted to keep it from being difficult. The meeting was planned for the following day for a casual lunch. Antonio encouraged Sabine to come as well, and she couldn't help but notice the wink he shot her way.

Dom and Gennie were delighted to see Annie and Sabine again so soon. When they came inside, Annie teasingly said, "Well, it looks like my cousin has the favor of yet another young man."

Sabine laughed and then responded, "You're one to talk."

Gennie looked directly at Sabine and said, "He is a wild one, that Antonio. Do not fall into the lure that comes with his good looks and his fame."

Sabine responded, "I truly do not think he's as bad as you all think. There is another side of him, although quite the *personage sympatique, je crois!*" They all laughed.

Annie looked at her now more seriously. "You both have been physically hurt...both in serious accidents. But this does bring home the reality of the dangerous sport these men participate in."

Reunited with her grandparents, as well as the glorious familiarity of Marbella's beauty, Annie's sense of nervous anticipation calmed. Sabine was still asleep when she got up to take an early morning walk along the shore. The rhythm of the waves breaking soothed her as always. The walk gave her time to contemplate how she would approach Ramone's mother. She thought about her father's revelation about Salvador's past and wondered whether Marguerite, or even Ramone, knew the whole story. Had Ramone told his mother and Antonio of her pregnancy? Surely Antonio would have said something if he knew.

Sabine was dressed when she returned. Annie took care getting ready to keep her appearance stylish yet casual. She could see the appreciation in Ramone's eyes as he glanced over her when he came to take them to his mother's house. In neutral colors, Annie had paired taupe linen pants with an ivory pullover top embellished with a hand-designed patchwork. On the other hand, Sabine chose a sleeveless black jumpsuit with a zebra-print accent at the waist.

Annie whispered to her, "Someone is going to be happy to see you!"

Sabine smiled. "Don't be silly. I'm just trying to get to know him a little..."

Annie's first thought when Marguerite answered the door was it was clear she had remained a Mediterranean beauty. Marguerite greeted Annie and Sabine with dark dancing eyes and open arms. She exuded a natural warmth, which set a welcoming atmosphere that immediately put Annie at ease. There was no denying how close the sons were to their mother, and the entire meeting was much more delightful than expected. Annie used the occasion to get to know Marguerite and decided to put her questions aside for the moment.

Antonio was naturally his charming self and made sure

Sabine was included in the conversation. There was no mention of Salvador, the baby, or bullfighting—simply an afternoon of enjoyable discussion about travel and an upcoming festival.

When they were leaving, Marguerite pulled Annie aside. "I would love to get to know you better and for you to know our background. My son appears to be quite infatuated with you. Perhaps a more in-depth conversation would be a good idea?"

Annie quickly agreed.

"Why don't we meet at the café on the boardwalk in the morning? I think it is walking distance from Don Marco's villa. Would ten o'clock work for you?"

"Yes, of course," Annie replied.

Ramone pulled up to the villa. Sabine got out, and Annie was about to follow.

"No, *querida*. Come with me."

Sabine smiled and blew them a kiss, then went inside. Annie was amazed at how happy she was to finally be alone with her man. This night was a complete contrast to the gentle lovemaking from that last night in Maine. Back at Ramone's flat, an intensity took over. They could not get enough of each other. The tighter they held each other, the closer they wanted to be. Finally spent, they collapsed with Annie wrapped around him.

She hugged him tight and said, "I have to go. Will you take me?" Grudgingly, they dressed so Ramone could take her back to the villa.

Marguerite was waiting the following morning for Annie at a table overlooking the sea. "*Hola*, Annie. Come sit with me."

The waiter poured tea and offered a few breakfast tapas. Marguerite smiled warmly at Annie. "Did you know I met your parents a long time ago? You look a lot like your father, but I also see your mother in you."

A perfect lead-in, Annie tentatively asked, "Is it too difficult for you to discuss Salvador? It must have been a shock when Ramone explained what happened in Paris."

"Not at all. I think I always knew things would not end well for him. I met Salvador in Barcelona where I was a relatively well-known flamenco dancer. The musical sounds of Spain have been ingrained in me since birth, but sometimes I like to think a little 'rhumba' beats in the heart of all women, don't you think?"

Annie nodded and smiled in agreement.

Marguerite continued, "The night I met Salvador, I had just finished a performance. He was so handsome and full of charm. I met Alex that night as well, but he didn't meet Celeste until several days later. They all came to watch me dance one evening. That was the evening the four of us went out together. After that, Salvador and I selfishly kept to ourselves. I heard Alex traveled to Marbella to see Celeste and that they eventually married, but we lost contact after that.

"We were all so young and impetuous. I didn't know about Salvador's matador lineage. He never talked about it. When Alex was reassigned to North Africa, Salvador hoped to follow. Instead, he was assigned to Hong Kong. Knowing he would be so far away, we decided to elope. Hong Kong was filled with excitement and mystery. It was easy to make a life there because of its wide variety of cultures and international residents. We settled in a Spanish-speaking area and were quite content, at least for a time.

"We had the two boys, first Ramone, then Antonio. Their early years were spent in Hong Kong. Salvador was a good father to them when they were young. Sadly, things changed once Salvador met Kung Li's activists. Thankfully, he sent the three of us back to Spain...this time to Marbella, where his older brother could look after us. It was only after meeting Pedro in Marbella that I learned about the generations of matadors in Salvador's family."

Marguerite shook her head, then continued, "From that first meeting with Pedro, with his stories of fighting the bull, Ramone was a young man obsessed with becoming a matador like his uncle. I think he resented that his own father had chosen a different path. Antonio was slower to catch the fever, but soon he was just as into it. When Salvador heard his sons signed up for matador training, he took a leave to try to dissuade them from pursuing this dangerous career. Salvador was furious with Pedro, and they had a serious falling-out. Eventually, the boys decided to follow Pedro's path against their father's wishes. It was then Salvador's personality shifted to a darker side. I hardly recognized him, and he was often gone weeks at a time.

"Before long, Kung Li's group enticed him back to Hong Kong full time, and I began life as a single mother to two matadors. Salvador and I were still married, but we lived apart. I wanted to remain here to be close to my sons. He came to see the boys occasionally outside of the ring...never watching them fight. However, Pedro was there for every fight of theirs. If one of them got gored or injured, it was Pedro who encouraged them to get up, nurse the injury, then want to do it again. They're fearless in that ring." Looking seriously at Annie, she added, "I am truly sorry for Salvador's treachery toward Alex."

Chapter 47

Choice at the Crossroad

Fascinated with this new insight, Annie accepted her apology. None of it had to do with Marguerite.

Annie added, "What an amazing life you have experienced. How did you feel about them becoming such popular fighters...knowing they could be injured at any time?"

Marguerite wisely answered, "I won't lie to you. It is not easy. But growing up in Spain, we have experienced bullfighting our whole lives. In ancient times, life was hard. So often, it was man against all odds. Seeing the physical struggle between man and a ferocious beast, with the man surviving, gave people hope that they too could overcome unsurmountable obstacles in their own lives. When they saw a defeat, they felt like it was their own. That is why they cheer the matador on so desperately.

Times are changing with the younger generation, though. There is a growing faction in Spain of animal rights activists who want to banish bullfighting altogether because of the cruelty to the bull. They do not abide by the old traditions."

Annie looked at her, appreciating her honesty. "I will be curious to learn how that affects the current traditional bullfight. Did Ramone tell you I am carrying his child?"

"Ramone did not tell me, but I suspected. That is why I wanted to share his background with you. When Ramone faced Salvador, betraying his own father, for you, I knew how serious he was about a future with you."

271

Annie could only briefly shut her eyes, sigh, and say, "I love him deeply from a depth I didn't know I had. But I just don't know if I can live with the fear of seeing him injured, perhaps fatally...or having my child see that. Think about what it did to Salvador."

Marguerite reminded Annie so much of her mother when she said, "Be true to the future you deserve, Annie. Make your choices, whatever they may be, to avoid future regrets. You must live with the decisions you make, but you also need to prepare for the impact those decisions have on those around you. Take your time..."

Even with the questions surrounding Annie and Ramone's future together, Marguerite and Annie formed a bond that morning, and they gave each other a genuine hug as they said goodbye. Back at the villa, Annie found out Sabine had baked cookies and left to take them to Antonio. That was good. Annie appreciated the chance for some alone time with Dom and Gennie. They knew about the baby now.

When they settled into a comfortable discussion, Dom cryptically asked Annie, "With all the countries you have been to and people that you've met, are there any special mementos you carry with you every day?"

Annie nodded and went to her room to retrieve a small satin pouch from her bag. Bringing it back out to the living room, she took out the amethyst she had loaned Sarah and gotten back, the note from Ramone she had shown her mother, the sketch of her rock climb Mara had given her, and the baby red rose. She had given the prayer necklace to the bride in Bali, but she thought of it often and mentioned it to Dom.

He took his time and studied each one. "What do you think it is that causes us to hold something so close that could simply be a trinket to someone else?"

Annie thought about his question and answered, "Faith, hope, inspiration, courage, endearment, clarity?"

Dom said, "That's good, Annie. I have one more for your

collection." He dug into his pocket and handed her a brilliant yellow-green stone. "This stone is peridot...it's meaning is connected to the sun and serves as a spiritual cheerleader. It was a favorite of Cleopatra in ancient Egypt. She wore it for its beauty, as well as to ward off evil spirits. Peridot is particularly beneficial in overcoming fear, instilling confidence in one's own abilities, and sustaining a sense of self-worth. I've carried it for years. Allow me to now share it with you."

Touched beyond words, Annie gave Dom a giant embrace. Back in her room, Annie contemplated her collection, which now included the peridot. Several hours later, Sabine came in with a note. Attached to the note was a long-stem red rose.

Sabine explained with a smile. "While you met with his mother, Ramone brought this over and asked if I would give it to you."

Annie opened it after smelling the rose.

'Meet me in the vineyard at dusk, querida.
Ramone'

"He must mean the vineyard not far from here. I think it belongs to his uncle's family. But first, tell me about Antonio. How is he feeling?"

Annie and Sabine fell into an easy rapport. Antonio's prognosis was good, and he was not only determined to walk again but also to fight.

Sabine gushed a bit, "Annie, *vraiment*, when Antonio smiles, those dimples just do me in! He is witty and makes me laugh. He wants to take me out dining and dancing but feels limited and frustrated. I understand how he feels. Believe me, I really like Robert, but Antonio is special too."

Annie said, "Well, dearest cousin, it sounds like you are on your own journey. Why don't we see if Ramone and Antonio are available tomorrow? All four of us should go somewhere fun. Ramone can maneuver the wheelchair."

Sabine agreed and went to read her book on the patio, leaving Annie to ponder what she would wear to a vineyard rendezvous. She pulled her hair up into a ponytail and put on her jeans and a red t-shirt with a short jacket in bronze with blue and red flowers. Coordinating earrings and necklace, and she was on her way. Fortunately, she wore her comfortable walking boots since the vineyard was a little farther than she expected.

What she also didn't expect was a Hansel and Gretel-like path leading to the vineyard. Instead of breadcrumbs, there was a mix of large and tiny red roses sprinkled sparsely along the way. Next, she heard the soft sounds of Spanish music. At the clearing, there was a large blanket, a picnic basket, and a small table beside a massive live oak tree covered in Spanish moss. Red roses were strewn all over. Annie smiled. Ramone had undoubtedly gone all out for romance!

He walked toward her to take her hands. She smiled up at him and noticed a more serious look on his face that belied this magical fairyland he had created.

Suddenly Annie was filled with a sense of panic! Her thoughts jumped around. *It's too soon...I'm not ready...I can't make this choice!*

Ramone noticed but began anyway, "The first day when I looked up at you from the ring, there was a radiance about you. Beyond your beauty, it was a magnetic pull that I felt, and when we danced, I knew I could hold you forever. Your inner spirit grew with each part of your journey, and I was privileged to be there to see it. *Querida*, you melted my heart that day at the waterfall when you turned around.

By the time we shared Greece, I already knew how strong my love was for you...but there was more. Around you, I didn't always have to be the strong one. You enabled me to feel how good life is in ways I have never imagined. When I thought I couldn't love you any more, knowing you carry my child has made my heart burst with joy and love."

Getting down on one knee, he reached over for a small box and opened it. Inside was the most gorgeous blue diamond ring. Continuing, he said, "This blue diamond symbolizes eternity, truth, peace, spirituality, and ensures a safe journey. In Greece, I told you I would have all of you. Before you today, I ask to have all of you. Be my wife, *querida*, the mother of my children. Allow your destiny to rest next to mine. Will you return my love and marry me?"

Annie, tears rolling down her cheeks, fell to her knees in front of him. "Ramone, I do love you with all my heart. You are a man of so many layers. It gives me great pleasure to unravel each one. Even in your strength, you have a gentleness that touches my soul. But, my darling, I cannot marry you. My father told me how Salvador changed after he saw his father fatally gored. I know it is your tradition, and I can't take that from you. It is me that is weak, and I am so sorry..."

Ramone held both of her hands, then reached over to hand her a paper. It was an advanced copy of tomorrow's Marbella newspaper turned to an article with the headline: "Spain's Most Beloved Matador Retires from the Ring!" With a look of total shock, Annie read on:

> RAMONE SANCHEZ has made the decision to give up bullfighting. He was quoted to say he hopes to marry, raise a family, and travel.

All she could do was look at him stunned for the sacrifice he was willing to make.

Kneeling there together, hands held, Annie studied this man who was ready to give up his profession, his family tradition, and his love of the sport to choose a life with her over all else. She saw the love in his eyes. *How can I live without this man, but also, how can I allow him to give up so much?*

"Ramone, my true love, my journey that allowed me to explore cultures around the world taught me the importance of tradition. Experiencing the villages of Dingle in Ireland and Olympos in Karpathos gave me an understanding of those who passionately want to preserve the past. Part of that is the tradition of bullfighting in Spain. You have it in your blood through your family. I cannot take that from you."

Ramone nodded and said, "You and my child are my world. If I can't have both you and my profession, I choose you, *querida*."

The sea had always held answers for her, but for once Annie allowed herself to be filled with awareness of the possibilities of a life with this man beyond the sea. She thought about the peridot gem Dom had just given her to overcome fear.

It was then she knew where her heart needed to reside. "And I choose you, my love. But I will not let you make this sacrifice. I must be willing to meet you halfway. I love you, and you fill my heart. The fear I feel is selfish, and I regret putting you in a situation where you felt you needed to make such a choice. Be my husband and my true love. Help me be strong for you."

Ramone's gentle kiss grew deeper and more passionate. He reached for the ring and slid it on Annie's finger. A blue diamond with such a significant meaning. Allowing true happiness with the hope of what was to be settling over them, they made love there in the vineyard. Every kiss, every caress was a prayer for their future together.

And the journey continues...in Crossing Paths

https://books2read.com/CrossingPathsNinaPurtee

About the Author
Nina Purtee

Nina Purtee is a worldwide traveler, philosopher, and award-winning adventure romance novelist. Growing up in Atlanta, Nina's father ignited her travel obsession with lavish family trips to exotic locations. Some of those experiences have found their way into her writing. Island-hopping with her family through the Greek islands on a 95-foot sailboat, the *Eleni*, gave Nina the inspiration for Don Marco's vessel, the *Porto Banus*.

While on safari in East Africa, she met a woman artist with her companion, a sculptor, living in tents, immersed in their artwork. They inspired the characters of Annie's friend, Sarah, and the sculptor, Sam, who we meet in Sarah's book.

Nina draws from her travels to embrace multicultural characters and couples seemingly from different worlds and allow them to compromise, co-exist, accept each other's traditions, and even find love.

Tammy Ruggles with Reader Views describes Purtee as "a natural storyteller, with the ability to transport readers into realms of imagination and possibility."

Nina now lives in Florida surrounded by family and friends when she is not traveling the globe seeking new experiences to write about.

www.ninapurtee.com

Crossing Paths

THE ROAD TO DESTINY

Compelling Sequel to *Beyond the Sea*

After a life-changing journey in book one, Annie's course is apparently set and she is ready to open the next chapter of her destiny with Ramone. However, amid the politically fraught British turnover of Hong Kong to Beijing, politics and suspense intervene, causing lives to be changed and plans to unravel.

The island of Mallorca off the coast of Spain offers the perfect refuge from the conflict. In the midst of the King's Cup Regatta and the Night of the Pilgrims Pilgrimage, a wedding is planned high in the mountains overlooking the sea. Annie's extraordinary journey has produced the man of her dreams and the happy couple welcome family and friends from their different worlds to celebrate their union.

Once gathered, one has to ask...is it fate that all these personalities have convened on this island at this moment in time? This combustion of characters have found themselves swept into Annie's journey and perhaps found destiny of their own with far reaching choices set before them.

*****

"There is an elegance to the writing, an allure of the locales and real-world situations, especially with the island and culture, that raise the book to a higher level in the romance genre."

-- READER VIEWS

Printed in Great Britain
by Amazon

57892095R00162